THE LIST

THE LIST

SHERRI L. LEWIS

URBAN CHRISTIAN

www.urbanchristianonline.net

Urban Books, LLC
78 East Industry Court
Deer Park, NY 11729

ISBN 13: 978-1-60162-892-3
ISBN 10: 1-60162-892-7

First Mass Market Printing February 2011
First Trade Paperback Printing March 2009
Printed in the United States of America

10   9   8   7   6   5   4   3   2   1

Distributed by Kensington Publishing Corp.
Submit Wholesale Orders to:
Kensington Publishing Corp.
C/O Penguin Group (USA) Inc.
Attention: Order Processing
405 Murray Hill Parkway
East Rutherford, NJ 07073-2316
Phone: 1-800-526-0275
Fax: 1-800-227-9604

Dedication

To my big sister, Joyce—thanks for all you've done and continue to do to support me as an author. There's no way I could say thank you enough for reading and editing every version, emailing your thoughts and corrections, and then being a great marketer and publicist. Love you!

Acknowledgments

Okay, so when your books come out so close together, you end up acknowledging the same people over and over. Since ain't much changed in my life since last year, this will be short.

As always, I thank you, God, for the gift of writing. I'm loving it more and more, and I pray that you continue to use me to affect the lives of others. You know my favorite days are those where I sit in my pajamas all day at the kitchen table, eating cereal, listening to jazz and sipping coffee, making my characters come alive. I'm trusting You to make that my full-time gig . . . soon. Oh yeah, and all the other stuff I dream about too!

To all my family and friends—I will definitely forget someone, so please consider yourselves all loved and thanked.

To Norine—I can't thank you enough for all the evenings you sat at the kitchen table with me, listening to me babble on and on about these five women like they were real people. You're the perfect sounding board. I thank God for your friendship, love, and support.

To Yvette—thanks for all the help with the television producer stuff. I didn't realize how much I had gleaned listening to your experiences over the years. One day, you'll be running black television and making it look like God wants it to look.

To Mommy—thanks for helping me birth these characters. Thanks for your tireless work as an assistant, publicist, sounding board, and being the world's greatest mom.

To Daddy, the little brown man—thanks for telling me it was too preachy. I fixed it!

To my best friend, Kathy—thanks for all your love and support and for all the books you've bought and gotten sold. I love you forever!

To Rhonda McKnight—you are invaluable as a sistah-writerfriend. You are becoming one of my favoritest people in the world. Thanks so much for your wisdom, endless resources, encouragement, reading/editing—I could go on and on. Your emails are the best; you have no idea how happy I am whenever I see your name in my inbox. Looking forward to your release and making this author journey together.

To Dee Stewart—you are amazing as a sistah-writerfriend, and even more amazing as a publicist. Sorry I'm so high-maintenance. I promise to answer all your emails and send you those interview questions as soon as I get this manuscript in the mail. Really.☺ I can't wait to see your books on the shelves. It's only a matter of time.

To Kristen Hemingway—thanks so much for reading and commenting and helping me bring the story together. Looking forward to seeing your words in print one day (you have to be a writer with that name.) To Erika—thanks for listening to me as I birthed the story. Thanks for letting me borrow your name.

To Victoria Christopher Murray—I know I mention you in every book, but as long as you're the wonderful mentor/godmother to me that you are, I have to give honor where honor is due. I know God will continue to bless you with awesome success and favor because you give so much to all of us that are following in your footsteps. Thanks for always being a blessing!

To my wonderful writing group, ACFW-VIP—it's great doing this writing thing with my sistah-writerfriends. Let's continue to love and support one another until everyone gets published.

To my pastors, Steve and Lindy Hale and Scott and Lacy Thompson, and my wonderful Bethel Atlanta family—thanks for your love and support and for pushing me to be everything I'm called to be in God.

To my cousin, Pastor Corey Kelly, and his beautiful wife, First Lady Tish—thank you so much for your love and support with my releases. I pray

God's greatest blessings on New Hope Baptist Church! Thanks to Garbo Hearne and Pyramid Art, Books, and Custom Framing for all your support with my releases.

To all my readers, book clubs, women's groups, and churches—thank you so much for your support of *My Soul Cries Out* and *Dance into Destiny*. I appreciate all the emails, guestbook entries and MySpace comments that let me know that what I'm trying to do is working.

one

Tick, tock, tick, tock . . .

There it was. The sound that had been growing louder and louder in my brain—until now, it was no longer background noise. Groaning, I rolled over in bed and pulled a pillow over my face. I peeked out and cast an annoyed glance at my nightstand clock, but it was digital, so it couldn't be blamed for the relentless ticking in my head. No, it was my own internal clock—the proverbial biological one.

And now there was an alarm to go with it. An alarm with no snooze button to make it stop. The AMA alarm. Today was my thirty-fifth birthday, and I was officially AMA—advanced maternal age. The age at which my eggs, encased in my ovaries since birth, started to get old and decrepit. If, by some magic, I were to meet Mr. Perfect tomorrow and we fell overwhelmingly in love and got married within the next six months, then got pregnant right away, mine would still be considered a high-risk pregnancy just because of my age.

I sat up on the edge of the bed and stretched my arms upward, resolving that today I would celebrate my life with thanksgiving, hope, and faith.

Hey, God. Thanks for waking me up healthy, beautiful and strong this morning. Thanks that I turned thirty-five today . . .

And then, for no apparent reason, I burst into tears. Sobs, actually. I rolled onto the floor and curled into a fetal position, crying like someone had died.

I guess someone had. The thirty-five-year-old woman I had dreamed I would be when I was a little girl. Married to a gorgeous, black Ken look-alike—plastic smile and all—with two beautiful children living in a castle on the hill with two ponies in our stable and a thriving career as a fire-woman or a ballerina.

Okay, so I was seven.

But still. I didn't expect to be thirty-five, single and childless. I was supposed to wake up to breakfast in bed cooked by my wonderfully loving husband and two beautiful daughters—all bouncy, bubbly and giggly. They were supposed to burst into the room and scream, "Happy birthday, Mommy" and cover me with kisses. My husband was supposed to kiss my cheek, say "Happy birthday, dear" and give me a knowing look that said as soon as the girls got off to school, he was going to really wish me a happy birthday.

But instead, I was all alone in my king-sized bed. Well, actually on the floor next to it. I grabbed a pillow, then pulled the comforter off the bed and snuggled underneath it. I could see God looking down from heaven shaking His head. He'd elbow

Jesus, who would roll His eyes. They'd both look at the Holy Spirit as if to say, "Please, go help Our pitiful child."

I imagined the Holy Spirit swiftly coming to my rescue. He'd come and get under the comforter with me and hold me in His arms, promising to love me until my earthly husband came along.

"God, for the millionth time—why can't you take it away? Just make me completely satisfied with you and you alone. If you're not going to fulfill it, then take away my desire for a husband and kids." I yelled at Him from under the comforter. I imagined the Holy Spirit hugging me tighter. I appreciated the fact that He wasn't moved by my angry outburst. He loved me no matter what.

I relaxed in His arms. Imagined myself snuggling into His chest, and instantly felt better. "God, why can't You send me a husband just like You? Send me You wrapped up in chocolate." How awesome that would be. To be married to a guy like God.

I must have fallen back asleep in His arms, because when the phone rang and I looked at the clock, it was two hours later. I wasn't in the mood for the onslaught of phone calls from people wishing me happiness for my birthday. I should have gone out of town like I'd originally planned. Instead, I had let my friends talk me into a "Girls' Day"— some big surprise they had planned. Much as I loved them, I wasn't in the mood for surprises.

All I wanted to do for my birthday was be alone with God.

The phone rang again and I ignored it. I thought about getting up to do a quick half-hour Taebo tape. Maybe some kicking and punching would get rid of some of my frustrations. Billy Blanks had become my best friend in the year right after my divorce. There was just something about being violent and calling it exercise. I had joined a gym with a big punching bag that I pretended, on a regular, was my ex and his mistress. I got a reputation at the gym as the girl no one wanted to spar with and would never want to meet in a dark alley.

My stupid ex. This was all his fault. My marriage should have never ended. After eleven years, he decided that twenty-one was too young to have gotten married and that he needed to see what else was "out there" . . .

Fresh tears flowed down my face. *What in the world?*

Was I really crying over my ex? Really? My divorce was final almost three years ago. I hadn't cried over him, or even thought much about him in the past two years. Had to check the calendar when I got up off the floor. This *had* to be my hormones.

I guess it wasn't my ex I was crying over. It was the fact that the marriage hadn't worked. That I was thirty-five, divorced, childless, and oh yeah, hormonal.

My cell phone chimed to indicate that I had gotten a text message. I picked it up and looked at the screen.

Get up off the floor. Dry your eyes. Get dressed and get ready to be celebrated. I promise the day will get better, but you have to get up first. Happy birthday. Please, girl—get over it. Thirty-five is not that old! Love you!!!

I had to laugh. My girl, Vanessa. I decided to take her word for it. Maybe the day would get better if I just picked myself up off the floor.

I pulled up at Vanessa's house an hour later—fresh faced and comfortably dressed as I had been instructed. As I got out of my car, I took authority over my hormones as I did every month. I could overcome most battles in my life, but once a month, the day before my cycle started, I wound up crying endlessly and reacting irrationally to the dumbest things. Amazing that a strong, successful woman—producer at the nation's newest up-and-coming black television station—and experienced spiritual warrior could be reduced to such ridiculousness by some estrogen. *Please, God. Not today.*

Vanessa must have been watching for me because, before I got out of my car, she threw open the door and held her arms out wide, walking toward me. It was rare that her petite frame was casually dressed in jeans and a simple blouse. She was one of those elegant suit ladies who wore shimmery stockings and four-inch heels with the perfect, short, sassy haircut. In spite of her casual attire, her make-up was flawlessly applied as if she was about to do a photo shoot. Wearing her signature brilliant smile, she sang out, "Happy birthday, Michelle!"

She looked so happy to see me and her eyes were so filled with love that I burst into tears. A look of horror flashed across her face. "Oh, no!" She shook her head slowly in disbelief. "Hormone day on your birthday? What was God thinking?"

I laughed a little. She took me into her arms and held me for a few minutes. Her comforting voice spoke directly in my ear. "Oh, Father, help us today. We take authority over estrogen gone awry."

I laughed a little more.

She broke our embrace and grabbed me by the shoulders. "Fix your face, girl, and snap out of it. It's your birthday brunch." She rubbed my arm and smiled. "Actually, you know what? It's your party and you can cry if you want to."

I laughed more and sniffled. I wiped my eyes as she led me into the house.

Vanessa was my *she*-ro. She had kept me alive and sane during my separation and divorce. She was the ministerial counselor at our church. Through our sessions, I decided that not only did I want to live, but that life could be good after divorce. Not too long after she released me from therapy, her husband died tragically in a car accident. I could only hope I was half the friend to her then that she had been to me. Our losses and relationships with God had bonded us together into one of the best friendships I'd ever had.

Vanessa's house was immaculate as always. I was amazed that a single mother of two teenagers, full-time counselor and minister could keep her five-bedroom house perfectly clean without a housekeeper. I, however—single with no kids—couldn't seem to keep my townhouse straight to save my life.

As we entered her two-story foyer, I looked above the winding spiral staircase and saw a huge banner reading *35th Annual Michelle Bradford*

Celebration Day. Simultaneously, I heard several voices cry out, "Happy birthday, 'Chelle!"

At the foot of the steps stood my girlfriends, Nicole, Lisa, and Angela. I burst into tears again. Lisa and Angela ran over to hug me.

Nicole stared at me. "Are you serious?" She looked over at Vanessa, who winced and nodded. Nicole picked up her purse. "I'm out. You know I can't stand her when she's like this." She got halfway to the front door before Vanessa grabbed her.

"Stop playing, Nicole." Vanessa put her hands on her hips.

"Who's playing? I can't stand being around her snotting and crying because a butterfly splattered on her windshield or Revlon discontinued her favorite lipstick color. Naw, I'm out. I'll meet you guys for the big celebration later." Nicole turned toward the door again.

"Nicole." Vanessa put on her mother voice and evil eye that always snapped her kids into perfect obedience.

Apparently, it worked on Nicole too, because she took her purse off her shoulder and came over to hug me. "Happy birthday, Michelle. You know I love you like a sister, but dang—can't you take the pills for this? I know God is a healer, but for real though, until your manifestation comes, you need some earthly medicine."

"Nicole." Vanessa said it like Nicole had one more time before she got sent to her room for a time-out.

Lisa and Angela disappeared into Vanessa's massive gourmet kitchen.

I had to laugh. It was funny to hear Nicole using spiritual lingo. She had just gotten saved two years ago and was still a little awkward when it came to using spiritual terms.

She gave me a big hug, which set off a new flood of tears. "Dang, girl." Nicole called into the kitchen. "Can y'all see if Vanessa has some olive oil or something? Shoot, some Crisco will do." She looked at Vanessa. "Can't you lay hands on her and cast out this estrogen demon so we can all enjoy our day?"

That sent me into a fit of uncontrollable giggles. When I laughed really hard, I couldn't stop myself from snorting. Snorting the snot from crying made me cough until I could hardly breathe. Vanessa pounded me on the back.

Nicole stared at me and let out an exasperated sigh. "What a crackhead." She disappeared into the kitchen to help Angela and Lisa with whatever they were doing.

I was glad Vanessa had only invited my closest sister circle for brunch. At least they all understood my condition. Premenstrual dysphoric disorder was what my doctor called it. Insanity was what my friends called it. Hell on earth was what I called it. Fortunately, it usually only lasted a day in my case. I hoped it would pass before the big celebration later that Nicole had mentioned.

Vanessa led me to the breakfast room table and sat me down. Angela, Lisa, and Nicole emerged from the kitchen a few minutes later, each carrying a tray. Vanessa fastened a tiara onto my afro, wavy from being let loose from two-stranded twists. "Today, we're celebrating you with your favorite things. Sit back, relax and enjoy."

I looked down at the trays my girls had brought from the kitchen. There were finger sandwiches—peanut butter, honey and bananas on wheat bread—chocolate-covered strawberries, mango slices, crab cakes, jerk chicken wings with rice and peas, fried plantains, and ginger beer to wash it all down with.

I clapped my hands and laughed. "All my favorites. Kind of weird together, but still. It's so nice to be loved and for you guys to know what I love." I looked up to see everyone holding their breath, as if they were afraid I was going to cry. "Loosen up, guys." I smiled. "This brunch is perfect."

I frowned at two capsules filled with greenish stuff on the side of my plate.

Vanessa answered before I could ask. "It's St. John's wort. The herb I told you about. I picked up some at the health food store."

I stared at the pills.

Nicole put a hand on her hip. "God gave us plants for natural cures, so it's not like you're not having faith for healing." She picked up the pills and shoved them at me. "Look, we're the ones that have to spend the whole day with you. The least you could do is try them."

Angela *tsked* at Nicole. "Girl, stop being evil. You'll only make it worse."

Lisa chimed in, "Yeah, Nicole. At least she can blame emotional craziness on hormones, and it only happens once a month. What's your excuse?"

Nicole shot Lisa an evil stare.

I obediently swallowed the pills, ignoring the organic taste in my mouth.

We filled our plates with my special treats. Everybody was silent for a few minutes as we started eating.

Lisa finally spoke. "So, Michelle, you're thirty-five today. How does it fe–"

She stopped talking when Angela elbowed her in the side and shook her head. Everybody kept eating.

After a few minutes, Vanessa said, "Michelle, we want you to know that . . ." Her voice trailed off.

Nicole rolled her eyes. "This is ridiculous. We're all afraid to talk because we don't want her to cry? I tell you what. Michelle, talk about what's bothering you—what we know you cried about when you woke up and in the car on the way over here. Let's get it out in the open and deal with it, so we won't be dancing on eggshells all day. This is supposed to be a celebration. Sheesh . . ."

Everyone stiffened a little and looked at me.

I stared past Angela and Lisa at the lake behind Vanessa's breakfast room bay window. The water moved slowly with the sun reflecting off it, creating a tranquil glow.

"Well . . ." I nibbled on a chocolate strawberry. The bitter sweetness of the dark chocolate blended with the natural sweetness of the strawberry. "I woke up alone this morning. No husband. No babies. And I'm thirty-five. This wasn't the life I dreamed of. But I have no choice but to accept it."

I took a bite of mango. Its tropical, tangy sweetness contrasted sharply with the strawberry-chocolate combination. I wondered if being hormonal made my taste buds more sensitive. I watched everyone waiting for the tears as I continued sampling the fruit. I was more surprised than they were when no tears came.

I decided to continue. "I've asked God countless times to send my husband, but I guess He's not listening. Or maybe He doesn't think I'm ready. I've done therapy. I've healed and forgiven and realized my mistakes. I think my heart is ready to love again. But I guess He doesn't."

I stopped for a minute to listen to the wind chimes tinkling outside the breakfast room door. It was a breezy, spring day, and I could imagine how sweet the wind would feel kissing my cheeks. I almost wanted to move the party onto the patio but didn't want to upset Nicole's allergies. Her sneezing and snotting and my crying and snotting would make for a very bad day.

"It's pure torture. Wanting something you can't have. Craving something, needing something and it not being there. I'm tired of begging. I want to not want it anymore. Just focus on my career, my friends, and chasing after God and let that be enough."

Angela and Vanessa nodded. Lisa shook her head like she couldn't get with me on that.

Nicole reached over and took my hand. "See? That wasn't so bad. If that's the worst, we can talk about anything now."

I smiled. "Yeah. Thanks, Nicki. You can be pretty all right when you want to be."

Everyone let out a collective sigh of relief, myself included. Maybe today could be a good day after all. Nicole squeezed my hand. As much as she could be evil and blunt, she was full of love—that ride-or-die chick a sista always wanted around, to have her back. I looked around the table and appreciated God for my friends. Maybe I didn't have a man, but I had some beautiful, strong women in my life that loved me. For now, that would have to be enough.

I looked out the window at the lake again. There was a long-necked duck with her babies trailing behind her on the water. "Look! Baby ducks." I pointed and everyone turned to look out the window. "They're so cute."

And with that, I burst into tears.

Nicole dropped my hand and shook her head in disgust. "Crackhead . . ." she muttered as she disappeared into the kitchen.

Vanessa passed me a napkin, and I wiped my eyes and blew my nose.

"Oh, well, it was nice while it lasted." Lisa got up and followed Nicole into the kitchen.

They both came back a few moments later—Nicole carrying champagne and orange juice, Lisa carrying Vanessa's crystal flutes.

Nicole set the bottles down on the table. "I'm not sure how smart it is to mix alcohol, herbs, and hormones, but it can't get much worse than crying over baby ducks."

Lisa cut her eyes at Nicole. "You were the one that wanted her to talk."

Nicole answered, "How was I supposed to know there would be ducks on the lake?"

Lisa said, "All we had to do was—"

"Ladies!" Vanessa interrupted. "Chill." Vanessa opened the orange juice and began filling the flutes. "Honestly, I think Nicole had a good idea."

Nicole crossed her eyes and stuck out her tongue at Lisa like she was five years old.

"In fact . . ." Vanessa topped off the glasses with a small splash of champagne. None of us were drinkers, but we always had a drop or two of champagne when we celebrated. I guess it made us feel grown, even though we always ended up throwing away almost a full bottle of the expensive stuff. ". . . I think it's a perfect idea for a birthday celebration. Instead of going to the spa, shopping, and eating cake, every woman's birthday party should be a look at her life."

Nicole muttered, "Oh boy, here goes the latest Vanessa psychobabbleology. Just when I thought this party couldn't get any worse."

Vanessa ignored her. "Yeah. That's exactly what it should be." Vanessa stared into space as she pushed the cork back into the champagne bottle.

"What?" Nicole tapped her fingers on the table.

"Shh, she's thinking." Lisa smacked Nicole's arm.

Vanessa handed each of us a mimosa glass and sat back down in her seat, the wheels in her brain ticking. "For a woman's birthday celebration, she should be surrounded by her sister-circle in a safe, loving environment. She should look at her past and see where she made it and where she missed it. Look at her present and see where she is and where she wants to be, and look at her future and if she's doing the right things to get there." Vanessa nodded and smiled to herself. "Then her friends should celebrate her by telling her wonderful things about her, giving her affirmations, blessings and prayers to press her toward her future."

Angela and Lisa nodded.

"I like it," Lisa said. She turned to Nicole.

Nicole shrugged. "Y'all know I don't like all that touchy-feely psychobabble stuff."

Lisa rolled her eyes. "Lord, Nicole, can't you get over yourself and help us celebrate Michelle's birthday?"

"I didn't say I wouldn't do it. I'm just saying." She pursed her lips together and glared at Lisa.

"Okay, then." Vanessa glared at both of them like they were about to get a beating. "Since Michelle has identified what's bothering her the most, let's focus on that. If there are other areas you come up with, we'll deal with that too. We'll break away for an hour or two and everybody take some paper and write something special for Michelle. Michelle—like I said, take an honest look at your past, present, and future and whatever else you need to get out, and then we'll reconvene. Pick your favorite spot—out by the lake, in the sunroom, by the fireplace, wherever you can get comfortable. Okay?"

"But I don't want to spoil whatever you guys already had planned for me just because I woke up hormonal and lonely," I said.

Nicole sucked her teeth. "Please, girl. We had planned to watch all your favorite movies. *Love and Basketball, Love Jones, Brown Sugar . . .*" She looked around the room. "There's not enough tissue in the house for that. Even though it's warm and fuzzy, touchy-feely, this is way better than you snotting and crying all day over a bunch of movies. And we still have your surprise for tonight." She looked at Vanessa with a nod of approval. "It's actually a good idea." She frowned. "Just don't expect to be psychoanalyzing me for my birthday."

Vanessa laughed. "I wouldn't dream of it. I don't think my years of training or experience have in *any* way prepared me for that."

Nicole's eyes widened with obvious surprise at Vanessa's dig.

Lisa laughed. "Good one, *V*."

"Whatever." Nicole lifted her champagne flute and indicated for us all to do the same. "To Michelle and celebrating her life. The good, the bad, and the ugly."

"Nicole!" Lisa, Angela, and Vanessa said in unison.

Nicole looked around at everyone and shrugged her shoulders. "What?" She lifted her glass again. "For real though, we love you, girl. I haven't known God long, but what I do know is that He's good. And faithful. And you're a beautiful example of Him living and breathing on earth. And no matter what, man or no man, your future will be bright and beautiful. I'm looking forward to being a part of it." She looked around the table. "Is that better?"

Everybody laughed and lifted their glasses. "To Michelle."

And, of course, I burst into tears.

two

I got up from Vanessa's hammock under the large elm tree by the lake and stretched. I almost got lost in the comfort of its padded cushions, the warm breeze, the sound of the water splashing against the rocks and the birds chirping. Thankfully, there had been no more baby duck sightings.

I had managed to focus for an hour or so and had jotted notes in a journal Vanessa had given me. I was usually introspective and stayed in touch with my feelings, but I hadn't taken a good look in the inner mirror for a while.

I walked through the patio door into Vanessa's bright sunroom and called out, "I'm ready."

Angela, Lisa, and Vanessa appeared one by one, each with notepaper in hand.

"Where's Nicole?" Lisa asked, frowning.

"I think she went upstairs to the guest room." Angela walked over to the staircase and yelled, "Nicole, it's time."

After a few moments, Nicole emerged at the top

of the steps, stretching, yawning and wiping her mouth. "I'm up. Here I come."

"You went to sleep?" Lisa voiced her obvious disgust.

"Yeah." Nicole descended the steps slowly like she was still tipsy with sleep and afraid that she might fall down the steep staircase.

Lisa put her hands on her hips. "Nicole, we were supposed to be celebrating Michelle. You said you'd participate."

"I don't need to sit around for an hour and think about one of my best friends to figure out how I feel about her." Nicole waved away their disdain. "When it's my turn, I'll come off the dome and from the heart. Okay?"

"Fine. Come on." Vanessa led us all back to her spacious family room, to her comfy sectional sofa with sink-in pillows. She turned on the television and flipped to a smooth jazz station on DIRECTV. She lit a few scented candles and placed them on the mantle and on the large coffee table in the middle of the sectional.

Nicole lay back against the couch, grabbed a pillow and a chenille throw and stretched out. After a minute, she leaned forward. "Humph, I better sit up. I worked about eighty hours this week." Nicole's career as an investment banker required long, exhausting hours, and she fell asleep if she sat still for too long.

We all made ourselves comfortable on the couch, except for Nicole, who sat on the floor, leaning against the couch.

"Ready, Michelle?" Vanessa asked.

I nodded and opened the journal. I grabbed a handful of my thick, wavy afro and pulled my fingers through the kinks. Going natural after my divorce was one of the best things I'd ever done. I took a deep breath before launching into my introspection.

"For the most part, I'm happy with my life. I love my job and feel like things are about to get even better. I can't say I'm always proud of the shows we produce, but I feel like God is about to put me in a position where I have more of a say in what we put out there. It would be awesome to be in a position to make decisions about programming on BTV. I could really make a difference in Black America." I had to stop before I got on my favorite soapbox. I would lose them if I started preaching on the evils of Black television.

I switched subjects. "I love my church, and I love where my relationship with God is right now. I can finally say I've recovered from my divorce and God has brought complete financial restoration. It's just the "man thing." I try to be okay with being alone, but it's not working. When I come home after a long day at work, I want someone there waiting for me. When work is frustrating or difficult, I want to call my man and hear him tell me it's gonna be all right, and then give me a big, strong, manly hug when he sees me."

Lisa nodded. I knew she was feeling me because she had confided some of the same things to me before. Angela was listening intently, and I could tell Vanessa was already thinking of her response.

I continued, "And I want babies. I can't imagine

leaving this earth without having children. I think about my nieces and my nephews and how they're little versions of my sisters and brothers and I want that. Maybe that's egotistical, but I do. I want to shape them and mold them into the image of God. And I know I do that through volunteering with the youth at church, but . . . I just want babies of my own, that call me Mommy instead of Auntie or Miss Michelle."

I gazed up at Vanessa's wall with pictures of her two kids, Angel and Michael Jr., at various ages. Angel was an exact replica of Vanessa, and Mike looked like his dad.

Vanessa followed my eyes to her kids and smiled with pride as she took in the images of them.

"And I have so many visions and dreams for impacting the world and saving the lost, but I can't imagine doing them on my own. I need my man, my protector, my covering to be there leading me. I know we have a pastor, but I want my own man, covering my own household."

I flopped back on the couch. "And let's not even talk about sex. I've been celibate for three years and six months. That's almost four years with no sex. That's pure torture. Why would God create me with these overwhelming hormonal surges twice a month where I climb the walls and everything makes me think of having sex and then tell me I can't have none? Why would a loving God do that to me?"

Lisa laughed. "I feel you, girl. But God is faithful. It's been nine years for me, and it gets better over time. Just trust Him. He'll keep you."

"Nine years?" I looked at her like she was crazy. "I don't want Him to . . . I ain't trying to wait that long before I get some." I looked up at the ceiling. "God, don't even play. You know Your girl better than that."

Nicole and Angela fell out laughing.

My voice softened a little. "Please, God, don't make me wait six more years." I sat there for a minute, totally perplexed at the prospect that it could be that long before I could have sex. "God, Your Word says You know how much we can bear. All I'm saying is . . . please, God. You know me better than that. Nine years? Your Word says You'll supply my every need. God, I need—"

Nicole laughed. "Wow, that's a new one. Begging God for some sex."

Lisa sat silent. I hoped I hadn't embarrassed her. I sat up and reached over to grab her hand. "I don't mean no harm, Lisa, but, for real?"

She nodded.

"How?"

She shrugged. "I don't know. When the feeling comes, I try to read my Bible or pray or go work out or watch a movie or do whatever I need to distract me until the feeling goes away. I definitely don't read, watch, or listen to anything that would get my juices stirring, so to speak. Over the years, the urge has decreased."

I looked at Vanessa. "I know how long it's been for you. And you, Nicole, a little over two years, right?"

She nodded.

I looked at Angela, who had suddenly shrunken

back into the couch. "How long has it been for you?"

Angela looked down at her hands. She said something low and soft.

"What?" the rest of us said.

I suddenly wished I hadn't asked her in front of everybody. Maybe she was caught up in fornication and didn't want to be put on the spot.

Angela looked up at us and spoke louder. "Never."

"What do you mean?" Lisa and I said together.

Nicole sat there, wide-eyed.

"Never. I've never had sex." Angela looked down and rubbed her hands together.

We all sat there quiet.

Finally, Nicole let out a low whistle. "Whoa. I can't even . . . I mean I know the Bible says . . . but . . . never?"

Vanessa put an arm around Angela. "That's something to be proud of."

"Please." Angela rolled her eyes. "Who wants to be a forty-one-year-old virgin?"

None of us answered.

"Yeah. That's what I thought." Angela sat back and crossed her arms with a sullen look on her face. She was the newest to our group. Lisa had met her at the church we all attended about a year ago. She brought Angela for one of our weekly girls'-night outings and she'd been hanging with us ever since.

Vanessa said, "I'm sure each of us—if we had gotten saved when we were young and never got married—would love to be a forty-one-year-old virgin."

Angela looked around at each of us. Lisa and I nodded, reluctantly.

"Nine years and never. I need a drink." Nicole got up and walked toward the kitchen.

I looked at Angela as if seeing her for the first time. She wasn't ugly or anything. Nice trim shape, shoulder-length bob, cute enough face. She was sorta shy and quiet, but certainly that didn't disqualify her from being attractive to a man.

I did have to admit, she was a brainiac that didn't get out much. And I couldn't really see her approaching a man. In fact, whenever she was with a bunch of people, she faded into the background. She was more vocal with us, but in large groups, I had seen her become completely invisible. But still . . . never?

I looked over at Lisa and wondered why it had been nine years for her. Lisa was gorgeous. She had a perfect body and had even done some modeling in her younger days. And she was smart and successful. She worked as a fashion magazine editor.

Nicole returned from the kitchen carrying a tray with juice, water, crackers and fruit on it. She set it down on the coffee table. "I believe we've gotten off the subject. This is supposed to be a Michelle celebration. Not an Angela crucifixion." She grabbed an apple off the tray and plopped down on the couch next to Angela, giving her arm a squeeze.

I turned a couple of pages in the journal, not wanting to go into the next topic I had written about. "I look back at my marriage and all the mistakes I made and the choices that landed me here, divorced at thirty-five. I know it's basically because I was twenty-one and naïve when I got married. I'm not the same woman now that I was then."

I took a deep whiff of the lavender-scented smoke spiraling into the air from Vanessa's aromatherapy candle and hugged a throw pillow to my chest. "I was a little girl, in love with my high school sweetheart, being pressured because it was 'better to marry than to burn.' To be honest, even though it's wrong, I would have rather fornicated than to have ended up in a divorce court eleven years later."

Lisa's eyes widened, and she covered her mouth with her hands.

Nicole chuckled. "Come on, church girl. She's being real. If a little premarital sex would have kept her from marrying the wrong man, ending up broken-hearted and financially devastated, I don't think God would have minded." She took a big bite of her apple.

Vanessa cleared her throat. "I beg to differ. God puts those boundaries in place for a reason. And He doesn't change His mind for our fleshly desires. And who's to say having sex would've kept them from getting married?" She looked back at me, dismissing Nicole's statement. "Michelle, keep going."

"I feel like I'm a better woman. In a better place, able to make a better decision." I closed the journal. "Otherwise, I'm happy. My life is good, and I have so much to be thankful for. It seems ridiculous that this one stupid little issue can so drastically affect the rest of my life."

Vanessa shook her head. "Don't beat yourself

up. It's not a stupid little issue. Even the Bible says it is not good for man to be alone. That encompasses the male *and* female. God gave us the desire to be in intimate, loving relationships. Think about it. God created man to have someone to love and be in relationship with. Marriage is a good thing. It's a beautiful, God-ordained thing. And there's nothing wrong with desiring it. So stop being hard on yourself." She focused on her husband's picture on the wall.

I felt selfish for making her have this conversation. I knew she had done a lot of work to overcome her loss and grief, but there was still some sadness in her eyes when she talked about him. I guessed that never went away.

Her eyes moved to her children's pictures. Her smile returned. "God created us in His image as His children—so guess where your desire to have children in your image comes from? There's nothing more beautiful than having kids. Pouring into their lives, speaking into their spirits, watching them grow into who God ordained them to be. So don't be upset with yourself." Vanessa pulled her eyes away from her family picture wall and focused on me again. "My question is, what are you going to do about it?"

I frowned. "What do you mean?"

Nicole tossed her apple core into the trash can in the corner. "She means, you whine and complain about not having a man, but what have you done to make things any different? You work almost as hard as me, because you *want* to, not because you *have* to. Which is insane." She rolled her eyes. "You spend your free time at church or at

home by yourself or hanging with us. So, how are
you gonna find a man?"

"I'm not supposed to be finding a man," I said.
"He's supposed to find me. A man that findeth a
wife, findeth a good thing."

Nicole said, "Yeah, but how is he supposed to
find you? He would have to throw himself in front
of your car on your way to work. Where do you actually go where you can be found?"

I shrugged. "I don't know. Church, I guess."

Lisa humphed. "Girl, please. You can't find no
man in church."

Angela said, "What do you mean? That should
be the best place to find a man."

Lisa shook her head. "The good ones in church
are already taken. A good, godly man who's committed to living holy ain't gonna be single long.
He's gonna find the right one, marry her and settle
down. Any man that's been single long is fornicat-
ing."

Vanessa laughed. "Lisa, that's not true. There
are plenty of men who live celibate for sometimes
as long as we do."

Nicole chimed in, "Plus, I've seen you shoot
down guys at church."

My eyes widened. "Shoot down guys? What are
you talking about?"

Nicole pointed a finger at me. "What's that guy's
name in the youth ministry who's always trying
to talk to you after service? Darryl? Derrick? He's
single, attractive, available, yet every time he's
around, you avoid him like the plague."

"Derrick's not interested in me. He's just . . .
he's . . ."

Nicole put her hands on her hips. "He always stares at you, makes a point of talking to you every chance he gets. He's definitely interested."

"And what about the guy in the bookstore?" Lisa added. "You guys always talk about your favorite books and music, but then you cut him off and rush away when he tries to take the conversation elsewhere. You don't give guys a chance."

"You two are reading into stuff," I said. "They're not interested. They're just being nice."

"How do you know, if you don't give them a chance? You make a guy afraid to approach you." Nicole folded her arms. "Guys gotta know they have half a chance to get the confidence to step to you. If they feel like they're gonna be rejected, you can forget it. You get labeled as unapproachable, and that's it."

I thought about it for a second. Was I unapproachable?

Vanessa looked at me intently. I could see the psychologist wheels turning in her head.

"What Vanessa? Psychoanalyze me, oh wise one."

She narrowed her eyes but then smiled. "You're whining about how much you're waiting and trusting God to send you a man, but sounds like He's sent you at least two possibles who you've shot down without giving a chance. I have to wonder how many others there have been, and why you're running them off."

I sat and pondered that for a minute. Was I self-sabotaging? "I guess I need to look at that." I grabbed a cluster of grapes off the tray.

Vanessa looked around at all of us. "Are any of you guys a part of the singles' ministry?"

Angela raised a finger at the same time that Nicole blurted out, "Please—who wants to be a member of the desperate-and-lonely club?"

I winced.

Angela said, "Why do you have to call it that?"

Nicole made an apologetic face. "I'm just saying. It's a bunch of women that ain't got no man who get together for various social activities and talk about how to catch a man. I can do that with y'all."

Angela answered, "That's not what it is. We . . . we . . ."

"What?" Nicole asked.

"First of all, it's not only women. I admit that it is mostly, but there are some men. Second of all—never mind, Nicole. We're talking about Michelle."

All eyes refocused on me. "I guess I don't go anywhere where I can meet men. Or be found by a man."

"When was the last time you went on a date, by the way?" Lisa asked.

Now I felt like Angela. "Never, really."

"Huh?" Lisa said.

"Well, me and my ex were best friends in church up until high school. Then we started going together, and next thing I knew, we were getting married. And since him . . . well, it's only been the past year that I've gotten over the bitterness and anger to even think about another relationship. I've just kinda been waiting."

"So, God is supposed to drop you a husband right out of heaven?" Lisa asked.

I shrugged. "That would be nice."

Nicole and Lisa looked at each other in amazement then looked back at me. Lisa said, "Surely you know that's not gonna happen."

"I guess I go on five-minute dates. I meet a man somewhere, strike up a conversation, and within five minutes, I know he's not anyone I would be interested in." I grabbed a bottle of water off the table and twisted off the cap. "Either he's not godly, or he's boring, or his eyes are roaming all over my body, or whatever. Something just lets me know."

"Are you one of those super-picky women who finds something wrong with every man?" Angela scrunched up her nose.

I shrugged. "I don't think so."

"So you meet a guy, shoot him down in five minutes, and then move on to the next?" Lisa asked.

Everybody was studying me like a science project.

"No, sometimes guys make it past the five minutes, but then something jumps out that's a big red flag. I don't know. I just haven't met anyone I felt like I had chemistry with, or that I would consider building a future with."

"You're hopeless." Nicole stretched out on the couch like she was finished dealing with me.

Vanessa almost looked like she agreed. "So, what exactly are you looking for?"

"I don't know."

Lisa threw up her hands and flopped back against the couch. "This is too much. She has no idea what she wants but has the nerve to be picky about it." She rolled her eyes and then asked me, "You mean you don't have a list?"

"A list?" I asked.

"Yeah, a list of what you want." Lisa looked at me in disbelief. "The essentials, the would-be-nice's, the icing-on-the-cakes, the not-so-desirables, and then, of course, the deal-breakers."

I looked at Lisa, totally perplexed. "What in the world?"

"Hey, I believe in knowing what I want. Maybe you haven't found the right guy because you don't know what you're looking for."

I pondered that for a minute and shrugged. "When I meet him, I'll know."

Nicole and Lisa stared at me like I had three heads. Even Vanessa was giving me a strange look.

"You've watched too many chick flicks. Girl, that's the only place where love at first sight happens," Lisa said.

"I'm not saying love at first sight. I'm talking about . . ." What exactly was I talking about? How did I really think it was going to happen?

The perfect man would ring my doorbell one day. I would open the door and stare into his eyes, and he into mine, and then he would tell me he'd been looking for me all his life and he was the man I'd been praying for and God had answered my prayers. And then we'd get married. And he'd be perfect with no faults and flaws, and we'd live happily ever after.

Not much more realistic than my dream life at age seven.

Lisa said, "You're asking God for a man, but not

telling Him what you want. Aren't you always saying we should be specific when we ask God for something?"

I took a long swig of water, thinking. "Okay, he couldn't be financially irresponsible, couldn't be a cheater, couldn't be a liar, couldn't be a—"

"Wait a minute." Vanessa held up a hand. "You're saying you wouldn't marry your ex-husband again. We know that. We want to know what you want, not what you don't want."

"Lisa mentioned deal-breakers. I'm telling you what they are."

"Let's start with the positive stuff first. What do you want?" Vanessa asked.

I lay my head back against the couch and closed my eyes. *What did I want in a man?* "I don't know."

"Okay, we'll give you one week. We'll reconvene for girls' night next week, and we expect a complete list. Essential must-haves, would-be-nice's, icing-on-the-cakes, not-so-nice and deal-breakers. In that order," Lisa said.

Nicole looked at her watch. "Okay, hate to end the fun, but let's get the rest of this touchy-feely junk out of the way so we can get on to the big birthday surprise."

three

The rest of my birthday turned out great. After giving me more affirmations than I could stand, the girls took me to my favorite artsy-fartsy clothing boutique in Atlanta's eclectic Little Five Points and bought me a brand-new outfit. Then they took me out to one of my favorite restaurants, Top Spice. We ended the evening with a concert featuring my favorite neo-soul gospel artists—Darlene McCoy, Christopher Lewis, and Leon Timbo at the C-room—our favorite Christian nightclub.

The entire evening, I found myself looking around the audience at men. Most of them had a woman on their arm. I realized that was the case most of the time I went out. At most of the places I frequented, the men were already attached.

After our finding-a-man conversation, I found myself paying more attention to the guys at church on Sunday morning. Most of them seemed paired-up as well. It was the same at work on Monday morning. Anyone I found even the least bit desirable had the golden band of commitment on his left hand.

"Michelle, did you get a chance to look at the promo I edited last night?"

See—exactly what I was talking about. Mr. Eye Candy popped into my office door asking about some stupid spot, not realizing he was the last person I needed to see. He took tall, dark and handsome to new heights, depths, and realms. His dazzling smile of perfectly aligned pearly whites, parenthesized by deep, cheek-puncturing dimples, almost blinded me. His deep, dreamy eyes with long, thick lashes any woman would pay for—shoot, give her firstborn for—were expressive and caring. And I dare not talk about his body. That would cause me to sin.

"Huh?" I kept my eyes on my computer.

"The promo you asked me about. Did you get a chance to look at it?"

Sometimes I thought he did that on purpose. Pop up at my most vulnerable times with a chest-hugging sweater and perfectly tailored slacks, smelling like—manliness. Was that pure testosterone cologne he was wearing?

Yeah, the good ones were always married. I allowed myself a brief glance at Jason Hampton. Brief because, as I said, he was married and I wasn't trying to sin so early in the morning.

I looked back at my computer. "Sure did. Looks great, as always. I appreciate your hard work."

"You okay?" He leaned in, hovering over my computer.

"Yeah, I'm good. Why do you ask?" I looked up at him for a moment. Those eyes. *Jesus, keep me near the cross.* I quickly refocused my eyes on my computer screen.

"I don't know. You don't quite seem yourself this morning." He sat down in the chair across from my desk.

Perhaps I wasn't looking busy and focused enough. I opened up a file folder and leafed through some papers. I didn't need him caring about how I was feeling right now.

Jason was one of those ultra-nice, sensitive guys that was easy to talk to. He seemed to sense when I was having a bad day or was frustrated with something at work. He'd pop in my office, and I'd find myself spilling my guts about the latest office drama, programming issue, or production problem bothering me. We'd talk and strategize for a while, and next thing I knew, my problem was solved.

No way was I about to open up about my personal issues. Especially guy issues. We had always kept things strictly and completely professional, and I planned to keep it that way.

I looked up at him and gave a reassuring smile. "I'm good, Jason. Just a little tired from my weekend."

"Oh, yeah. Happy birthday. How was it?" He crossed his legs and leaned back in the chair, obviously not planning to go anywhere anytime soon.

"It was great. Spent an awesome day with my girlfriends. They celebrated me extra special. I couldn't have asked for a better day." *Except maybe to have had my husband and two daughters come into the room, bringing me breakfast in bed singing, "Happy birthday to you—"* I cut off the little fantasy before it got to playing in my head good.

"I'm surprised you didn't spend it with that special someone. How did your girlfriends rank higher than him?"

He clearly didn't know there was enough residual estrogen running through my body to either make me burst into tears or rip him a new one with a sleight of my tongue. He had never crossed the line between personal and professional like that before.

I looked at his dimply smile, its attraction fading at his blatant social violation in pointing out my lack of a man. He clasped his hands together and that's when I noticed.

His wedding ring was gone.

"Um, Jason, please don't take this as rude, but I cut out early on Friday to get ready for my birthday, and now I'm paying for it. I got a bunch of stuff to finish and can only hope to get out of here by eight tonight."

"Anything I can help with?" He leaned forward, flashing a perfect view of his pearly whites and almost anesthetizing me with his cologne.

"No, it's all stuff I gotta do." That was my last polite sentence. If he pushed me any further, he would get to see the ugly side of Michelle.

"All right then. Call me if you need me. You know where I'll be."

"Thanks, Jason."

He slowly rose as if he was waiting for me to

change my mind and remember that there was something he could help with.

I wheeled my chair around to the file cabinet behind my desk and pretended to look for a folder. When I turned back around, he was gone. *What in the . . . ?*

I tried to give Jason the benefit of the doubt. Maybe he'd taken off his ring over the weekend to complete some chore his wife had asked him to do. Maybe he had sent it out to be cleaned. Whatever the case, surely he wasn't trying to cross any lines with me. He had been my editor for the last two years, and we were a great team. He had never done or said anything out of line. He hadn't mentioned any problems with his wife, but then again, he never talked about his personal life either.

I repented for all the times I had told God I wanted a man like Jason. Sweet, sensitive, dedicated to his family, dedicated to his job, and conscientious. And we won't mention *fine*.

I forced myself to concentrate. Even though it wasn't as bad as I'd told Jason, I did need to get some serious work done. I had a deadline creeping up on me for a show idea for the next pitch meeting. I tried to focus for a few minutes, but the lingering scent of his cologne was a huge distraction.

My assistant popped her head in the door. "Going to get lunch. What you want?" She closed her eyes and sniffed. "Ummm, Jason was just here?"

I laughed. "Yeah, girl. He does leave a scent behind, doesn't he?" I tried to look normal, like that same scent wasn't about to drive me out my mind.

She walked into my office and sat down in the chair Jason had just occupied. "Ooh, girl. I don't see how you stand it. I could not have that man up in my face all day." She closed her eyes and took another deep whiff.

"Girl, you are too silly," I said. I really wanted to tell her to stop sniffing up all my Jason air.

She put a finger to her lips. "You know, you and Jason would make the perfect couple. You should go out with him." She nodded. "Yeah, you guys would be great together."

"Ummm, hello. Earth to Erika. Has the cologne killed off your brain cells? That man is married. You *know* I don't roll like that."

Erika stood, stuck her head out my door, looked both ways then shut my door and sat back down in the chair. "Michelle, where have you been? Jason's wife left him over a year ago. His divorce was final eight months ago."

My eyes flew open. "Jason's wife left him? He's divorced?" My heart started to flutter. "What! How do you know that?"

Erika squinted her eyes. "Everybody knows that. She left him for some Atlanta Falcons rich dude. He was all messed up. Don't you remember when he took that sudden vacation last year and came back looking a mess? Everybody was joking that he needed a vacation after his vacation. For months after that, he was looking crazy every day for a while. How did you miss all that?"

I scratched my head. I did remember his vacation last year and him coming back looking worse than I'd ever seen him. He blew off my concern by saying that he should have gotten more rest.

"How could all this happen and me not know about it?"

I felt like a bad friend. Jason had been going through pure hell, and I hadn't been there for him. In fact, I had pulled on him to help me solve my little problems here at work when he was experiencing a man's worst nightmare.

Then again, we weren't friends. We were co-workers who were careful about observing professional boundaries. Still, seems like I would have noticed something.

"I can't believe you didn't know all this. I guess y'all really do be working like you say when y'all be all huddled up in the edit suite for hours, huh?"

I raised an eyebrow at Erika's suggestion that something improper was going on while Jason and I were working behind closed doors. Maybe we needed to keep the door open or something.

"So, are you gonna scoop him up?" Erika was almost salivating. "Talk about a great catch."

I shook her suggestion out of my head. "Girl, don't be silly. That would never work. First of all, we work together, and it would be unprofessional. Second, he's fresh out of divorce court and needs some time to heal and put this all behind him before he even thinks about another woman. Third of all—"

"Okay, you keep adding to your list of reasons. In the meantime, some other smart woman will snatch him up, and you'll be sitting next to me at his wedding. Men ain't like women. Women get divorced and spend a year or two in therapy and crying to their girlfriends. Men find them a new woman and get remarried. They can't handle being alone after they been married. Their primary goal is to fill that spot so they can get on with their life."

I shook my head, more to get rid of the thought than to say no. "Erika, you know how the boss lady is. She strongly frowns on intimate relationships between co-workers."

"So." She sucked her teeth. "That didn't stop Randy from knocking up Brittany, now did it? And quiet as it's kept, everybody knows Richard and Sheryl are kicking it. So, you need to go 'head and get yours."

"That's different. Randy is a free lancer. Brittany is an administrative assistant. And Richard and Sheryl aren't upper level. They're under the radar. Ain't nobody paying attention to them." I lowered my voice a little. "And you know the deal. I want this promotion, more than anything. I can't afford to mess up."

Erica nodded slowly. "I guess so." She took another deep whiff of my Jason air. "Whatever, girl. You can get a new job. Where you gon' find another Jason Hampton? He is truly one of a kind. Sleep if you want to. I guarantee we'll be at Jason's wedding within a year. Now whether you'll be carrying the bouquet or catching the bouquet is up to you."

Erika took one final sniff, got up and left my office. As she closed my door, I heard her humming the wedding march, *"Dum da da dum. Dum da da dum."*

I looked back at my computer screen at my treatment, begging to be finished. *Yeah, right. Like there was any way I could concentrate for the rest of the afternoon with this new bit of information.*

I clenched my teeth, grabbed my mouse and scrolled up to the last thing I had written.

Reality television is the latest trend in programming . . .

Jason was divorced. Jason was no longer married and unavailable. Jason was single.

Viewers enjoy it because of the "anybody-can-be-famous" factor . . .

Jason is gorgeous. Jason is smart. Jason is sweet. Jason smells good.

This show would highlight individuals who are . . .

Jason is saved and attends church regularly. Jason keeps a Bible in his desk drawer that I've seen him take out and read on many occasions.

I had to concentrate. There was too much riding on this show. It could be the key to my promotion into a position where I had more input about programming. I decided to answer the nagging voice in my head.

Jason is freshly divorced. Jason is three years younger than you. You NEED this promotion.

Unfortunately, none of my thoughts overpowered the scent of his cologne still hanging in the air.

I pushed back from my desk and marched to the restroom down the hall. I grabbed the air freshener off the little shelf, concealed it in my suit jacket and marched back to my office. Once I got inside, I sprayed and sprayed and sprayed until I was sure there was no remnants of Jason left behind.

Of course, that was too much. My eyes watered, and I started choking. I tried to catch my breath, but every time I inhaled, my lungs filled up with the chemicals.

I stepped into the hallway, coughing. Erika looked up from her desk. I was sure I looked crazy—tears flowing from my eyes, stooped over wheezing, trying to get some fresh air.

She came running over and pounded me on the back. "What's wrong with you?"

I waved her away. "I'm fine," I gasped.

"You're not fine. Are you choking on a peppermint? Do I need to do the Heimlich?"

"Really, I'm okay." I tried to stand up and look normal. I took a deep breath and set off another coughing fit.

Erika took me by the arm and headed toward my office. I was creating a stir in the hallway.

"No," I croaked.

She stepped inside and attempted to pull me in. Instantly, her eyes started watering, and she started coughing. "What the . . . ?"

We both stumbled back into the hallway, in coughing fits.

"Why did you"—Erika's question was cut off by a cough. "Why in the world would you"—She coughed again.

I shook my head, not even trying to answer.

She walked toward the break room and waved for me to follow. When we got there, she grabbed a cup and filled it with water. She handed it to me, then poured another. We both drank. The coughing died down.

"Why in the world did you empty a can of air freshener in your office?" Erika looked around and leaned in close to whisper. "You had a bean burrito for breakfast again?"

I laughed. "No, silly." I took a big sip of water, crumpled my cup and threw it away. I walked back toward my office to avoid answering her question. But before I got out the door, I knew I was busted.

"Oh," I heard her exclaim. "Oh, uh-huh. I get it."

As I walked down the hallway, Erika broke into song again. *"Dum da da dum. Dum da da dum."*

Somehow I knew that stupid song would be in my head the rest of the day, as would the nagging thought—Jason Hampton was single and available.

four

Angela, Lisa, Nicole, and Vanessa sat around the table staring at me, waiting for me to spill it. My stupid list.

We were at Nicole's for girls' night. Her luxury penthouse condo in Buckhead pretty much said everything one needed to know about her. The two-bedroom palace felt like something a celebrity should live in. High ceilings, hardwood floors, a small, sexy kitchen with stainless steel appliances, granite counter tops and recessed lighting made us feel like we were cosmopolitan girls in a scene from *Sex and the City*. We crowded around her small breakfast table.

Nicole never cooked. She always picked up something from one of her "she-she-pooh-pooh" restaurants with elegantly named foods that exercised the taste buds, things like goat cheese and sun-dried tomatoes, and spices like rosemary, dill, and cilantro.

Nicole set out some glasses and pulled a bottle of San Pellegrino out of the refrigerator. I frowned.

I knew it was supposed to be chic and all, but I never understood why she paid so much money for some sour-tasting fizzy water.

Angela poured herself a glass and squeezed a lemon wedge into it. Lisa did the same. I gave Nicole a look, and she pulled me a bottle of Dasani out of the refrigerator. Vanessa held out her hand, indicating that she wanted one, too.

"Well," Lisa said, "tell us about Mr. Wonderful."

All eyes were on me. I felt ridiculous, but I knew they weren't going to let me out of it.

I flapped my piece of paper and cleared my throat. "To begin with, the essential must-have's." I twisted the cap off my water and scanned my short list. "He has to be a man of God, completely submitted to God, in love with God and all about God. I think that shrinks my choices to a very small pool right from the jump."

Vanessa frowned. I couldn't tell if she disagreed with my statement, or whether she didn't like the appetizer tray Nicole placed on the table. "I wouldn't say that. There're plenty of godly men out there." She looked over at Lisa. "And they're not all married." She looked at me again. "Remember, let's not be negative about this."

I nodded. "Okay, number two—he needs to be financially stable. He doesn't have to be rich or anything, although I wouldn't send him packing if he was. But he *has* to be able to manage finances. Third, he has to be a good father to his kids or potential father to my future kids."

Lisa's eyes widened. "You'd marry a man that already has kids?"

"Uh, yeah. I'm trying to be realistic. I'm thirty-five years old. I'm not sure of the likelihood of me finding a man without kids."

"Yeah, but you're supposed to be putting what you want, not what you'd put up with because you think you'd have to."

I thought for a minute. "I love kids, though. I feel crazy that I don't already have some. So, if he has some, that would be okay with me."

Lisa shook her head and gave me a look of pity. "Clearly you've never dated a man with kids. You wouldn't be saying that if you'd ever dealt with some crazy baby mama drama." She looked around the table for someone to agree with her.

Angela was her usual quiet self, and sat munching on one of the funny-looking appetizers from the tray. Vanessa shrugged like she had no idea what Lisa was talking about.

Nicole shrugged too. "I've dated men with kids. Let me remember." She scrunched her eyebrows and thought for a moment. "None of them had full custody. One of them had a cool relationship with his child's mother, so it was never an issue. Wait a minute—they were too cool, and it was an issue, because they ended up getting back together." Nicole frowned. "And the other, his ex-wife had moved out to California, so he didn't get to see his kids often."

Lisa grabbed a couple of appetizers from the tray. "All I'm saying is I've dealt with enough baby mama drama and bad Bebe kids that my list requires that a man have no children."

We all looked at Lisa like she was crazy.

"No children? As in, kids are a deal-breaker?" Vanessa asked.

She nodded.

"Ummm, Lisa, you're thirty-eight years old," I said. "What are the chances?"

"It's possible. Look, I believe in telling God what I want, then trusting Him to bring it." She folded her arms resolutely, as if there were no further discussion on the issue.

Nicole rolled her eyes. "I thought Michelle had a disconnect with reality. Anyway, Michelle, how many kids would you put up with?"

Vanessa frowned.

I shrugged. "I don't know. I'm guessing no more than two. Or if they're grown and gone, he can have as many children as he wants. Or if he's a great guy with three well-behaved children, I could see dealing with that. It depends on the situation."

"Okay, that's fair. What else?" Vanessa asked.

I had tried to wait, but I was starving. I picked up an appetizer—a weird, triangle-shaped, breaded thing with some type of filling. "He has to be intelligent, so we can have great engaging conversations." I took a bite. Wasn't bad. Tasted like teriyaki something.

"College-educated, professional degree?" Angela finally joined in the conversation.

"Uh, I guess. I mean, I would think he would need a college degree to be intelligent enough to keep up with me."

"What if he didn't, though? What if he never went to college, but is a smart guy who reads books all the time, and learned everything in the school of hard knocks?" Angela leaned forward, as if challenging me with the question.

"I never thought of that," I said. "I guess I wouldn't require a college degree, if he was smart enough."

"Are you sure about that? Like, would you date a bus driver or a cook or construction worker?"

I always wondered what made Angela decide to talk. She'd sit silent for up to an hour sometimes then, suddenly, something would interest her and she'd come from that private little world of hers and become totally engaged.

"Sure. As long as he's intelligent, well-rounded, and godly."

"Yeah, right." Lisa gave me that look of hers again. "You would date a construction worker? You would date a man that makes less money than you?"

All of us stared at Lisa. I said, "Ummm, yeah. Once again, I'm trying to be realistic. I make a nice bit of money and plan on making much more. It's possible that I'll make more than him. As long as he's not insecure and can handle it, I'm cool."

Lisa shook her head. "Call me old-fashioned. I think a man should make more money than a woman."

Nicole opened her mouth with disbelief. She started to say something, but then shook her head.

"What?" Lisa asked, as if she didn't sound completely ridiculous.

Vanessa looked at Lisa as if she had new understanding about her singlehood. "What else, Michelle?"

"That's about it. I'm not too hard to please," I said in Lisa's direction.

"That's all?" Nicole asked. "What does Mr. Right look like?"

I shrugged. "I don't know. I'm not particular about looks. It's more of what's on the inside of a man that matters to me."

Nicole chuckled. "Really, now?"

"Yeah. I mean, he should be pretty all right-looking, I guess. I can't see finding a perfect man who's godly, intelligent, financially stable and great father material and rejecting him because he might have a few extra pounds around his waist or because he doesn't look like Taye Diggs."

Vanessa nibbled on a teriyaki triangle and then said, "So if he was three inches shorter than you and weighed four hundred pounds, you'd love him just the same?"

I winced. "Uh, I guess."

Angela broke her silence again. "That's what you think now—that you're not shallow enough to be concerned about a guy's looks. Just wait until you date someone and he's not the cutest in the world. All of a sudden, everyone else will look cute and sexy, and he'll look uglier and uglier to you."

Everyone turned to look at Angela.

"What? I'm being honest. I know I'm not the prettiest girl in the world and don't have the most outgoing personality, but still, I want a guy that I find attractive. He may not be a model, but *I* need to think he's cute."

Vanessa put on her concerned therapist face. "You don't think you're pretty, Angela?"

"I don't have a Halle Berry face and Beyoncé body like Nicole. And I don't have perfect skin, a great smile and exciting hair like Michelle. And I'm certainly not a model like Lisa. Like Michelle said, I'm trying to be realistic. A guy I can pull won't be as cute as what any of them could pull."

Now we all had concerned looks on our faces.

"Angela, you're pretty. What are you talking about?" Nicole looked almost disgusted.

"Yeah. Okay. Let's face it. I'm a pretty nerd," Angela said.

"Well, there has got to be some fine nerds out there. We'll just have to find you one." Nicole leaned over and hugged Angela.

Angela laughed and pushed Nicole away. "A fine nerd?" She thought about it for a second. "Okay, I could do that."

We all laughed.

"Well, I ain't gon' lie." Lisa put her hands on her hips. "I want me a fine man. He has to be at least six-three, athletic and chiseled, great face, nice skin, nice hair or shiny bald. We'll be one of those stunning couples with beautiful children."

"How deep does the rabbit hole go, Alice?" Nicole asked Lisa.

"Huh?"

"This wonderland of yours. No *wonder* it's been nine years."

Lisa's eyes widened. She looked as if Nicole had slapped her. Funny how none of the rest of us reprimanded Nicole. It was another one of those times when she said what everyone else was thinking.

"I guess I'm an equal opportunist when it comes to men," I said. "I like them in all shapes, sizes, and colors. Just as long as he feels like God to me."

"Feels like God?" Angela asked.

"Yeah." I wrapped my arms around myself. "Whenever I spend time with God, He feels so sweet. I can feel how much He loves me. I always tell God I want Him to break off a piece of Himself and come down here and marry me."

Nicole looked at me like she had looked at Lisa only minutes before. "Ummm, Jesus already came and died, and unless you're buying that 'DaVinci Code' mess, he didn't have a wife and kids.

"I don't mean Jesus Himself. I'm just saying, someone who's so full of the Spirit of God, who has died to himself and let Jesus take over—so much so that he feels like God. He'll love me like God loves me. I hope I'm not sounding like Lisa, but I don't think that's too much to ask. Is it?"

Everyone sat silent for a few minutes, pondering my words.

Vanessa finally answered. "I know what you mean. That's how Michael was. When he held me in his arms and told me how much he loved me and would never let anything happen to me or the kids, or when he would wake me up with sweet kisses every morning, telling me how beautiful I was and how blessed he was to have me as his wife . . . I always felt like God had sent a part of Himself to earth to love me." Vanessa sighed. "It's not too much to ask, sweetie. In fact, make sure you hold out for that. That kind of love is the most precious thing on earth, and everyone should get to taste it. Even if only for a little while."

Nicole arose and slid into the seat next to Vanessa. She took her hand in hers and squeezed it tight. Vanessa laid her head on Nicole's shoulder. Angela took Vanessa's other hand and held it.

The room was silent. We could almost feel Vanessa's pain, raw and hollow, hanging in the air.

Vanessa sat up. "Lisa, you know I love you. But I think you should let go of this ideal man you've got made up in your head. I know God is a miracle worker, but what you're asking for isn't realistic. He sounds like something in a book or in the movies. You have to be willing to accept a man with flaws who may not look perfect, be rich, and have no children or issues from previous relationships. I think Michelle has the right idea in looking first and foremost for him to have the heart of God."

Vanessa turned to me. "Michelle, I think you've got a great start on your list, but it's missing some things. I guess you'll fill things in as you go, but try to be open and not rule out guys in five minutes. You may have great instincts, but you have to be careful about underlying internal stuff, like fear making you reject someone before you even give them a chance."

She turned to Angela. "And you, my sweet beautiful Angela, I want you to look in the mirror every morning and tell yourself how beautiful you are until you believe it. From this point on, you're not allowed to say anything bad about yourself or compare yourself to anyone in this room or on television or anywhere else. Okay?"

Angela nodded. "Okay."

Vanessa turned to Nicole. "And what about you?"

"What about me?"

"Underneath that tough, raw, honest, blunt exterior of yours, you are one of the most loving people I know. Are you gonna keep that all for yourself and us?"

Nicole shifted in her seat. "I . . . I'm just . . . I've just been . . . I don't know."

Vanessa squeezed her hand. "I know you think you're a strong, independent black woman who doesn't need a man, but what about some man out there that needs you—his helpmate? Loving, strong Nicole, who won't pull any punches, will always tell him the truth, but will love him so much, he'll believe he can take over the world. Think of what you're depriving some wonderful man of. Just because you're afraid of being hurt again."

"Hey! No psychobabbleology on me. You promised, remember?" Nicole got up and picked up the appetizer trays. She walked over and set them down on the counter and opened the oven.

Vanessa sat quietly, as if she knew that was all Nicole would take for the evening.

Angela took Vanessa's hand again. "What about you, *V*?"

"Huh?"

"Do you think . . . could you ever—"

Vanessa shook her head. "I don't think so. I can't imagine I would. For one, I have the kids to think about. To me, there's nothing worse than a woman bringing men in and out of her children's lives. And—"

"And what?" Angela asked gently.

"If by some miracle, I met someone as wonderful as Michael, I don't think I could ever chance suffering that kind of loss again. I'd drive him crazy with fear. He'd have to check in at least six times a day, couldn't drive at night or in the rain, no long trips. What man would deal with that?"

"So, then, I guess we're both in bondage to fear?" Nicole brought over a tray with little black cartons with steam smelling of lemon grass and Asian spices rising from them. She slid back into her seat next to Vanessa.

Vanessa took her hand. "Since you put it that way, I guess so, Nicki."

Nicole squeezed her hand tightly. "I guess we should do something about that, huh?"

Vanessa nodded. "You first. Talk."

Nicole leaned back in her chair. "Me? Are you serious?"

"It's only fair," Lisa said. "We've all been spilling our guts. Nine years and never, remember?"

Nicole let out a deep breath. "Okay." She looked around at each of us. "Okay." She sat fidgeting with her napkin for a few seconds. "My life before Christ was . . . was not so clean. I've been in a lot of relationships. I've had a lot of sex. And I've been hurt a lot of times. Love has always ended with me getting my heart broke."

Angela and Lisa looked shocked. Second to Vanessa, Nicole was my closest friend in our group, so I knew all her dirt.

"Yeah, me. Gorgeous Nicole with the Halle Berry face and Beyoncé body." She looked at Angela. "You might think you want it, but honestly, it's a curse. Men can't see past the way I look. And when you got a booty like this, and boobs like these, all men want is to sleep with you. They don't know that I'm smart or funny or loving or whatever else I may be."

I had never thought of it from that standpoint. I had to admit that, like Angela, I had compared myself to Nicole and wished my butt was bigger and my face prettier.

Nicole opened each carton of food on the tray, releasing a variety of steamy scents into the air. "And so, now, I feel like I'm good. I just got saved and I'm figuring this whole God thing out and I don't need anything to complicate my life right now. Quite honestly, I kinda hate men right now and don't want one anywhere near me. So . . ." Nicole opened a pair of chopsticks and shoveled some rice and vegetables on her plate.

Vanessa said, "Why don't we both work on our hearts then? I'll finish working through my grief and my fears, and you work through your bitterness and man–hatred. And maybe one day, we'll both be ready to try again. But until then, we'll be happy being single."

Nicole nodded and gave Vanessa a hug. "Okay, enough psychobabble for me. When my birthday comes around, remember tonight."

Everybody laughed. Nicole passed out chopsticks to all of us. "So, it's official. Angela, Lisa, and Michelle are on a mission to be found by their husbands. Me and Vanessa are gonna allow God to heal our hearts."

Angela heaped a noodle dish onto her plate. "In that case, you guys gotta come to the singles ministry meeting with me next week. It's a special meeting they do every year, and it always gets rave reviews. The topic is 'Things Your Momma Should Have Told You About Marriage.' They invite guest speakers from other churches in the city, and it's usually packed out. You guys gotta come with me." Angela was almost begging.

"Sounds interesting. I can think of hundreds of things I wish my momma had told me before she pushed me to get married," I said. "I'll go." I tossed the chopsticks and got up to get a fork from the kitchen. I was too hungry to be playing with some wood sticks.

Lisa nodded. "I'm in. When I get married, I ain't ever trying to get divorced, so I'm trying to learn everything I can."

"If you ever get married . . ." Nicole said under her breath.

Lisa smirked. "So, you going, Nicki? You never know, God may work a miracle and quickly heal your evil heart. You might be closer to marriage than you think."

Nicole rolled her eyes. "No way. Did anything I just said indicate that I have any desire to be a part of the desperate and lonely club?"

"Nicole," Vanessa and Lisa said together.

"Please, Nicole. Please go with us," Angela pleaded.

Nicole rolled her eyes and let out a sharp breath. "I hate it when you do that, Angela. You know I can't say no to you."

Angela clapped her hands together. "Good. We're all in then."

five

I stood outside our church, New Destiny Christian Center, waiting for Nicole. She was running late as usual. No way I was going into a meeting of the desperate and lonely club without her. I finally saw her Mercedes convertible drive up. She whipped into a parking space and rushed out of the car.

"Sorry, girl. Had this stupid meeting that didn't want to end. Had to fake cramps to get out of it."

I laughed and followed her into the church building. When we entered the large sanctuary, we saw Angela seated at the front. She must have been watching for us, because she immediately smiled and waved for us to come up to sit with her.

"Dang, now we gotta look *real* desperate and lonely," Nicole said, as we tipped down to the front trying to be inconspicuous, since the program had already started.

Angela reached over to squeeze our hands and

mouthed, "I'm glad you guys came. Lisa's on her way."

Our first lady, Stephanie Jackson, was already on stage, seated with four other women in comfortable-looking armchairs surrounding a coffee table—all particularly set up for our discussion tonight. I guess that, and the fact that they were all casually dressed in jeans, was supposed to make us all feel comfortable. First Lady continued speaking, "For some reason, when you're single, marriage is this perfect magical paradise women fantasize about. We want to present the reality of marriage—things you should know before you say, 'I do.' I don't want any one of you to ever say, 'Nobody ever told me marriage was like this.' Let me introduce to you tonight's guests."

She held the hand of the woman sitting next to her. "As most of you know, this is my best friend of many years, Stacia Bennett. She co-pastors with her husband at our sister church, Light of the World. She joins us every year, and as you know, she always tells it like it *t-i-is*."

Everyone cheered as Pastor Bennett waved at the audience. First Lady held out a hand to the second woman. "This is Cynthia Martin from Grace Church. She's a long-time friend as well." She pointed to the last woman. "And this is the newest addition to our panel, Cassandra Peyton."

Lisa came down the aisle looking flushed and harried. She slid onto the seat next to Angela. They exchanged a quick hug, and then Lisa reached to squeeze my and Nicole's hands.

First Lady Stephanie said, "We're going to start by having each guest speaker tell who she is and why she's here sharing with us tonight. Listen to their stories carefully."

Stacia Bennett took the microphone first. "As she mentioned, I'm a pastor, married to Pastor Tyrone Bennett for eighteen wonderful years now."

We applauded.

"I say eighteen wonderful years new, but they definitely weren't all wonderful. I left my husband four times within the first three years of our marriage."

A few gasps arose from the audience.

"Yeah, chile, I was convinced that my husband was the worst husband in the world and didn't know how to love me. Funny thing was, every time I prayed about it, God only told me about me. Looking back, I realize that most of the problem was me, not him. He's just as sweet and wonderful now as he was then. I was the one who was selfish, stubborn, and completely un-submitted. God had to change me, or our marriage never would have lasted."

She paused for a second and leaned forward in her chair. "My message to you single women tonight is make sure you're prepared for marriage." She paused again, I guess, to make sure it sank in. "The most important thing you can do while you're waiting for God to bring your husband is to get ready. The perfect example is Esther in the Bible. She was cleansed and purified for a whole year to be sure she was fit to be a queen prepared for her king. Should we do any less? Stop looking for the perfect man, and make sure you're the most perfect woman you can be for him. If I was my husband, I would have killed me about fifteen years ago." She looked out over the audience. "Right now, I want each of you to take a good, hard look at yourselves. Think about your character, flaws, and faults. What things do you do that would drive a man crazy? Are you selfish and self-absorbed? Are you a strong, independent woman who has no intention of submitting to a man?"

Everyone was silent.

She continued, "What is your attitude like? Are you depressed? Irritable? Demanding? Some of y'all are looking for a man with money. Where are you financially? What does your credit look like? Do you keep your house clean? Do you cook?

"How often do you lay yourself on the altar and ask God to purge you of everything that's not like Him? When was the last time you climbed up on God's surgical table and asked for a divine character operation? Begged Him to cut everything out of you that's not like Him?"

I could hear the pastor in her coming out. She acted like she was ready to get a good preach on.

"I drove my husband crazy because it was always I, I, I. One day my husband got frustrated and told me over and over that he wished I would die. 'I wish you would die. Just die.'"

Murmurs arose from the audience.

"Yeah, y'all. That's what I said too. Is this man gon' try to kill me in my sleep? Of course, that wasn't what he meant. He just wanted the selfish, self-centered woman in me to die, so Christ could live. Took me a while, but when I started to die, my marriage started to live."

Her voice softened. "What areas do you need to

die in? Are you completely submitted to the Lordship of Christ? Because if you're not completely
submitted to Christ, you can't fully submit to a
man."

She nodded that she was finished, and First Lady
motioned for her to pass the microphone to Cassandra Peyton.

"Good evening, ladies. I'm Cassandra Peyton
and I just celebrated two years of divorce after
five years of a horrible marriage. I hope that, from
what I have to share, you can avoid the same pain
in your life."

Shoot, I could teach this segment myself. But
then again, could I? Did I really understand what
went wrong? More importantly, did I know enough
not to make the same mistake again?

I perked up to listen closely to see if Cassandra
Peyton had learned something I might have missed.

Cassandra smoothed her fingers over her short,
natural hair. "I met this wonderful man who I just
knew was God-sent. We had a whirlwind dating
period and were married three months after we
met. The dating was great—every woman's ro-
mantic fantasy. Even the first year of marriage was
wonderful, but eventually, the real man came out,
and my life became a nightmare."

Murmurs rose from the audience.

Cassandra went on, "The worst part is, just like
these ladies, my husband was a pastor. Looking
back, for everything that ended up happening,
there was a little red flag sometime while we were
dating that, if I had paid attention, I would have realized who he was and gone running as fast as I
could. There are no surprises in relationships."

Cassandra lifted a finger to punctuate her point. "My message to you tonight, women of God, is *choose well*. Once you make sure you're prepared, make sure you choose a man who is adequately prepared as well. And I don't care how lonely you think you are or how bad you want to have sex, don't ever settle for less than God's best for you. You'd rather be alone and horny than married to the wrong man."

It would have been funny if she wasn't so serious.

"I let my biological clock talk louder than the Holy Spirit. If I had listened to Him, my marriage would have never happened. But I was lonely. And I was getting old. I wanted to be married and have babies like all my friends. So I ignored me, the Holy Spirit, my mom—everyone who had enough wisdom to know that I had no business marrying that man."

She picked up a bottle of water from the coffee table in front of her. She took a long sip, I think, to give us time to focus on what she'd said.

"Don't be so afraid of being alone and childless that you end up worse off. I was left completely devastated, broke, hurt, bewildered, betrayed, confused—every bad emotion you can name. I won't go into the details of what happened with my husband because he's still pastoring, and I wouldn't want to speak badly against a man of God."

Nicole leaned over and whispered in my ear. "Isn't there a Pastor Peyton in that big church out in College Park?"

I nodded.

"Didn't he just remarry, and he and his new wife are putting on a big marriage seminar in the fall?"

I nodded again. I was sure she was wondering, as I was, if this was Cassandra Peyton's ex. I respected the fact that she didn't want to speak badly of him, but couldn't help wondering what had happened.

Cassandra continued, "Ladies, asking some simple questions can save you a world of hurt. What kind of family did he grow up in? What was his childhood like? What past hurts has he not dealt with that could one day be an issue in your relationship? What is/was his relationship with his parents like? How many serious relationships has he been in, and how and why did they end? Has he ever cheated? What is his philosophy for managing his finances? What does his credit look like, and how did it get that way? What's the worst thing that ever happened to him, and how did he come through it? What is his prayer life like?"

I guess the questions she was telling us to ask gave us some clues into what happened.

"Don't be so googly-eyed in love that you don't see what's really there. I know it's hard because love and romance feels so good. And you can be blinded to the truth, or you see the truth but ignore it because you love the way it feels. Introduce him to your friends, your parents, your pastor. Maybe they'll be able to see the truth you're choosing to ignore. Is he submitted to the Spirit of Christ? When someone points out some area in his character that needs fixing, does he listen and seek the Lord to change, or does his pride get in the way? A man may not be perfect, but as long as he's willing to be perfected, completely submitted to the Lordship of Christ in his life, you've got something you can work with." She paused for a moment and then looked out over the audience and finished with, "Ladies, choose well."

She passed the mic to the last speaker. Everyone was completely silent.

I guess I needed to take Lisa's list thing a little more seriously. As if she heard my thoughts, Lisa leaned past Angela and looked down the row and raised an eyebrow at me. I nodded, acknowledging her I-told-you-so.

Cynthia Martin was the last to speak. "Good evening, ladies. I'm Cynthia, and I've been married twice. The first time ended in divorce after six years. I remarried five years after my divorce and have been married now for eight years. I have the wisdom of having been in a bad marriage and in a good marriage. I can tell you what made the difference in the two. My first marriage ended because I wasn't prepared *and* because I didn't choose well. I was twenty-two years old and didn't know who I was. I met what I thought was this great guy, but honestly, I didn't know who he was either."

She stood up and walked to the edge of the stage. "Some of you need to be focusing on who you are, what you want out of life, and who you are in Christ. Sometimes when we get married too early, we haven't had time to develop and figure out what we want out of life, let alone what we want or need in a husband. Who has God called you to be? What is your purpose? If you can't answer these questions, you're not ready for a husband.

"Second, make sure you take the time to heal whenever you end a relationship. The first year after my divorce, I dated several men, and all the relationships ended in disaster. Each one reminded me of my ex-husband. So, for the next three years after my divorce, I didn't date, or even think about talking to a man. I wanted to allow God to heal my heart, so I wouldn't carry any baggage into a new relationship. The worst thing you can do is punish a new guy for the sins of the previous one."

I nodded. That was the last thing I wanted to do.

"During my healing period, there were times I would sit on the floor and cry, yelling and screaming at my ex over the things he had done to hurt me. I then made sure I completely forgave him and dealt with the bitterness in my heart. I spent time in prayer and worship, allowing God's presence to heal me and make my heart new and ready to love again."

Cynthia put her hand on her hip. "Then, I spent time getting to know me, figuring out what I wanted out of life and getting to know God's perfect will for my life. Then I spent time figuring out what I wanted in a husband. I put together a list of everything I wanted and everything I didn't want. Ladies, if you don't have a list, don't go another day without making one."

Lisa leaned forward again. I rolled my eyes at her to say, "Okay, I get it." She smiled like she knew she had won the argument.

Cynthia walked toward the podium and leaned against it. "Make sure you have a realistic list, though. Some of your lists are so unrealistic, Jesus Himself couldn't live up to your expectations."

I leaned forward and gave Lisa the same look she had just given me. She answered my I-told-you-so look by holding up a hand.

Cynthia continued, "Once you have your list, don't compromise. I don't care how cute he is, how rich he is, how wonderful he seems—if he doesn't line up with what you want, let him go. Lowering our standards is what gets so many of us in trouble.

"And make sure he fits with your destiny. The last thing you want is a man to distract you from reaching God's purpose for your life. You should be able to come together and chase destiny as one. Instead of finding out how tall he is, how much money he makes, and what kind of car he drives, find out who he is in God. Does he know what his purpose is? Does he live a Matthew 6:33 life, always seeking first the Kingdom?"

Cynthia handed over the mic to First Lady Stephanie. She stood and said, "Ladies, let's give these awesome women of God a hand."

Everyone stood and applauded. After the applause died down, First Lady Stephanie spoke again, "To sum things up for the evening, women of God, it's so important that first you make sure you're prepared for marriage. It's not just about going to the gym to lose that thirty pounds so your body can be right. Some of you need to lay aside every weight and get your spirit right. Instead of going to get that new outfit that will blow his mind, outfit your spirit with the fruit of God's Spirit. Get your credit straight, your finances right, keep your house clean, learn how to cook, and get your attitude right. In every facet of your life, make sure you reflect the image of Christ."

The preacher in her was starting to come out as well. Some people said it was just a matter of time before she would be ordained as a minister in the church.

"Ladies, make sure your heart is healed from past relationships. Take the time to clear your heart of old wounds, hurt and bitterness. And, finally, know who you are in God, what your purpose and destiny is, and where you're going. And then when you're straight, make sure you know exactly what you want and need in a husband. Make a list and check it twice, and whatever you do, don't compromise. Be prepared and then choose well, so God will have something to work with in making your marriage strong and lasting.

"To take this 'choose well' advice one step further. The Bible says a woman is supposed to submit to her husband. Many women today are so independent and headstrong that they don't want to submit. But submit doesn't have to be a bad word. Marriage should mirror the relationship between Christ and the church. Christ loved the church so much that He gave His life. It's not about control and domination—it's about love and the ultimate sacrifice. I have no problem submitting to my husband, because I know he's completely submitted to God. I trust him with my life because I know how deep his love for me goes. Women, choose a man that you have no fears about submitting yourself to, because it's just like submitting to Jesus, the one who gave His life for you."

She stood at the podium. "The divorce rate in this country is more than fifty percent, and the church is no different from the world, where divorce is concerned. The devil is attacking the family, God's foundational institution for His kingdom in the earth. If Satan can get rid of strong godly families, then he has already destroyed the foundation for our society. Let's fight back by making sure we become strong families of God."

She gestured to the women on the podium. "I'd like to take some time now for questions and answers. There's a wealth of wisdom here that you single women can glean from."

The four of us gathered in the parking lot after everything was over and we had spent some time mingling and talking to other friends from the church.

We were all kinda quiet. Nicole finally broke the silence. "Y'all got this marriage stuff. I may not ever get married."

"Yeah, that was a little heavy for me, too," I said. "It goes deeper than being lonely and wanting a man. This thing is no joke."

Angela answered, "That's why I thought it was important for you guys to come. If we're on a mission to be found by our husbands, that was essential stuff."

Lisa said, "Everything they said was good information. Especially the 'choose well' and submission stuff. Girl, I don't know about all that. That seems like a bad word. I been living on my own for the past twenty years. All of a sudden, I gotta turn over my life to a man?"

"You said you wanted to get married," Nicole reminded her. "And I know you want to do it God's way, don't you? That's why y'all got that. I'm just learning to be submitted to God."

I kinda felt them. Even though I wasn't a neck-twisting, mouthy, headstrong woman, I had gotten used to my independence over the past three years. Submission did seem like a bad word.

Angela spoke up, "Yeah, but you guys got so caught up on submission that you missed the most important thing she said. If a man loves you as much as Christ loved the church, then it should be easy. Imagine a guy that loves you enough to die for you."

"Girl, when you find that man, let me know." Nicole held up a peace sign. "All right. I did my duty and came like you asked me to. I'm out."

"Yeah," I said. "I'm tired and need to take it on home."

We all hugged and headed to our cars. As I started up my car, my phone beeped, indicating that I had a text message. I looked at the screen and saw it was from Lisa.

Girl's night at my house next week. Bring your laptop!

Oh, dear. I couldn't even imagine what foolishness Lisa had dreamed up.

six

On Monday morning, I sat at my office desk and said a silent prayer. The day had come for me to pitch my show ideas at the programming meeting. I had dreamed about them for years, worked on them for months, and refined them over the past few weeks.

God, I believe it's Your will to change the way Black television looks. Please give me favor in this meeting. Help me not to be nervous. Touch their hearts and cause them to hear Your heart. I know this is You. Go with me.

I grabbed my treatments and headed down the long hall to what I hoped was a new future for me and programming for our station. I entered the room and knew all the other producers wondered what I was doing there.

Especially Rayshawn Jennings. She gave me one of those up-and-down, you-ain't-nothing, what-do-you-think-you're-doing-here looks that only a sister can give.

I ignored her and headed toward an empty seat

near the head of the table. I got other glances from some of the other producers—not as evil as Rayshawn's, but still a closed-door, you-don't-belong-here type of look. Their faces made it clear—I was a promo producer that did spots to promote their shows. I had no business in this meeting.

I got a smile from the one person in the room who counted—Phyllis Carter, the VP of programming. She had come to my office weeks ago and said she had been looking over my spots and liked my eye. She mentioned what I already had heard. A large chunk of money had come to the station that would allow us to do more original programming. So, in addition to the music video shows, syndicated sitcom favorites, and church programs on Sundays, the station would be creating more of its own shows. We already had a few talk shows and news shows of our own, but now we'd be able to really create our own niche in the market. We were still a small network, but this chunk of money could allow us to enter the ranks with BET and TV One.

I sat down at the table, a few seats from Phyllis Carter. She nodded to acknowledge me.

Clearing her throat, she indicated that the meeting was to begin. "Okay, everyone. As you all know, we're getting ready to produce more original programming for our fall line-up. I've asked each of you to come up with at least two show ideas to pitch. Let me hear what you've got." She looked over at one of the senior producers. "Mark, you first."

Mark presented a sports talk show idea and a sports reality show idea. I didn't particularly care for either one of them, seeing that I wasn't into sports. The guys around the table seemed to like them, though.

It was hard to read Ms. Carter's face. She simply nodded and said, "Thanks, Mark. Sounds good. Rayshawn?"

Rayshawn put on her best fake smile. She was such a brown-noser. She was evil as a snake to her production assistants and editors to the point where no one wanted to work with her. Around Ms. Carter though, she was sickeningly sweet. I had to admit she was a great producer, which I guessed was why she thought she could get away with her diva, serve-me attitude. Right now, her shows were the highest rated at the station, and she made sure no one forgot it.

"In looking at the market right now, reality shows are hot. I think we would do well to continue to ride the wave. They're cheap and easy to produce. They're also quite engaging for the audience because they appeal to the 'anyone can be a star' in all of us."

She pulled out her treatment. "My first idea is a reality show about girls who want to become music video dancers. In the tradition of *American Idol* and *America's Next Top Model*, we get girls from all over the country who want to be dancers. They go through the audition process, learning how to dance and dress to fit the videos. They'd compete with each other, eliminating one person per show. At the end, the winner gets to be in the latest video by the hottest rapper at the time. We can have rappers as the judges, which will increase our ratings because of the star factor. I've already got connections with Nelly, Young Jeezy, and Ludacris, who could be potential judges."

I looked around the table to see if anyone else was as disturbed by her idea as I was. Just what we needed. Another television show to degrade Black women. What would we call it, *Pimping My Hoes*? I shook my head in disgust.

"What?"

I looked up to see Rayshawn looking straight at me. My eyes widened. Nicole always said I needed to learn how to have a poker face. I hoped my look didn't express what I was thinking. "Huh?"

"You look like you have a problem with my idea." I could tell Rayshawn was having trouble keeping her nasty attitude in check. She glanced at Ms. Carter and smiled a little.

I shrugged and shook my head, hoping to deflect everyone's attention from me.

No such luck. Ms. Carter put me on the spot. "Michelle, if you have some thoughts, don't be afraid to speak your mind."

Should I lie and pretend I liked the idea to keep the peace and avoid the wrath of Rayshawn? I could almost see the Holy Ghost glaring at me, arms folded, tapping His foot, saying, "Speak *My* mind. I put you here for a reason. I got your back."

I took a deep breath. *Then help me, Holy Ghost.* "Well...I...I'd have to say..." I took another deep breath and pretended my sistergirls were around the table rather than cutthroat producers vying to have their shows picked up. "I think music videos have done a lot to affect the way Black women look at themselves. And the way society looks at us. We've become sex objects dressed in scant clothing, dropping it like it's hot. No brains, just sex. Our value is in having big booties and boobs and being able to shake them until a man loses his mind. And young girls are buying into it. We owe it to our youth not to continue to promote these images. I volunteer with a church ministry for inner city youth, and the way some of the young girls dress is ridiculous. Sometimes I have to stop them from imitating dances they see on television. They're twelve years old and want to dress and dance like strippers. And I think Black television is responsible for it. So, to have a television show that promotes it . . . I don't think . . . I think we have to be accountable for what we put on TV."

Silence. I could almost hear crickets.

Rayshawn glared at me. None of the other producers said a word. Ms. Carter didn't say anything either. Which made me most nervous. I guess her silence gave Rayshawn the confidence to speak.

"I appreciate your concern for the youth, but I think it's important at this stage of the game to go with what sells. BTV is at a point where we need to break into the market to compete with the well-established Black stations. And regardless of your opinion, Black music videos are hot. I don't think it's smart to bring your personal, religious, holier-than-thou views into decisions we make about programming."

Perhaps I shouldn't have mentioned volunteering with the church youth ministry. Even though that was my foundation, it didn't have to be a Christian issue. Just plain old self-respect. Respect for Black women.

I could tell, from Rayshawn's holier-than-thou

slam, that I had offended her. I studied her. She probably didn't think there was anything wrong with the girls in the videos. She was the only woman I knew who could make Prada look sleazy.

"Any other thoughts?" Ms. Carter looked around the table.

No one even breathed.

"Rayshawn, your other idea?"

Rayshawn glared at me as she pulled up her other treatment. "My second idea . . ."

I tried not to pay attention. That way, if I didn't like it, it wouldn't show on my face and I wouldn't be forced to voice my opinion. I blocked out her voice and reached for the Holy Spirit on the inside. *Did I say the right thing? What did Ms. Carter think? Will she like my show ideas? Should I just leave now?*

He didn't answer with words, but I felt His peace wash over me. My soul was flooded with confidence.

"Michelle, you're up next." Ms. Carter nodded at me.

The Holy Spirit graced me with one more wave of peace, and it was on. "My first idea is also for a reality show. As Rayshawn said, it's what's popular in television now and it's cheap and easy to produce." I smiled at Rayshawn as if to say I appreciated and respected her wisdom. She fake-smiled back.

"My first show is called *Destiny's Child*. We would go into the inner city and audition youth who would normally be at risk for teenage pregnancy, drugs, gang violence, and highlight their talents. We would have them compete in the areas of dancing, singing, music, producing and allow them to be mentored by some of the best in the industry. The show would go in-depth into their lives and the obstacles they have to face to make it. Deal with their difficult family issues, poverty, drugs, but show their strength in being able to overcome it to succeed at their dreams."

Ms. Carter nodded, as did some of the other producers around the table.

Rayshawn was, of course, the first to speak. "I don't know. It's . . . it's kinda . . . ." She wrinkled her nose and frowned. "It's cliché."

Like video hoochies weren't.

She went on, "I mean, it's a sweet little idea and all, good bleeding-heart stuff, but I'm not sure it would be strong enough to grab and hold people. They might watch it once and think it's cute, but it may not draw them enough to want to watch it every week."

Mark spoke up. "I disagree, Rayshawn. It could be gripping. Show some kid whose mom is on crack and father is in prison but he has this dream to sing or be a producer. A young girl who wants to dance, but instead of wanting to be a video girl, she wants to do ballet or dance on Broadway. I think it could work. I would watch it."

I wanted to hug Mark. Not only was he supporting my idea, he was also agreeing with my dislike for Rayshawn's video girl show. In a subtle way, but clear nonetheless. Other nods around the table assented as well.

Ms. Carter nodded. "Michelle, your second idea?"

I squared my shoulders, more confident since

my first idea had done fairly well. "When I first moved to Atlanta, one of my favorite things to do was go out to listen to live music in some of the jazz and neo-soul clubs here. There are a lot of independent artists who are extremely talented—better than some nationally released artists—but who haven't gotten that big deal to put them in the national limelight. I'd love to do a show called *Indie Artist* to highlight independent artists. We'd have them perform live before an audience then do brief interview segments—what made them choose music, their struggles with making it and whatever else makes their story unique. We could start with artists here in Atlanta, but I'm sure they have underground enclaves in Philly and DC and other metropolitan cities, as well. The show would have a real artistic, eclectic vibe to it."

This time, I got nods from almost everyone at the table. Even Rayshawn looked interested, in spite of herself.

"I like it," Ms. Carter said. First opinion she'd expressed all day.

Thanks, God. I tried not to smile too big.

There were a few other producers to present after me. A couple of them had cool ideas. The other sounded like a Rayshawn disciple. Stick with what's already selling in the market and promote negative black stereotypes.

When we all finished, Ms. Carter spoke, "I like some of what's been presented here, and I'm confident that we'll have more than enough good ideas for our fall lineup. I do want to say that I'm not necessarily looking to duplicate what's already out there. I'm looking for fresh ideas that will give our station a brand different from the status quo. I'm also not looking to propagate already existing stereotypes of what Black television is. I think we should be cutting edge. This is the vision of our CEO—to do something different. Know that some things will be changing around here."

My ears got hot. Was she saying what I thought she was saying? I looked up to see Rayshawn glaring at me. Apparently, she'd heard the same thing I did. I looked up at God. What had I done? I was *not* trying to be enemy #1 of the station's top producer.

But then again, if I got a chance to represent God and change Black television, maybe I was.

Jason and Erika were waiting for me in my office when I got back. I closed the door, sat down and took a few deep breaths.

"How did it go?" Erika put a cup of chamomile tea on my desk.

I inhaled the sweet, tangy steam. I could tell she had put the perfect amount of lemon and honey in it. "I think okay." I picked up the mug and blew on the tea.

"You think okay? What happened? What did they say? Did they like your ideas? What did Rayshawn pitch?" Erika seemed exasperated at having to pull the information out of me.

"Give her a sec, Erika. I'm sure it was a tough meeting." Jason sat in the chair across from my desk. I could tell he was as anxious to hear about the meeting as Erika was, but knew I needed a minute to calm down.

I gave him an appreciative smile and then ran

down the details of the meeting, discussing the different show ideas and people's responses. "Ms. Carter collected everyone's treatments and will get back to us in a few weeks."

Erika sat on the edge of my desk. "That Rayshawn is such a skeez. Video hoochies? She looks like she may have taken a dance on a pole in her early days. And no telling how many people she slept with to get to where she is now."

"Erika . . ." I gave her a disapproving look.

She sucked her teeth and rolled her eyes. "What? Girl, I'm just saying what you know. I know you a Christian and can't say bad stuff about people, but think about it. How did she get to be top producer around here?"

I knew she was referring to the rumors that Rayshawn was sleeping with one of the station's owners.

I frowned. "She's a good producer. She may have a nasty attitude, but she's good at what she does."

"Please. She ain't that good. She hoards the best assistants and editors and terrorizes them into doing their best work. The people around her make her look good." Erika folded her arms. "Tell her, Jason."

Jason had worked with Rayshawn before switching over to promos. Seemed like a step backward to me, but he had requested it. Jason said, "I wouldn't say that exactly. I would agree that the people around her work hard and it reflects well on her. And I agree she's not the easiest person to work with."

I could tell he was choosing his words carefully. "Is that why you switched over to promos?" I realized I had never asked before.

Jason rubbed the back of his neck. The conversation was obviously making him uncomfortable. "Sort of."

Erika put her hands on her hips. "Why don't you tell the whole truth?"

Jason sat quietly.

Erika glared at him and turned to me. "Let's just say that in their late-night edit sessions, Rayshawn wanted to get busy at more than editing."

Jason winced and stared out the window.

"What do you mean? She hit on you?" I asked. "Weren't you married at the time?"

"So." Erika sucked her teeth. "That don't mean nothing to man-eating Rayshawn. And she's used to getting what she wants around here."

We both looked at Jason. He finally let out a deep breath. "She was . . . flirty at first." Jason looked like he had a bad taste in his mouth. "And then I guess because I ignored it, she got . . . bolder." He grimaced. "I told her over and over I was married and not interested, but that didn't mean anything to her. So, I went through all the proper channels, but for some reason, everyone wanted to look the other way and didn't take me seriously. So I decided to switch departments. It's in the past now, and I'd like to keep it there."

Erika smirked like Jason had proved her point about Rayshawn and the station owner.

We all sat silent for a few minutes until Jason finally said, "I'm glad they liked your ideas. I'd like to see some changes around here, and you're the perfect person to bring it. I'm sure God is gonna hook you up with a senior producer spot. Don't forget about us little people when you move up in the world."

"I have every intention of taking you guys with me. If I get to do a show, I'll still need a production assistant and an editor."

"Yeah, but that doesn't mean you get to pick. You're not Rayshawn," Erika said.

"We'll see." I patted Erika's arm and glanced over at Jason. "I can't imagine working in this place without you guys, so God's gonna have to work it out."

After the two of them left my office, I flipped through the pages of my treatments and thought about the meeting. *God, please let them choose one of my ideas. I know it's Your will for me to get this promotion. Isn't it?*

seven

M e, Angela, and Nicole took our shoes off as we entered Lisa's house for girls' night. Vanessa couldn't make it because Mike Jr. had a game.

Lisa's house reminded me of a high-priced art gallery. Dark hardwood floors, large windows, neo-modern furniture, abstract sculptures and artsy photographs everywhere. Models in high fashion, still life photos of gripping scenes, and an amazing Gordon Parks collection.

Lisa dressed in themes, depending on her mood. Tonight, she must have been in what she called her peaceful Zen mood, because she had on a pale green, silk kimono with her long hair held up with those plastic stick things. She led us down her long hall filled with pictures of a recent photo shoot of herself and a set of her own amateur photographs she took with her latest new camera.

When we got to the kitchen, she gestured toward a stack of paper plates, cups and plastic forks on the counter. "Tonight we have to talk about where we're going to be found by our husbands." Lisa removed aluminum foil covering trays of food on her stove.

"This should be fun." Nicole's sarcasm cut through the air.

Lisa ignored her. "If we only go to work, church and then hang out with each other, we'll never get married. We have to strategically place ourselves in situations where we can be found."

"Such as?" I was starving.

Lisa had one of the restaurants she used for her photo shoots send over dinner. There were grilled chicken breasts with some sweet-smelling orange sauce, pasta with vegetables, fresh salad, fluffy rolls, and huge brownies.

Angela hovered as if she was as hungry as I was.

"The question is, where do saved single men go?" Lisa indicated for us to go ahead and fix our plates.

Angela and I grabbed our plates, and I stabbed a chicken breast like I thought it could get away. Angela raked a heaping dose of pasta onto her plate and then attacked the salad. Nicole stood back from our feeding frenzy, acting like she was afraid to get in harm's way.

"The same place everybody else goes. You act like they're some precious endangered species with special habits. They go grocery shopping, to the movies, out to eat . . ." Nicole picked up a plate and inched toward the counter, checking to see if Angela and I were done fixing our plates.

Angela sat down at the kitchen table. "My friend, Tonya, says there are three great places to pick up men. The grocery store, later at night. The married men are home with their families, so if you see a guy after eight, he's probably fair game. She also says Lowe's or Home Depot. These guys are homeowners and care about working on their house. She says to go there after work while you're still dressed in your business clothes, looking sexy and successful. And then she said coffee shops, especially ones in bookstores. Men there are either readers or they're meeting someone for business. Whichever the case, they're probably intelligent."

I looked at Angela with newfound respect and sat in the seat next to her. "Wow. That's pretty impressive."

Angela nodded, cut off a huge chunk of chicken, and stuffed it into her mouth.

Lisa joined us at the table. "So, have you tried it?"

Angela frowned and shook her head, still chewing her chicken. She strained to swallow, and for a second, I was afraid she would choke.

"Why not?" Nicole sat in the empty chair next to Angela.

Angela shrugged and finally swallowed. "I'm not like that. I'd never go up to a guy or introduce myself, and I'm not the kind of girl who guys notice and introduce themselves to. I tried it once—at the Starbucks in the Barnes & Noble—for hours. I saw a lot of cute guys. And a couple of them actually talked to other women while I was there. But nobody approached me."

I could hear the pain in her voice. I sensed that Angela was worried she'd never meet anyone. I wish I knew someone perfect I could introduce her to.

"A lot of married people I know were introduced by someone," Nicole said. "They said to tell everyone you trust that you're looking and to think about someone they know that you might hit it off with."

Angela cut another huge bite of chicken. "It's still hard for me when I first meet someone. You guys know I'm shy. I scare guys off because I don't know what to say."

"Then what I have planned for tonight is perfect." Lisa got up from the table and disappeared down the hall. She returned with her laptop in hand and sat back down.

Angela, Nicole, and I frowned.

"Online dating." Lisa turned on her laptop. "You guys brought your computers, right?"

Nicole sucked her teeth. "Please. You could have saved me the trouble. There is no way—"

Lisa waved a hand at her. "We know you're not going to do it." She looked at me and Angela. "I'm talking to them. You guys up for trying it?"

I shook my head. "No way in the world. I ain't no desperate girl who has to go plastering my face all over cyberspace to find a man. That doesn't even seem godly."

"Why not?" Lisa challenged. "Think about Angela here, who's too shy to meet a guy in person. It's a perfect chance for her to get to know someone ahead of time, share some conversation in a non-threatening way, and meet someone she may have never met. What's so ungodly about that?"

"And what's up with you and Nicole calling me desperate all the time?" Angela's lower lip trembled.

"We never called you desperate." Nicole leaned closer to Angela and slipped an arm around her.

"You said I belonged to the desperate and lonely club at church, and Michelle just said I was desperate for trying online dating."

Lisa's eyes flew open. "You've tried it?"

"Yes, I have." Angela sat up in her chair. "For a couple of months now. Can't say that I've met anyone magical, and I haven't gone on any dates from it, but I've gotten a little more comfortable with the whole dating thing. Guys see my profile and tell me I'm beautiful and that they want to get to know me better. Granted, some of them are twenty years older or can't spell worth a darn and obviously missed grade school grammar, but at least I'm out there trying."

Angela shrugged off Nicole's arm and pulled out her laptop. "I'll show you my profile."

I sat there amazed. Angela dating online? Who knew? Nicole bit her tongue. I could tell she was afraid to say anything for fear of hurting Angela's feelings.

"What?" Angela saw right through her. We could all tell when Nicole was itching to say something, but decided not to. It was rare, but it did happen—usually for Angela's sake.

"I don't care what you guys think." Angela cut her eyes at Nicole. "I'd rather be in the desperate and lonely club than the old, bitter, and lonely club."

Ouch. I winced.

Lisa chimed in, probably to defuse the situation. "I've been wanting to try it and actually created a profile on different sites, but haven't responded to anybody yet. Angela, you've inspired me."

I shook my head. "I don't know. It seems weird. What kind of guy has to find a woman online? I can't imagine anyone I'd fall in love with having to find a woman that way."

"Why do you say that? It's the computer age. We do everything else on the Internet—buy clothes, books, cars, you name it. Why not date?" Angela's voice had more courage and defiance in it. "Especially for busy women like us. It's much more time efficient than hanging out at Lowe's or in coffee shops for hours."

"Seems like something's wrong with them if they have to do it that way." I pushed my plate away and rubbed my stomach.

"Is there something wrong with me?" Angela put a hand on her hip.

"No. You're shy—like you said." I tried to think of a time we had seen Angela this fiery. This was definitely the most I had ever seen her talk.

"Are you powered up? Let's see your profile." Lisa peered over Angela's shoulder. "Which service did you try?"

"Match.com, Christianpartners.net, Blacksingles .com, and Yahoo personals. Oh, and eHarmony."

Nicole whistled. "Dang, Angela. You're a regular cyberho."

Angela giggled and elbowed Nicole. Obviously, she was forgiven. Angela said, "The Bible says to cast your bread upon many waters."

Lisa said, "I'm trying eHarmony. I figured if I

went high budget, there'd be a better caliber of guys on there. Plus, I like the fact that they match you on your personality."

Angela nodded while typing on her computer. "Took me forever to make it through all the questions. It's intense."

"Exactly," Lisa said. "Makes me all the more confident that the guy I might meet could be the right one."

"Yeah, but what if you answer one question the wrong way and end up getting paired up with the wrong guy?" I asked, still not convinced it was anything I wanted to try. I couldn't imagine plastering my picture and personal information on cyberspace for all the world to see.

Desperate and lonely girl seeks any man willing to have her.

What if someone I knew saw me on there? How embarrassing. It didn't seem like trusting God. A Christian woman posting an ad to sell herself on the Internet? Nah. I couldn't do it.

Angela turned her computer around for us to see. Lisa sat next to me, and we both leaned forward to look at the screen. There was a fuzzy picture of Angela, in a white coat, working in her lab.

Lisa used the touch mouse to scroll down, shaking her head the entire time. "This is all wrong, Angela."

"What?" Angela's eyes widened.

"First of all, you've got this terrible picture on here. No one can tell how pretty you are, and you look like a nerd in the lab." Lisa held up a hand to ward off Angela's protest. "I know you are a nerd in a lab, but that's not the first impression we want to give. We're gonna have to take some better pictures of you to post."

Lisa stared at the screen for a few seconds more. "And you shouldn't put your PhD or your income on here. It invites predators and scares off men intimidated by a woman who makes more money than them. Put *you'd rather not say*."

"Yeah, but it's the truth. If they're intimidated by it, I'd rather not be bothered."

Lisa shook her head. "And you didn't answer any of the questions at the bottom to give them a better look at your personality."

"That's because Tonya said men never read, they only look at the pictures," Angela said.

"Exactly—those are the men you don't want. The ones that actually take the time to read your profile are the ones you'd more likely be interested in. And if you know they're only looking at the pictures, why would you put such a yucky picture on there?"

"Because I want them to be attracted to me for me. That way, they don't have to be disappointed when they meet me. If I put some glamour shot on there and then show up looking like my regular self, they might turn around when they see me."

Nicole frowned. "Have you been doing those affirmations Vanessa told you to do?"

Angela shrugged. "I just believe in being realistic."

Lisa patted Angela's hand. "Sweetie, you must remember men are visual creatures, ruled by what their eyes can see. You have to dazzle them with your looks first, then they'll realize how wonderful you are once they get to know you. Looks first. Personality second."

I didn't like how that sounded.

"So, you're saying I should project some false image of myself to get a guy interested, then reveal who I really am?" Angela asked.

Lisa shook her head. "I'm not saying a false image. I'm saying your best image."

"What if my best image isn't how I look every day?"

"I guess I'd have to ask why not. Why don't you look your best every day?" Lisa walked over to the kitchen counter and grabbed a huge brownie off the tray. She split it in half and gestured to each one of us to see who wanted it.

I had never been one to turn down chocolate. I started to accept it, but decided I wanted a whole one. I pointed to the plate for her to pass me my own.

Angela accepted the other half of Lisa's brownie. "I like how I look every day. I know it's not necessarily what guys would think is beautiful. So it's my best, but not their best."

I'd had enough. "Why don't we glam ourselves up and auction ourselves off on eBay? I can't believe we're having this conversation. I can see worldly women talking like this, but not Christian women."

"What do you suggest? I'd love to hear your plan," Lisa said, with Angela nodding in agreement.

I looked at Nicole for support.

She shrugged. "I got nothing."

"That's what I thought," Lisa said. "When you come up with a better plan, let us know. Otherwise, you can remain dateless, while we put ourselves out there to be found."

Lisa typed on her laptop. "Check out my matches so far on eHarmony. I deleted most of them because they didn't meet my requirements, but there are still a few I'm thinking about communicating with. I like this one the best so far. Only problem is, he's in D.C."

Curiosity got the best of me. Lisa turned her computer around, and I looked at the screen. A gorgeous cutie smiled back at me. I read his profile. Lawyer, committed to God and serving in his local church. Last good book he read was *The Audacity of Hope*. I had to admit he looked interesting.

"Well?" Lisa asked.

"There has to be something wrong with him." I looked down at the screen again. "A good-looking lawyer in the Chocolate City who can't find a woman? Please."

"Maybe he's like us. Maybe he's looked and can't find the right one. Maybe he's tired of dating chicken-heads and gold-diggers and is hoping the computer will match him with someone more suited for him. Maybe he's shy and doesn't approach women well. Who knows?" Lisa looked down at his picture and raised an eyebrow. "I'd say it's definitely worth finding out."

Angela chimed in. "What can it hurt? At worst, it's doing research to see what's out there and what's available. Maybe the Black man crisis isn't as bad as we think. I've seen a lot of seemingly nice guys online that are successful and available. Maybe there's more of a problem of hooking up than anything. If nothing else, it's a fact-finding mission."

Nicole rolled her eyes. "There goes Angela, researcher extraordinaire. A science project for the sisters, huh?"

Angela nodded, looking like she was proud to be helping the race. "Yeah. I like the way that sounds, Nicki."

I shook my head. "Sorry. I just ain't down with it."

Lisa waved her hand in disgust. "Do you, then. We promise to pick nice bridesmaids' dresses that you can wear to other events."

I made a face at Lisa. Nicole put her hand over her mouth to cover up her laughter, and I made a face at her, too.

Lisa said, "Tell you what. You try your way. We'll try our way. We'll talk next week about who we've met and perhaps even had a date with. We'll see what works. I think we should at least try to meet one guy a week."

"One guy a week?" My mouth dropped open. "If I could meet one guy a week, I wouldn't be sitting here with you ladies on a Friday night."

Angela looked intimidated, too. "Yeah, that's a lot, Lisa."

"I'm not saying you have to have one date a week. I'm saying at least have some interaction with one guy just to find out what's out there. Have a phone or email conversation. Even your silly five-minute dates. If you're ruling out one guy a week, it shouldn't be long before you run across a worthwhile guy. Right?"

Me and Angela nodded slowly at each other, still not convinced.

Lisa continued, "The main point is to get out there. Meet people, experience dating. All I know is nine years is a long time. Instead of sitting back and waiting for something to happen, I'm gonna be proactive."

"You're gonna help God out, huh?" I asked.

"I think it helps to give Him something to work with. Why make Him work a miracle by sending the perfect man to your front door? He's out there somewhere, looking for you. You could at least do your part to make it a little easier for Him."

Nicole smirked. "This is gonna be rich. I can't wait to hear the stories."

Lisa turned to her. "Yeah, Nicole. You get to be the judge."

"The judge?" Nicole asked.

Lisa nodded. "Yeah, of whether each of us has made an honest effort or not."

I folded my arms. "What is this now, a game? I didn't sign up for all this."

Lisa shrugged. "Fine. Don't do it then. I'll make sure I throw my bouquet in your direction."

"Where am I supposed to find a guy a week?" I whined.

Lisa shrugged again. "Oh, I don't know. You might want to try the Internet."

Lisa stood and beckoned to Angela. "Come on, Angie. I'ma let you borrow a red top, 'cause it's such a great color on you. We'll put on some makeup—the bare minimum, and we'll bump your hair. I'm gonna take some nice pictures for you to post on your profiles."

Angela followed Lisa back to her bedroom.

Fine. She could get cute to be auctioned off on the Internet like a slave. I wanted no parts of it.

The whole discussion had me thinking, though. I didn't have time to hang out at Lowe's and was always too preoccupied with getting in and out to meet someone in the grocery store and didn't really like coffee enough to hang out at Starbucks.

Now that I had a halfway decent list of what I wanted, where *was* I supposed to meet this perfect man?

eight

If we weren't meeting at my house this week, I would have definitely skipped girls' night. Of course, I hadn't met one guy all week. I thought of making one up, but I couldn't lie to my girls. Still, there was no way I could stand any more of Lisa's wedding day jabs.

It wasn't like I hadn't tried. There was this cute guy in the produce section at the grocery store. I'd lingered around squeezing peaches and smelling cantaloupes, waiting to see if he would talk to me.

Right when I got up the nerve to say something to him, his cell phone rang. I could tell the call was from the woman he loved. His whole countenance changed. Can a guy glow? He talked in a low, sexy voice and then let out this sexy laugh that made *me* tingle.

And it made me sad. Sad that there was no one in my life who I made glow and smile and laugh. That there was no one who made me glow and smile and laugh. So, I grabbed a stupid melon, shoved it in my basket, and hurried to check-out.

And, okay, so I even went to Lowe's. I had been thinking about painting my kitchen. Really, I had.

They were wrong when they said it was full of available men. Everyone I saw was with some woman. And they looked happy together. Excited about painting their bedroom, or building a deck, or finishing their basement. Why did they all have to be holding hands and smiling at each other? One guy was rubbing his pregnant wife's belly as they looked at paint colors for their nursery.

Made me sad again. I was starting to feel desperate and lonely.

And, okay, I even went to the Starbucks in Barnes & Noble. I picked out some books to make me look intelligent and then magazines to make me look not overly intelligent, ordered some Tazo Passion tea for inspiration and sat down to read.

I met eyes with this good-looking, brown-skinned guy. He looked like he might come talk to me, but then another guy showed up and they sat together. At first, I wondered if they were gay—this was Atlanta, after all—but the guy kept stealing looks at me, so I guessed not. The second guy pulled out his laptop, so I figured they were having a business meeting.

I decided to wait until they were finished. If he kept sneaking peeks at me, I would take it as a sign that I could introduce myself. Unlike Angela, I wasn't shy and had no problem approaching men. I could always play it off as networking.

I pretended to read for about an hour—total waste of time—and they finally finished. Laptop guy left, and cute guy stayed at the table. I should have used the hour to think of a good opening line for conversation, but the thought hadn't occurred to me until it was too late. Had to work on some witty icebreakers.

He looked up and caught me looking at him and smiled. I took it as a sign. I trusted my brain to come up with something clever by the time I made it to his table.

"Hi." Yeah, that was clever. *Think, Michelle.*

"Hey. How are you? You look like you got some pretty intense studying going on over there." He eyed my stack of books.

"Not intense. Just picking out some reading for the weekend." *Great, Michelle. Show him how boring you are.*

"Cool. You love to read. That's a plus." He glanced over my shoulder like he was looking for something.

Oh my, he was a cutie. Thick lips, big eyes, and a nice athletic physique.

He looked back at me. "Maybe we could get together sometime to discuss your favorite books and mine. You have a business card or something?"

Wow, that was easier than I thought. "Oh. Okay. Um . . ."

"Hey, baby."

I turned around to see who the velvety female voice behind me was talking to. She faced Mr. Cutie, but was looking straight at me with that why-you-talking-to-my-man look.

I hated stereotypes, but her picture was probably in the dictionary by the entry for *ghettofabulous.* Her cleavage left little to the imagination, and her jeans were so tight, I couldn't imagine how she could breathe. She was begging for a yeast infection. Her long, ratty weave was beyond tacky, and her make-up overdone. Why in the world would an intelligent businessman be with her?

Mr. Cutie held out his hand to shake mine. "It was great to meet you and let me know how my company can be of any service to you." He grabbed Miss Hoochie Mama around the waist and led her out of the store.

I wondered if he feared her starting some drama in the middle of Barnes & Noble.

As they walked away, I realized why he was with her. She had a huge round behind that made me look at God and ask Him why I got cheated. Bigger than Nicole's, even.

I subconsciously smoothed my hand over my backside, knowing that, although it was a decent black-girl butt, it didn't begin to compare.

Men. I couldn't believe he had the nerve to say reading was a plus. She didn't look like she'd read a book since she dropped out of high school.

When I looked down, his business card was in my hand. I didn't bother to read the details. Just crumpled it and dropped it in the trash. Did he really think I would be interested in talking to someone who would try to pick me up with his woman on the way? Even more, did he think I would be interested in talking to someone who would be with someone like her? Please.

I looked down at my watch. I had wasted almost two hours on some foolishness with nothing to show for it. There had to be a better way. For half a second, I considered the dreaded online dating. At least I could do it on my time at my own leisure. But there was no guarantee it would be any better.

Why do I have to deal with this, God? Why can't you just send him to ring my doorbell?

The next evening, as I stuffed a week's worth of dirty dishes into the dishwasher, hid the stack of untouched mail in the already overflowing kitchen drawer, and ordered pizza for the girls' arrival, I had to stop and think. Was I really ready for marriage? If I was too busy to cook, do laundry and keep my house clean, how was I going to take care of a man? I would be embarrassed for any man to see my house as messy as it was. And that was the norm for me.

Maybe my man wasn't ringing the doorbell because God knew he would go running once he saw what was inside.

"Pizza again? Michelle, do you even try?" Nicole frowned when she saw the Papa John's boxes on the counter.

"You're welcome to fast if you don't like what I'm serving."

Her eyes widened. *"Raaarrw."* Nicole clawed at me as she made a cat noise.

I knew my comment was rude, but instead of hearing her voice saying it, I heard my husband and two daughters asking me for a home-cooked meal. Maybe it *was* my fault God hadn't brought him yet.

"Sorry, girl. Had a busy week. I promise I'll do better next time."

Nicole sucked her teeth. "You know I love you, 'Chelle, but you say that every time. Which is why I brought reinforcements."

She pulled a brown paper bag out of the huge Coach duffle she carried everywhere.

"Fine. Whatever." I tried to slam the plates onto the counter, but Styrofoam didn't slam very well. I think she got the point that she'd upset me, though.

Nicole studied my face for a second then went to answer the doorbell.

Lisa and Angela entered. Angela took a deep whiff. "Pizza again? I should have called ahead. I could have picked up something on the way."

Lisa said, "That's why I ate before I came."

I let out an exasperated sigh. "You know what? Next time I'll let you heifers starve."

Lisa and Angela's eyes widened, and they looked at Nicole. She shrugged.

"And no, it's not hormone day," I added to my tirade.

The doorbell rang again. Lisa went to get it and led Vanessa in. Vanessa stared at the pizza boxes on the counter. "Pizza again?"

Angela, Lisa, and Nicole all held their hands up to keep Vanessa from saying anything further. Vanessa looked at them, then looked at me. I must have looked crazy, because she inhaled and said, "Smells great."

We all sat around my dining table. Nicole pulled out some kind of green wrap sandwich with sprouts and other vegetables sticking out of it. I bit into a piece of pepperoni pizza. Lisa sipped some ginger ale, and Vanessa and Angela reluctantly grabbed their own pizza slices.

Lisa said, "So, how'd it go this week, ladies?"

"Yeah, how'd it go?" Nicole asked. She looked directly at me like she couldn't wait to hear about my week's failure.

"You guys go first. I'm starving." It would at least give me a chance to make something out of my pitiful attempt at being found this week.

"Umm, did I miss something?" Vanessa asked.

She frowned while Lisa filled her in on our man-finding pledge.

"Okay. I guess that's healthy. Gotta start somewhere."

"Lisa neglected to mention that they're looking online for men." I expected Vanessa to share my view and talk them out of participating in such ungodly behavior.

"Cool," she said, biting into her pizza.

"Cool?" I wrinkled my eyebrows. "You're okay with it?"

"I don't see anything wrong with it. In fact, a good friend of mine met her husband on eHarmony about four years ago. They're happy, and she says it was the best thing she ever did. And one of the other girls on staff at the church just got engaged to a guy she met through an online Christian dating service."

"Ooooh, which one?" Lisa bounced on the edge of her seat.

"I can't believe this." I rolled my eyes and looked at Vanessa like she had betrayed me.

"Really? Tell us how your dating week went then," Lisa said.

"That has nothing to do with it," I sulked.

"That bad, huh?" Nicole tried to catch some vegetables falling out of her wrap. Yellow sauce dripped down her arm.

I got up to get her a napkin and a fork. "Yeah." Might as well be honest. They'd see through any lie I tried to fabricate. I sat back down and plopped the napkins on the table. "Pretty horrible, actually. I swear everyone in the city is married or has a girlfriend."

I told them about my week. I finished by telling them about Mr. Cutie in Starbucks.

"What a dog." Nicole had a disgusted that's-why-I-hate-men look on her face. "Actually, though, I think that counts. You had an encounter with a guy. You took the initiative to step to him. You found out about him and quickly ruled him out. I'm the judge, and I'd say that qualifies as your one for the week." Nicole patted my shoulder.

"Really?" I looked at Lisa. I knew Nicole was trying to make me feel better.

"I guess I agree," Lisa said. "Especially since you approached him with the intention of getting to know him. You didn't know Miss Hoochie Mama was on the way. Yeah, 'Chelle, you're in there for the week."

I smiled. This wasn't so bad after all. "So how 'bout you guys?"

Lisa rolled her eyes. "My week wasn't much better. I *met* three guys. One was the eHarmony cutie I showed you guys last week. Total dud." She sing-songed, "*Bor-ing*. With a capital *B*."

"Really? He looked too cute to be boring."

Nicole and Lisa looked at me and rolled their eyes.

"Too cute to be boring?" Vanessa asked.

"Yeah, with those snazzy pictures and his good looks, you'd assume he had it going on. Anyway, what about the other two?" I asked.

"The second one I met on Blacksingles.com. He lives here in the ATL, so I figured, cool, no long-distance issues. And his profile was kinda poetic, so I figured he might be smart. Girl, somebody must have wrote his profile for him. The first time I talked to him—"

"You talked to him?" My eyes flew open.

"Yeah." She gave me a funny look.

"You gave someone you met on the Internet your phone number? That's crazy. And dangerous."

"How is it any more crazy or dangerous than giving someone you meet in Starbucks your number? You don't know anything about them except what they look like in person. At least I've read these people's profiles," Lisa said.

"Yeah, but they could lie on their profiles," I said.

"As could a guy you meet in person. It's all taking a chance. You have to use good judgment, plead the blood, and trust God that you don't meet an axe murderer or serial killer—whether online or in person."

I shook my head slowly. "I guess so."

"How do you know Mr. Cutie from Starbucks wasn't a rapist or child molester?"

"I guess I don't."

"My point exactly. Anyway, do you want to hear about this or not?"

I nodded for her to continue.

"So, I talk to the guy, and he's going on and on about how he's so excited that I called him and he can't believe I'm interested in him and that he promises he's going to do everything in his power to make me know how much he loves me and he's a good man and not like all the rest, and if I give him enough of a chance, he'll prove that to me and on and on and—"

Nicole put down her wrap sandwich. "He loves you? He just met you."

"Exactly," Lisa said. "My first clue that something wasn't straight. So the next day, this nut calls me at midnight—yes, twelve p.m.—because he needed to let me know he was thinking about me and couldn't get me off his mind and thinking about me made it impossible for him to sleep."

"Midnight?" Vanessa asked.

"Yeah, girl. I promptly told him I wasn't having any trouble sleeping and that he should try counting sheep. I hung up the phone, thinking he would get the message how inappropriate that was. So, of course I didn't call him back and had no intentions of calling him back ever. Three days later, he sends me a text—at five in the morning—and I had to save it to show you guys."

Lisa flipped open her phone and pushed a few buttons. "Check this out." She passed the phone to Angela, and Nicole leaned close to read it.

In a few seconds, both their eyes bugged out. Angela put a hand over her mouth to stifle her laughter.

Nicole shrieked, "Are you serious?"

I reached out my hand. "What? Lemme see."

Nicole passed the phone over, her mouth still gaping open.

I stared at the small screen and leaned over, so Vanessa could see as well.

I awake this morning with you perspiring my soul. I search the whole worl for the one and I felted that I founded it in you but the lack of cumulative time together is creating distance my soul cannot bear. Open your heart to embrace my love and you will never look for love agin.

I screeched, "No way."

Vanessa's eyes were wide, and her eyebrows knit together.

"Yeah, girl. So I called him and left a voicemail to let him know how inappropriate his calls and texts at such odd hours were and that I really thought he should look elsewhere because I wasn't the one. Apparently he was texting while I was calling because I got another text asking me to 'open my heart and could we meet for a ride on the clouds later that day.' So I texted him back and simply said, 'Please do not call me or text me anymore. Delete my number from your phone.' This fool sends back a message that says, 'Whatever' . . . and then this . . ." She scrolled through the text messages on her phone again and then held it out to Angela and Nicole.

This time, Nicole's mouth flew open in horror, and Angela covered her mouth.

"Oh, no, he didn't." Nicole went into full neck-swinging, finger-snapping, sister mode. She flipped the screen around for us to see.

My eyes widened. "He cussed you out by text? He called you crazy? He's clearly the one who needs medication. And y'all wonder why I don't want to Internet date. Please . . ." I sucked my teeth. "What made you even communicate with him in the first place?"

"Chile, I don't even know," Lisa answered. "He was cute and said he worked in the legal profession and made a lot of money. Turns out he's a paralegal, and the salary he put on the page is what he's trusting God to one day attain."

"They put their salaries on there?" Vanessa asked.

"Some of them. Most put that they'd rather not say."

I got up to grab the garlic sauce from the pizza box. "Girl, ain't no way you can convince me to try that Internet stuff. Should we even ask about the third guy?"

Lisa shrugged. "He wasn't so bad, but there was nothing special about him. I think he felt the same way, because we talked on the phone for about fifteen minutes. There was no connection, no chemistry, no nothing. Then he said he had to answer another call—even though his phone didn't beep—but would call me back later. I haven't heard from him since. Which is good, because I would have ignored his call had I seen his name on the caller ID."

I sat back down and put my head in my hands. "I'm not built for this dating stuff. I'm convinced there has to be an easier way." I looked around the table. "Why did they do away with arranged marriages?"

Everybody laughed. Vanessa rubbed my back.

Angela's soft voice spoke up. "Don't you want to hear about my week before you draw your conclusions?"

All heads whipped in Angela's direction.

For the first time all night, I noticed there was a little something different about her. A glow, maybe. When she smiled a shy little smile, I knew something special had happened. "Do tell."

We all leaned toward Angela to get the details.

She leaned back like all the attention was too much for her. "Well . . ." She giggled.

Not that she never laughed, but she sounded . . . girlish. I was even more intrigued.

"Well, I met this guy on eHarmony, and basically, the way it works is that you answer a bunch of questions back and forth and then you can email each other. So we did, and then we finally talked on the phone . . . after I was pretty sure he wasn't crazy," she said in Lisa's direction, rolling her eyes. "So, the first time we talked, it was amazing. Like talking to someone I'd known for years. We stayed on the phone all night, for like six hours, and we've talked every day since." Her eyes glazed over. "He's wonderful."

"My, my, my. Look at you." Lisa leaned back and stared at Angela. "So, tell us about him."

Angela grinned. She looked twenty years younger. Not that she was old-looking, but she had a bubbly adolescent look that was so un-Angela.

"Well, he's forty-four. He's a computer geek—

works in IT and also builds computers. He's very involved in his church and teaches Sunday School. Has been divorced for three years and has a son and daughter in college. And he's sweet and godly and smart and is serious about a committed relationship and getting married again." She paused and batted her eyelashes. "He wants to come visit next weekend."

"Come visit?" Vanessa raised her eyebrows. "Where is he from?"

"Augusta. Two hours away. I told him he'd have to stay in a hotel."

"Darn skippy he has to stay in a hotel. He surely can't stay with you. And make sure you meet him out in public." Vanessa snapped into mother hen mode. "Don't be having that man in your house at all."

"Yes, ma'am," Angela said.

I was afraid her face would crack from smiling.

Lisa sat back against her chair. "Wow, you met somebody. You think it was the new pictures?"

Angela shook her head. "I started communicating with him before we posted the new pictures. He liked me even when I had the boring picture on there. Me in the lab. He liked the fact that I was smart and so different from all the women he's met recently."

"Is he cute?" Nicole asked.

I wanted to ask the same thing, but didn't want to embarrass Angela, if he wasn't. Leave it to Nicole.

"I think so. At least from his pictures, anyway. 'Chelle, where's your laptop? I'll pull up his profile."

I scampered back to my office to get it. Once inside, I almost broke my neck tripping over a huge stack of papers in the middle of the floor I had been meaning to sort through.

I looked up at the ceiling. "Okay, God, I get it. I'll do better. I'll be neat and clean from now on. I promise. But do you have to break my ankle?"

I could see God looking at Jesus like, *"I broke her ankle? Who left the papers in the middle of the floor?"*

"Okay, you're right. My bad. I'll do better." I unplugged the cords from the computer to take it back to the table. I dodged a stack of books in the hall on the way back.

I set the computer down in front of Angela.

In less than a minute of typing and clicking, she turned it around to us and said, "That's him." Her voice was half- excited, half-nervous.

"My, my, my," Lisa said.

Vanessa smiled in approval as well. "Well, now. I say."

"Lemme see." I reached for the computer. "Oh, my."

Nicole grabbed the computer next. "Talk about answered prayer. A fine nerd, indeed."

Angela giggled.

I pulled the screen back around from Nicole. "Girl, he's cute." He was caramel-colored with squinty Chinese-like eyes, and a broad smile. His low haircut was sprinkled with gray at the temples. He had that older, classy-handsome, Billy Dee thing going on. "You go, Angela."

She covered her face with her hands. "I know. I

can't believe it. So, you think I should let him come visit?"

"Girl, are you crazy?" Lisa pulled the screen toward her. "You better."

Vanessa pulled the computer toward her. "He seems to have a kind, gentle spirit. Okay. I guess I approve. He still can't come over your house, though."

"Yes, mother." Angela couldn't contain her grin. She clapped her hands together and bounced in her seat. "Okay, tonight when I talk to him, I'm gonna tell him he can come." Her glee faded. "Oh, no. What am I going to wear? What am I going to do with my hair?"

Lisa put a hand on her shoulder. "Girl, you know I got you. I'ma hook you up to where he ain't gon' know what to say."

"Don't hook her up too much." Nicole sucked her teeth. "She's got years of pent-up passion locked up in her loins. We don't want nothing lettin' loose."

We all laughed. Angela blushed.

"Did you tell him?" Vanessa asked gently.

Angela's eyes widened in horror. "Of course not. I don't want to run him off by telling him I'm some inexperienced virgin."

"Did you at least tell him you were celibate and planning to be so until you get married?"

Angela sat silent.

"I take that as a *no*," Nicole said.

Angela shook her head. "He's saved. He's in church and loves the Lord. He's one of the leaders in the men's ministry, and he knows the Word of

God. Why should we have to have that conversation?"

Lisa rolled her eyes. "Girl, everybody saved ain't livin' saved. You know that."

"Well, he's a mature Christian. I shouldn't have to tell him that," Angela said.

"You may not have to tell him that, but you should see what his views on the subject are." Vanessa brushed back a large curl that had fallen over into Angela's face when she bent her head down.

"I don't want to run him away." Angela's voice was so low, we could barely hear her.

"Sweetie, I beg to differ," Vanessa said. "If he doesn't have the same commitment, you *do* want to run him away. If he does, then at least you'll both know where you stand."

Angela nodded slowly. "Okay. I guess I'll talk to him about it. When though? How soon in the whole dating thing should we have that conversation?"

"I always tell them on the first date. I think they need to know. It's unfair to let them expect something they're not gonna get." Lisa flipped her hair over her shoulder. "And of course, when they see all this, they start salivating and imagining what it would be like. I can't have them all excited for nothing."

Nicole rolled her eyes. "Girl, please."

I looked at Vanessa. "When do *you* think is the right time to tell? I mean, like Angela said, if they're saved, they should already know that, but like Lisa said, everybody saved ain't living saved."

"Girl, you are asking the wrong person. That is *so* not an issue in my life right now." Vanessa took a sip of her soda.

We all sat there quiet for a minute.

I looked at Angela. "I'm happy for you, girl. I hope this turns out well for you."

She nodded. "Me too. But if it doesn't, it's worth the experience. I've learned things about myself already. About what I'm looking for in a relationship. I mean, he's not the only person I've ever talked to from eHarmony. He's like one of three guys I communicated with this week. But there was something about him. Like this magical connection. I can't explain it. If it doesn't work out, well, at least I got to enjoy him for a moment." She rested her head on her hand and sighed.

Angela's cell phone rang. She looked down at the screen and then back up at us. "It's him." She started flapping her hands like she was trying to be airborne. "It's him."

"Well, answer the phone, Tweety," Nicole said.

Angela picked up the phone and answered it. "Hey, you." She paused a second and giggled. "I was just thinking about you, too." She pushed her seat back and got up. She started down the hallway toward my bedroom.

"Noooooo!" I flew down the hall after her and stood to block her from going in.

She frowned at me but kept talking. "Yeah, I was thinking about that. Where do you want—" She started for the office, but I didn't want her to go in there, either.

I moved to block the door.

She stared at me like I had lost it.

I pointed her toward the bathroom. I always kept it and the public areas clean when I knew company was coming over.

She said, "Hold on a second," and put her hand over the phone. "What is your problem? Can I have a few minutes of privacy?"

"Go in the bathroom, my room is a mess."

"It can't be that bad." She bolted around me and opened the door. She started in but backed out. "Okay, maybe it can." She went into the bathroom and closed the door. She popped her head out. "Be back in a sec. Oh, and uh, you really need to work on that. God can't send you a man with your life looking like that."

I hung my head and returned to the table. Everybody was shaking their heads when I sat back down.

Nicole grabbed my arm. "You know I love you, girl. But you got to do better. She's right. God ain't sending you no king and you can't keep his castle clean. And that doesn't mean you gotta be the one doing all the cleaning. But you gotta do better than this. And you need to start cooking some decent food, too. You can't feed your husband and kids fast food every day."

"I know. Things have been crazy busy lately."

Vanessa pursed her lips. "'Chelle, I've known you for almost five years. It's always like this. Do what you got to do. Hire somebody if you have to."

Lisa nodded. "Yeah, girl. Don't block your blessing."

"All right. I hear you." I got up from the table and snatched up the pizza box and stuffed it in the refrigerator. I took a rag and wiped the counters.

"You ain't got to do it now. You got company," Nicole said. "And you ain't got to be snippy about it either. We're just giving you the truth in love."

"I know." I slid back into my seat. "I'm sorry. I—"

"He's coming. He's coming." Angela emerged from the bathroom and skipped back to the table. "Next weekend. He'll be here Saturday morning, and we're going to spend all day together, and then he's coming to church with me on Sunday. He said he was excited about meeting me, and next weekend was gonna be extra long getting here." She fell into her chair and hugged her arms around her waist. "He likes me."

Vanessa patted her back. "Of course he does. You're beautiful, smart, compassionate, godly— just all around wonderful."

"Really, *V*?"

Vanessa frowned. "Have you been doing your affirmations? I think you need to do them four times a day this week. Don't be worried about whether he likes you, or trying to make sure you don't run him off. Make sure you like him. Okay?"

Angela reached over to hug Vanessa. "Yes, mother."

Lisa said, "Good. He's coming to church with you on Sunday. That means we can get a look at him. And . . . we can do the worship test."

Angela frowned. "The worship test?"

"Yeah," Lisa said. "You can tell a lot about a guy and his relationship with God by how he behaves during praise and worship. If he sits down while everyone else is standing and praising, you definitely don't want him. If he stands out of obligation but doesn't sing or lift his hands or participate, you probably don't want him. If he actually knows the words to the songs, lifts his hands and worships God, then he's a keeper. And if he sheds a tear or ends up prostrate on the floor, girl, you better marry that man."

I stared at Lisa. "Where do you get this stuff? Is there some how-to-catch-a-man book you sit up reading all night, or is this all especially created by you?"

"This is dating, according to Lisa Brooks. Watch, I'm gonna write a book one day."

"Yeah, that's only if you actually meet a man and get married," Nicole said. "If that never happens, you have to call it how *not* to date, according to Lisa Brooks."

Lisa narrowed her eyes and glared at Nicole. Angela giggled. I glanced over at her.

Who would have thought Angela would be the first one? Not that she shouldn't. And not that she was getting married next week. I was glad Angela's experience our first week was so much better than mine and Lisa's. I might have gotten discouraged otherwise. But the glow on Angela's face and the sound of her teenage giggle was enough incentive to keep trying.

I pulled the computer over in front of me and stared at the face on the screen. He was a looker. Why was he on eHarmony? He shouldn't have any trouble finding a good woman. Especially with the number of desperate sisters out there his age.

And if he was on eHarmony, what other good-looking, saved men were on there?

nine

I woke up the next Sunday and he was there in bed with me.

My archenemy. The horny monster. I could feel him reaching out to engulf me and knew this was going to be a particularly bad day. I rolled over toward the nightstand and grabbed the calendar I'd kept there since I'd become a slave to my hormones.

Yep. Exactly fourteen days after my last cycle began. I had a hormone surge because I was ovulating. I knew the horny monster kept a calendar of his own so he would know the exact times I would be most vulnerable to his attack.

I didn't waste any time jumping out of bed and into my exercise clothes. It was definitely a Tae Bo kind of day. As I punched and kicked, I called out my most "keeping it holy" scriptures. If I could head off the attack before it got on me good, I'd be all right. At least it was Sunday, and I could get into God's presence to chase it away.

On Sundays, I had God, a good service, and my

friends afterward. On weekdays, I had work to keep me occupied. But Saturdays? I had at least sixteen hours to fill up with something strong enough to keep my mind off the "burning in my loins," as Nicole called it.

After I exercised, I showered, put on a pantsuit and grabbed a bagel to head out to service.

When I arrived in the sanctuary, I met Nicole at our usual section in the middle of the sanctuary.

"I haven't seen them yet," she said as I settled into my seat next to her.

"Who?"

She frowned at me. "Angie and her new man. Did you forget?"

"Oh. Yeah, I guess I did." Going ten rounds with the horny monster that morning had knocked it out of my brain. I scanned the sanctuary.

A few minutes later, Lisa slipped into the seat next to me. "They're here. And he is too fine. Even better than the picture." She clapped her hands together. "Angie got her a fine man."

"What's his name? I forgot to ask the other night," I said.

"Gary," Lisa said.

"Where did you see them?" Nicole craned her neck toward the vestibule.

"Girl, I was waiting out in the lobby for them to walk in," Lisa said.

I shook my head. "You are too much."

"Please. I had to see what my girl was working with." She turned around and put her hands on her lap. "Here they come. Don't look."

Yeah, right. That was like saying, "Don't think of a pink elephant."

Nicole and I turned our heads around, and we scanned the crowd pouring down the aisle until we saw them.

Angela was glowing even more than she had last Friday night. She looked cute in a pair of black slacks and a red short-sleeved sweater. Her hair fell to her chin, the ends bumped. Lisa must have wrapped it for her. I didn't recognize the clothes and figured they must have gone shopping, too.

Behind her trailed Gary. He was about six foot one, broad shoulders, nice smile, and a handsome face. Better than the picture. And like Vanessa said, the gentle friendliness to his spirit could be felt as he smiled down at Angela and put his hand in the small of her back as he followed her to a row a few ahead of ours. I knew Angela was sitting there so Lisa could conduct her worship test.

They sat talking for a few minutes as we all waited for service to start. Angela's eyes were bright and her smile shy. Every once in a while, he leaned closer to her to talk, and her eyes softened and she giggled. They seemed oblivious to everyone else around them. Was it possible that she had found the one already?

I had to fight the jealous monster. I rebuked him quickly, reminding him that after my spar with the horny monster that morning, he didn't want any parts of me.

The band started playing softly, and the praise and worship team walked out onto the pulpit. Everyone stood up. Gary stood as well. Not like he was following everyone else, but like he was familiar with praise and worship and knew it was time to stand.

When the praise team starting singing their first upbeat song, he clapped his hands. I knew we were all watching his mouth.

When we got to the chorus, he sang along, even when the words projected on the screen lagged behind by almost a full ten seconds. He knew the words. Sure it was an Israel & New Breed song that anyone active in any church probably knew, but so far, Gary was passing the worship test with flying colors.

I knew God had to be looking down at me, Lisa, and Nicole like, "Can I get some attention here? This is supposed to be about me, after all."

I know, God, but this is our girl, Angela. We gotta make sure she's straight with the worship test.

I could almost hear Him say, "Oh, yeah, that's so much better than asking me if he's the right man for her."

I felt convicted and changed my focus from Gary and Angela to worshipping God. Especially since after service, I still had the horny monster to contend with. I needed to get as much of an outpour of the Holy Spirit as I could get.

As the team switched over from praise to worship, I closed my eyes, lifted my hands and focused on God.

Just as I sensed His presence flooding over me, Lisa elbowed me. "Look," she whispered loudly.

Gary was lifting his hands as well. His eyes were closed, and as much as he was focused on Angela a few minutes before, he wasn't thinking anything about her right now. His mouth moved slowly, and a tear streamed down the side of his face.

So much for me getting into the throne room. There was nothing sexier than a man worshipping God from the depths of his heart. The three of us stared at Gary, our mouths open.

"You go, Angela," Lisa whispered.

She couldn't possibly realize how loud she was. She sounded like a kid when they first learned how to whisper, not realizing they were almost as loud as they were when talking.

You go, God. I thought it was real sweet of Him to honor Angela's request first. Maybe He was honoring her faithfulness at having maintained her virginity for so long. I wasn't sure I could have done it. And that's the honest truth. I didn't think she'd have to worry about the celibacy thing either. He seemed like a godly man.

Well, at least one of us was happy. I worked hard to focus on the service, but between watching Angela and Gary, and trading the occasional jab with the horny monster, I wasn't paying much attention.

It was the usher's fault. He was tall and thick—muscular thick. I didn't think it was very godly of him to wear such close-fitting black pants and a closer-fitting black shirt as his *church* usher uniform. I could tell he made regular use of the gym.

And then there was the guy sitting two seats down from Nicole on my right. He wasn't extra special cute or anything, but he had the sexiest hands. Well-manicured and strong-looking—like he could hold my hand and I'd never be scared of anything in life again.

And then there was the entire tenor section of the choir while they were singing their Sunday selections. And the entire usher board as they received offering.

I loosened the top button on my blouse and fanned a little. Was it men's day or something?

"You okay?" Nicole leaned over and whispered.

"I'm fine. It's just a little warm in here." Hot was more like it. I looked up at the ceiling and closed my eyes. *God, please don't send me to hell for lusting in church this morning. Why do I have to live like this?*

It was the worst possible test. Forget the trials of Job. Fill Michelle's sex-starved body with super abundant levels of estrogen, surround her with good-looking, godly men and command her to live holy. Forget the fruit in the garden. Do not choose of any of the men surrounding you, for in the day you taste of it, you shall surely die. Forget Jesus' temptation in the desert or in Gethsemane. Okay, maybe that was taking it too far.

After Pastor Kennedy preached what was probably a great sermon, he led an altar call for anyone needing prayer in any area of their life.

I almost crushed everybody on my row's feet, stepping over them to get to the aisle.

"Lift up that thing before the Lord—whatever you're struggling with—and commit it to His hands." Pastor came to the edge of the stage and lifted his hand out over the congregation.

I imagined hoisting the horny monster up over

my head to throw him onto the altar for God to destroy.

Pastor Kennedy said, "There's someone standing next to you in need of prayer. Let the body heal the body today. Reach out to the one next to you. Hold their hand, put an arm around them. Let them know a fellow citizen of the Kingdom is fighting with them."

I reached out for the hand of the person next to me. Instead, I felt an arm go around my shoulder. A strong, thick, muscular arm. I froze. A strong, thick, muscular hand squeezed my shoulder and pulled me into a strong, thick, muscular side.

For a second, I wondered if God hated me.

Of course, I knew He didn't. But He was taking this test too far. Way too far.

I peeked through a closed praying eye and saw none other than usher–man. *I guess he decided to give me comfort in my time of need and show me he was a fellow Kingdom citizen, fighting the good fight of faith with me.* What he was really doing was making the very struggle I was praying about all the harder.

And, honestly, it wasn't even the horny monster that was bothering me so much at the moment. It was being touched by a man. I was up close and personal with a man of God. Something I wanted more than anything.

And it was pure torture.

I couldn't remember the last time a man held me. Of course, there was the usual "arms around the shoulders, butt poked out so nothing could possibly touch" church hug with some of my male friends after service ended. This was different.

Close. Intimate in a spiritual way. And even though I didn't know this guy from Adam, I felt comforted, covered, and loved.

I lifted my head toward heaven and said my simple prayer, "God, you know." I should have been praying that altar time would end, so usher-man could let me go and I could go back to the safety of my girls.

Mercifully, prayer ended, and I broke away from his embrace to return to my seat.

I turned to see Angela and Gary standing in prayer with his arm around her. Something in my spirit said he was the one for our Angela.

I said a silent prayer for them, for me, and for love-starved women everywhere. Every woman of God should be able to experience what I had just experienced and what Angela was experiencing. A godly man who loved them and was committed to covering them in prayer.

I was so busy watching Angela and Gary, I walked smack into a broad chest.

"Sorry." I stepped to the side to maneuver around the man in my way, but he stepped in the same direction. I stepped in the other direction to go around him, but instead of it being a mishap, it seemed like he was intentionally blocking my way.

"I don't get a hello?" A set of strong hands planted themselves firmly on my shoulders to keep me from side- stepping again.

I looked up.

It was Jason.

ten

"Wha . . . wha . . . what are you doing here?" I sputtered.

"Ummm, the same thing everyone else is doing here." He eyed me strangely. "Worshipping God and getting some good Word."

"But why here? You don't go here. You go to . . ." the name of his church escaped me.

He dropped his head and looked past me. "Can you meet me out front after the benediction? There's something I should tell you."

I nodded and headed back down the row to my seat next to Nicole.

She leaned over to me and whispered, "What's with you today? Clinging to the usher during prayer then hugging Mr. Hottie in the aisle. Do we need to get some anointing oil?"

"I wasn't clinging or hugging," I hissed back.

Her eyes widened. I guess I was a little rude. She made one of her cat-claw gestures at me and mouthed her little cat growl. I laughed and elbowed her.

After the benediction, I was torn between standing around to be introduced to Angela's new guy, or meeting Jason on the front steps. It would be rude to leave him out there waiting. And I had already seen enough to know what I needed to know about Gary.

"Meet you guys out front," I said to Nicole as I attempted to scoot past her toward the aisle.

"Aren't you gonna stay and meet—"

"Gotta take care of something. I'll meet him in a minute."

She nodded and let me by.

I spotted him before he saw me coming. It was definitely not a good day to be seeing Jason. Not looking as good as he always looked. I didn't remember smelling his cologne during our brief bump in the aisle, but I couldn't imagine him leaving home without it. Sure enough, as I stepped closer to him, I smelled it. His pure testosterone cologne and the super potent estrogen flooding my veins were not a good combination.

He gave me quick hug. He had never hugged me before, but I guessed being at church made him feel like it was the appropriate thing to do. It must have felt like hugging a board because I made no attempt at hugging him back.

"Good to see you, Michelle. You okay?" He looked into my eyes in that way of his, and I cast them downward so he couldn't see what was lurking beneath.

"Yeah, I'm great—praise the Lord. Blessed and highly favored." Lovely. I sounded super-religious. "I'm fine. How are you? What are you doing here?"

I wished I could take back the question, to

avoid the conversation it would lead to. I guess we had to have it some time, but I'd rather it was within the professional boundaries of work rather than here, after church, where Jason felt like it was okay to hug me.

"I don't know if you know this or not, but my wife divorced me." He said it like he was embarrassed.

I started to pretend not to know, but that would seem like a lie. On the church steps. "Someone mentioned it, Jason. I did notice your ring was gone." *Great, Michelle.* Must *learn to think before we speak* and didn't want him to realize I made a regular practice of eyeing men's ring fingers. Especially his.

Was that a smile? Was he smiling because I admitted I noticed his ring was gone? Oh, God help me.

"Yeah. It's true. So, I figured I needed a new church. Even though my ex didn't go much, I didn't want to be at the same church anymore. You always talk about how great yours is, so I decided to check it out."

This is what I get for being an evangelist at work?

"It is great and I'm glad you came. Did you enjoy the service?" *Please say no. Please say no.*

He nodded and grinned. The dimpled, perfect-teeth grin. "Yeah. It was better than you described. I know I'll definitely be back."

"Oh, how wonderful. I'm glad you enjoyed it." *Oh, how terrible. I wish you had hated it.*

He looked around for a second and loosened his tie. "So, what do you usually do after church?"

I froze. *Oh, God, please don't let Jason ask me out.*

"Wanna grab a bite to eat?"

God, are You listening to me at all today???

As if God suddenly understood His need to demonstrate that He was paying me some attention, Nicole and Lisa emerged through the church doors.

I tried not to exhale my relief too loudly. "Me and my girls always go out for dinner after church. Every Sunday. It's our tradition. For years now." I pointed to them. "Here they come."

He looked over my shoulder in the direction I had pointed. "Oh. Okay." He tugged at his tie again. "I guess I better get home anyway. Latrice will be bringing the girls home soon, and I need to get ready for the school week."

It took a second for his words to register. "You have your girls?"

He nodded. "Yeah. I got full custody. When she left, she left all of us. She picks them up for the occasional weekend, when she's not traveling with . . ." He looked down at his feet. "But it's okay. I've got enough love for my girls to make up for it. They are definitely Daddy's girls. Even before all this happened."

I wanted to hug him. To embrace away the pain I knew he had experienced in the last year. It was the same as mine, except he was left taking care of his two daughters. My respect for him jumped twenty points in the last five minutes. Unfortunately, so had my attraction to him. Would it be so bad to date someone from work?

Yes, Michelle. It would be bad.

I reached out to touch Jason's arm. It seemed cold-hearted not to offer some sort of comfort after such a conversation.

Bad decision. Felt like Jason had been working out his pain in the gym like I had in the year after my divorce.

Do Jesus. All of a sudden, cold-hearted didn't seem so bad compared to hot-in-the-pants.

Since I had already reached out and touched, I went ahead with my attempt at comfort. "Sorry for all you've been through, Jason. I know how hard it must be. Well, the divorce part. I can't imagine raising two kids on my own." I rubbed my hand up and down his thick bicep. Comforting Jason was going to have me up all night, fanning. "I'm sure you're a great father, and I know God is taking care of all of you."

"Thanks, Michelle. That means a lot coming from you." He looked at me with those deep eyes of his.

I stood there staring into them for a few minutes. I think I would have fallen in if I hadn't heard Nicole's voice in my right ear.

"Michelle, who's your friend?"

I ripped my eyes away from Jason's and had to blink for a few minutes to focus on Nicole's face to answer her question. "This is Jason. My editor. Actually, my right hand at work. I don't know what I'd do without him."

"Is that so?" Nicole smiled and reached out to shake Jason's extended hand.

I turned out of Jason's view to glare at her so she would know she needed to be on her best behavior because the wrong words from that mouth of hers could end, or at least badly damage, our friendship. Her eyebrows rose slightly as she acknowledged my non-verbal threat.

"Jason, this is Nicole and Lisa. Two of my best friends in the whole world."

"Great to meet both of you." Jason shook Lisa's hand after he let go of Nicole's. "I'm taking off. You guys, enjoy your lunch."

"Our lunch?" Lisa frowned and looked at Jason, then at me.

Thoughts of murdering Lisa on the church steps raced through my mind.

Jason grinned. "Yeah. You guys probably didn't know it, but you're going out to lunch with Michelle today. You guys always go out to lunch together after church. It's your tradition. For years."

Was that mischief in his eyes? Yes, it was. And pure amusement at busting me in a lie.

He sauntered down a couple of steps then turned around. "I guess we'll have lunch tomorrow at work, Michelle. See ya then." He gave one last dimpled smile, waved and turned back around and left.

As soon as he was out of earshot, I glared at Lisa. "Our lunch?" I mocked her voice. "You couldn't play along? You had to bust me out like that?"

Lisa put a hand on her hip. "How was I to know you were out here lying on the church steps after such an anointed service?"

Lisa and Nicole spoke at the same time. "Who is he? . . . Editor? . . . Girl, he is too fine . . . How come you never told us about him before? . . . Right-hand man? . . . Is he taken? . . ."

I held up a hand to ward off their questions. "It's

complicated, and I don't want to talk about it. Where's Angela? Did you guys meet Gary?"

They both stood there with their mouths open.

"Don't want to talk about it? Oh no. That's in total violation of every girlfriend rule there is. You can't have a cutie like that up in your life and not share some details." Lisa's neck was twisting and her finger pointing. "No secrets among girlfriends. Nine years and never, remember?"

Nicole laughed. "And I thought you were working long hours because you were so dedicated to your job."

I closed my eyes and rubbed the back of my neck. "Fine. I'll tell you guys about it over lunch." Probably wasn't a good idea for me to go home with the feel of Jason's bicep still pulsing through my fingers. Cold pizza and hot loins was not a good combination.

"Oh, yeah." Nicole smirked. "We wouldn't want to mess up our tradition."

"Ha, ha, ha." I sneered at Nicole.

Lisa grabbed me by the arm. "Let's go back inside and say goodbye to Angela and Gary, and then we'll go to Paschal's."

I resisted. "What if she doesn't want us to meet him? To avoid having to go through what you just put me through."

Lisa's eyes widened. "Put you through?" She rolled her eyes. "We already met him. Angela was looking for you, too. She didn't understand why you left." Lisa pulled me up the steps. "Wait 'til I tell her why."

eleven

The next day, I came to work armed with my excuse for why I couldn't join Jason for lunch. And this time, it was the truth. Sort of.

Sorry for lying yesterday, God. And on the church steps after an anointed service. Perhaps having no idea what the sermon was about due to my drooling over men all morning had something to do with it.

At noon, when Jason gave his usual rap on my door to signify that it was time for lunch, I didn't look up from my computer.

He stuck his head in the door. "Ready?"

I waved a hand, still focused on the screen, pretending to be overwhelmingly distracted. "You go 'head. I'm in a flow and I don't want to break my concentration."

"Really? Whatcha workin' on?" He stepped his full body into my office.

So much for my concentration. Even if it was fake. "The promo for Rayshawn's next show. I need it to be flawless 'cause I have a feeling she's looking for a reason. If I stay focused, I can finish it by tonight."

"Or if we go grab some lunch, you can fuel your brain while we talk about it, and we can come back and finish it together."

He was relentless today. Usually, if I said I was working on something, he'd ask if I wanted him to bring something back, take my order, then leave.

Most of the time, I went, though. Jason, Erica, and I ate lunch together at our favorite little sandwich shop down the street at least three times a week. Gave me some much-needed time to unwind and for us to toss ideas around. Me and Jason bantered back and forth while Erika took notes between bites of food. By the time we got back to the office, we usually had completed whatever the project of the day was.

But that was when we were just co-workers. Before he became single and available.

"Jason, why don't you grab me my usual sandwich, chips, and a drink. That would be a big help." Not once had I taken my eyes off the computer to look at him. I had pretty much taken the horny monster out in prayer last night, but didn't want to give him a chance to rise up again.

Instead of leaving like he should, Jason shut my door and walked over to my desk. He stood there for a second. When I didn't look up, he put his face directly above the computer screen. "What's with you lately?"

"Huh?" I said, still typing away. I prayed he wouldn't look down at the screen. If he did, I'd be totally busted. I had been typing the same sentence over and over since he entered the room.

"Michelle." He said it firmly, almost demanding my attention.

At that point, it would have been rude not to look up. So I did. Right into his eyes. I thought of all the poems I'd read about eyes being pools of this, or rivers of that, or deep wells of the other, all references to bodies of water I could drown in. That's how Jason's eyes felt to me.

"Huh?" I said again.

"What is up with you? You've been acting strange lately." The concern in his eyes made my heart flutter a little. I wondered what it felt like to have a man care about me like his eyes said he did.

"Nothing's wrong, Jason. Just want to make sure this is straight. Don't want to give Rayshawn any reasons. Not that she needs any. Remember that time she came in here ranting and raving about—"

"I know all that." He waved a hand at me. "Are you sure that's all?"

"Yeah. Of course. You know my work is my life." *Great, Michelle. Way to sound lonely and desperate.* How in the world did I let this guy—married until last week for all I knew—get to know me so well?

"I know that. Not sure it's healthy, but I do know. Okay, if you say that's all it is." He walked over and put a hand on my door to leave. I thought I was home free until he said, "So why'd you lie about your Sunday after-church lunch tradition with your girlfriends yesterday?"

"Huh?"

"Don't *huh* me. Your girlfriend—the tall one—

had no idea what I was talking about when I said, 'Enjoy your lunch.' Can't be much of a tradition."

I let out a deep breath. Tried to think of a lie Jason would actually believe.

He sat down in the chair again, a tiny grin forming in the corners of his mouth.

Oh, God help me.

And mercifully, He did. The door flew open. It was Erika. "Michelle, get yourself together, girl. Ms. Carter asked to have you come to the conference room. I think it's time to announce the fall lineup."

The other producers and I filed into the conference room, all trying to be cool but anxiously awaiting Ms. Carter's arrival. I sat with my hands folded, trying not to make eye contact with anyone. Especially Rayshawn. She had a smug look on her face that said she expected to continue reigning as the queen of BTV.

After what seemed like forever, Ms. Carter finally entered. She had a large file folder in her hands and moved slowly, as if she wasn't carrying our future in that durn folder.

I took a few deep breaths. I felt the Holy Spirit nudging me like, "Here comes the great news. You're in there." I imagined myself elbowing Him back, telling Him to calm down and not get too excited, just in case my shows weren't chosen. Kinda silly, seeing that He knew everything about everything.

Ms. Carter took her seat at the head of the table, sat for a few moments, then opened the folder.

The air was tense with anticipation. She smiled a calm, even smile. "Good afternoon, everyone. Sorry for the short notice on the meeting. I'm flying out to New York tomorrow to meet with the investors and the other VPs. I wanted to have this discussion before we left, so things can start moving. First off, I want to say thanks to everyone for your hard work on your treatments. I appreciate the time and creativity that went into every one. Secondly, there were many great shows presented and if you're not in the fall lineup, that doesn't mean that your show won't be used at another time."

I tried to prepare myself for my show not being picked, but the Holy Spirit wouldn't allow the sinking feeling to settle in my stomach.

Ms. Carter continued, "Finally, as you know, even with the funds coming in, we're still on a very tight budget for production. If you're assigned a show, I want you to think long and hard about what it will require. A lot more hours with not much increase in pay. I hope you can appreciate the fact that we're building something special in this station and any shows chosen will be foundational for the network. It can lead to other opportunities within this network and elsewhere. Hopefully, that thought will be enough to carry you through the long hours that will be required to pull this off. If you count up the cost and decide it's not for you, we'll understand. If you do produce a show, know that your work won't go unrewarded and that, as the company grows, you will be compensated." She looked around the table to see our responses.

Everyone nodded. No one spoke. They probably all felt the same as me. Enough with the speech. Get to the shows.

"All right, then. The fall lineup . . ."

I held my breath as she announced the shows. To kill us with further suspense, she didn't announce them one by one. She had to stop and discuss each one, making production assignments. I tried to be patient, but after the third show, I started to wonder how many they had chosen. What if I didn't get picked? I'd have to go back to promos and produce spots for these shows she was announcing.

"Next. *Indie Artist.* Michelle Bradford will serve as producer with the oversight of Mark Jackson as senior producer. I think you'll work well together, and I think it has the potential to be a great show. Michelle, if you'd like, you can keep your production assistant and editor, or we can assign someone else if there's anyone you'd prefer."

I tried not to sound too excited. "I'll stick with Jason and Erika. We work well together. Thank you." I pretended not to hear Rayshawn clear her throat.

I faded out as Ms. Carter announced the next shows. The wheels in my mind were spinning. I had a show. I was going to produce my own show. I looked over at Mark. He would be cool to work with. And I'd get to keep Jason and Erika. I started thinking about the artists I would call first. I could hardly keep still. I wanted Ms. Carter to hurry and finish with the show announcements, so I could share the news with Jason and Erika.

"Is that okay with you, Michelle?"

I looked up to see Ms. Carter and the other producers looking at me.

"I'm sorry." How embarrassing to be caught not paying attention in the meeting.

Ms. Carter smiled. "I guess you tuned me out, thinking about *Indie Artist*. I said I really liked the idea for *Destiny's Child*. I want to launch it in the fall lineup as well. I think it would be too much for Mark to do three shows, so I wanted to you to produce it, with Rayshawn as the senior producer."

That would explain Rayshawn's need to pick her face up off the table. I was speechless. Both of my shows were being picked? I never imagined I'd have two. But to have to work with Rayshawn? To have her produce a show she tried to squash at the pitch meeting? The one nearest and dearest to my heart? It was almost like asking someone else to raise my child. An evil person with no morals or scruples that I had no respect for.

It wasn't like I was going to say no. "Wow. Uh, sure. That sounds great. I could learn a lot working with Rayshawn." I gave her my most admiring face. Tried to focus on the fact that I respected her as a producer. It was going to be challenging. I'd have to look at it as an opportunity for spiritual growth.

The scowl on Rayshawn's face made me realize something else. She'd be producing my show because neither of hers had been picked. Ouch. I wasn't going to be her favorite person for a while.

I looked at the two other producers whose shows hadn't been picked. They did a better job than Rayshawn at hiding their disdain, but I could tell they weren't too happy with me either. It would be hard enough working long hours to produce the shows on a tight budget. I didn't need hateration from the other producers I was so glad to be joining the ranks with.

I squared my shoulders and sat up. The favor of God had gotten me here, and I wasn't about to shrink back. He put me here for a reason. To fulfill His vision to change the face of Black television. I had His mind, and that's why my ideas got picked. I wasn't about to be sorry for that.

After Ms. Carter finished the meeting with final comments and instructions, we all stood to leave. Mark came over to congratulate me. One of his shows had been picked, so he'd be working on his and mine. We made plans to sit down and start some budgeting and planning. A few of the other producers congratulated me and patted me on the back. Ms. Carter nodded in my direction and then left the room.

I knew the right thing to do would be to go make nice with Rayshawn, but the evil glare she shot me wasn't the least bit inviting. She was huddled up with her girl, and they were talking fast and looking in my direction.

I decided to be the bigger person and walked over to where they were. "Rayshawn, I'm really looking forward to working with you. You're a great producer, and I'm glad to have the chance to learn from you." I hoped kissing her tail would work. She seemed to like it when everyone worshipped the ground she walked on.

She narrowed her eyes. "Yeah. I'm sure you'll be spending most of your time working on your other show with Mark. Why don't you have your assistant send me a copy of your treatment and I'll take it from there?"

"Oh, I wouldn't dream of it. I plan on working very closely with you, so I can learn all I can. I'm sure you enjoy sharing your wealth of knowledge on producing." No way in the world I was going to turn over my show to her to twist it into whatever she wanted. She'd turn all my inner city kids into video hoochies.

She scowled again as I walked off. I wanted to tell her to be careful making those ugly faces because her face would get stuck like that. I bit my lip and walked out the door, eager to find Erika and Jason and tell them the good news.

twelve

I scanned the audience at Wednesday night service, looking at the men. I wasn't in a hormonal, lusty mood this time. I just needed to have at least a minute of conversation with some guy, so I could report it at our next girls' night meeting. For the last two meetings, I had no guy encounters to report. With everything going on at work, I didn't have time to be man-chasing.

I didn't feel like watching Angela giggle and glow or hear about Lisa's three men a week, then her repeated slams about me never finding a man.

I glanced down the row at a light-skinned brother. I didn't have much time. We had switched girls' night to Thursday nights because, almost every weekend, Angela was either going to Augusta or Gary was coming here. Lisa also went out regularly on Friday nights, too. She always had some funny story to share about a date gone wrong. Somehow, even with her crazy list, she picked the wrong guys. If it wasn't for Angie, I would have given up on dating altogether.

Light-skinned brother raised his hand in response to something Pastor was preaching, and I noticed a wedding band. I wished there was a rule that married men had to have a big "married" stamp across their forehead. That way I wouldn't have to work so hard to get a look at their ring finger. Looking all desperate and lonely.

After service, I went to the church bookstore to see if they had Micah Stampley's new CD.

"Hey, Michelle. Long time no see. Looking for something in particular?"

Perfect. It was Kelvin, the guy Nicole and Lisa swore was trying to get next to me. I decided that I would chat and flirt for a few minutes, find some reason to rule him out, and have something to report at tomorrow's meeting. *Thanks, God.*

I must have overdone it. Next thing I knew, I was giving Kelvin my number, and we were making plans to go see a movie on Friday night. *Thanks, God. Really. Thanks.*

I was sure God was gonna strike me one day for being sarcastic with Him. I could see Him looking at Jesus and shrugging His shoulders like, "What did I do? She's the one down there batting her eyelashes and giggling when nothing's funny."

Maybe it wouldn't be so bad. He was nice enough looking—butter-cream colored with nice eyes and a great smile. And he seemed godly enough, working at the church bookstore. He had to be in church every time the doors opened. Certainly it had to have some effect on him. Maybe this would be good for me. I needed to get out there and date, instead of whining about being manless but not taking action.

* * *

The girls were excited when I told them about my date at the meeting the next night. Angela was all giggles, more so because of the Gary effect than being happy for me. Lisa was full of dating advice—what to wear, meeting him instead of letting him pick me up, not being an independent Black woman and letting him pay for everything. I felt like I should be taking notes. Nicole smirked the whole evening like she knew there was no way it could go well. I ignored her and made up my mind that no matter what, I was going to have a good time.

Before I knew it, it was Friday night. I realized it was my first date since . . . since forever. I wanted to dress cute, but not like I was trying too hard. I wanted my make-up to look natural and not too overdone. I took out my two-stranded twists and let my hair fly high and wavy. I put on a blue-jeans-turned-blue-jean skirt with African mud cloth trim and a brown T-shirt. My cowry shell choker and earrings finished off the outfit. When I was done, I winked at myself in the mirror. *Don't hurt him, girl.*

Me and Kelvin met at Stonecrest to see a movie. When we got there, he realized he had gotten the time wrong and the movie wasn't due to start for another hour. At least it would give us a chance to talk and get to know each other better. We strolled through the mall, and I had to admit, it felt good to be with a guy. I knew I was looking good, and he looked cute in a pair of nice jeans and a black T-shirt.

We chatted easily for a few minutes while we were walking. This wasn't so bad. Tonight would be fun, and maybe we'd go out again next week. Maybe I would be the one glowing and giggling by the next meeting.

He cracked a few jokes and I laughed. They weren't very funny, but I felt giddy. Whenever I laughed, he smiled real big like it made him happy to make me happy. Which, of course, made me laugh at the next corny joked he cracked. I didn't know why Lisa's luck was so bad. I should've done this weeks ago.

"You look really nice, Michelle. Your hair is real cool like that. I love the natural look."

"Thanks, Kelvin." I blushed a little. I wasn't sure if I was supposed to compliment him back or just say thanks. I should have asked Lisa more dating questions.

He stopped and stood in front of a kiosk that sold vitamins and health products. *Oh good, he's a healthy guy.*

He browsed for a second and then the sales lady came over. "Looking for anything in particular?"

"Yeah. You got anything for stamina and longevity?" He elbowed me in the side and winked.

My eyes flew open. Was he serious? I didn't move or speak while the lady sang the praises of ginseng.

When we walked away, he elbowed me again. "You know I was just playing, right?"

I nodded and forced a smile.

We walked around to a few more stores, and I tried to make myself relax. *Don't rule him out too quick, Michelle. Give him a chance. He's a nice guy. A godly guy. He was just joking.*

His face lit up. "Oh, there's my favorite store. Do you mind if we stop?"

I looked up at the sign. "Shoe-4-Less. All shoes $6.99 and under." Without even thinking, I glanced down at his shoes. Looked like he only had about $1.99 worth of wear left in them. I followed him as he browsed the men's aisles.

He pointed toward the ladies section. "You don't want to look?"

I shook my head. *Do I look like I want to have bunions by the time I'm forty?*

We looked at a few more bargain stores that I never realized were in the mall, and finally, it was time for the movie to start. When we got to the ticket counter, he pulled out an old card and flipped it onto the counter. "Two tickets for *I Am Legend* on a student discount."

The young girl at the counter sucked her teeth and pushed the card back toward him. "We don't do student discounts."

He leaned back and looked at the sign where the movie prices were listed. "No student discounts? Why not? I always get a student discount at Atlantic Station."

She cracked her gum and let out a loud breath. "This ain't Atlantic Station. We don't do student discounts here." She pulled the card toward her. "And this is about ten years old. Ain't you out of school?"

He slid the money across the counter. I wanted to sink into the floor.

I guess he could tell I was embarrassed.

"Sorry about that. I'm a little strapped for cash at the moment. I had to borrow forty bucks from my boy for this date."

He said it like I should be flattered. So, of course when he gestured toward the concession stand, I shook my head—glad I had eaten before I left the house.

After the lights dimmed in the movie, I felt his hand slide onto my right thigh. He couldn't be serious.

I shifted a little, hoping he'd take the hint and move it. He didn't.

I shifted again. He squeezed my thigh, I guess, misinterpreting my squirming.

I finally got disgusted and lifted his hand and pushed it over onto his lap.

He leaned over and whispered, "Yeah, I guess I better keep my hand off your leg. We wouldn't want my nature to rise."

All I could think of was Nicole's face when I shared at the next girls' meeting.

I leaned away from him. He leaned toward me. I leaned further away until I was almost in the empty seat next to me.

He whispered loudly, "What's wrong?"

"What?" I whispered back.

"Why you all the way over there?"

"My side hurts because I slept funny last night." What'd I say that for? Next thing I know he was massaging my side.

I pushed his hand away. "That makes it worse."

He pulled his hand back and scowled. I swear his face stayed like that for the rest of the movie. He kept letting out long disgusted breaths like I really made him mad. Maybe I hadn't dated in a while, but I didn't think his hands all over my body when we just met was the least bit okay.

After the movie ended, we walked out to the parking lot. I held out my hand to shake his. "Thanks so much for such a good time. I really enjoyed the movie." *In spite of you groping me.*

"You're ready to go home so early? I wanted to show you a good time, and I feel like we got off to a bad start. Plus, I still got money left."

I wanted to tell him to save his last twenty dollars. Was I being difficult and unapproachable? I remembered my girls telling me to not rule guys out too fast and sucked in a deep breath. "What do you have in mind?"

"Well, I know you like music, so I figured I'd take you to listen to some jazz."

I thought it was sweet that he considered that I liked music. We talked about the latest gospel CD releases whenever I went into the bookstore, and he played samples for me all the time. I hadn't been out listening to live music in a while, and I could scout some talent for *Indie Artist*. "Okay. Sounds good."

"We should take one car. I'll drive."

I thought about Lisa's rule list, but followed him to his car anyway. It didn't make sense to take two cars to the same place. I bumped into him when he stopped at this ratty, broke-down car. Certainly, it wasn't his. He took out his keys and opened the door. Oh dear, it was.

I wasn't really into cars, but I couldn't imagine getting into his ride. It looked like it was being held together by safety pins and duct tape. The girls were not going to believe me when I described that the hood, side panels and driver's side door were three different colors. I could tell he was friends with whoever owned the junkyard he frequented.

If only I had gotten in my car and driven off then. But I was committed to trying this dating thing. *Right?*

I directed him to one of my favorite jazz spots I used to hang out in.

When we got there, he started to pull into the parking lot. "Valet parking? How much is it?"

"Oh, just five dollars," I said.

"Five dollars? Are they crazy? We can do better than that." He pulled out of the lot and down the street.

I pointed to another parking lot. "There's one. Three dollars for the rest of the evening."

He shook his head. "I think we can do better." He drove another two blocks to a bank parking lot. "See, I told ya. This one's free."

Yeah. It'll just cost my feet four blocks of pain walking in these shoes I was stupid enough to wear trying to be cute for you.

"How much does this place cost to get into anyway?"

If I had driven my own car, I would have left at that moment. Actually I would have left after the parking fiasco.

"I don't know. I used to come before nine when ladies get in for free."

He looked down at his watch. "Dang, we should have skipped the movie and come straight here. It's almost ten."

I wanted to tell him I'd pay my own way, but according to Lisa, that was the worst way to hurt a man's pride.

When we got to the entrance, he asked the woman at the door, "Can ladies still get in for free?"

She rolled her eyes and cast a pitying glance in my direction. "No, sir. It's after nine. It's ten dollars per person."

I was too aggravated to be embarrassed. Or to care about his manhood. I pulled a twenty out of my pocket, pushed it into her hand, and walked through the door before he could say anything.

He followed close behind. "Hey, you didn't have to do that. But thanks. I appreciate you having my back."

I walked toward the tables closest to the jazz stage. The waitress stopped us. "These tables are for dining customers. Will you all be ordering from the menu?"

He looked at me. "You're not hungry, are you?"

I glared at him and bit my tongue. *We met at six, cruised every bargain store in the mall for an hour, watched a movie for two hours, drove here and took an hour to find a parking spot, then walked a mile to get to the club. What do you think?*

I hissed, "Yes, I'm hungry. But, don't worry, I'll buy myself something to eat."

The waitress bit her lip, probably trying not to

laugh. She grabbed two menus and held out her hand. "Right this way."

I was glad she sat us close to the stage. Hopefully, the music would drown out any attempts at conversation. I perused the menu.

He studied it with a pensive look on his face. "We could share some wings. Or an order of fries and something to drink. Or we could split a burger." He looked up at me.

I ignored him.

When the waitress came to the table, I ordered grilled chicken, vegetables, and garlic mashed potatoes. His eyes bugged out when he looked over at the prices on the entrée side of the menu.

I handed my menu to the waitress and said to him, "Don't worry. Like I said, I got it."

He smiled. "Oh, yeah. In that case, I'll have the same thing." He folded the menu and gave it to the waitress. He leaned over and whispered. "You got me, too?"

I looked up at the waitress. "That'll be on separate checks." Luckily, the music started as soon as she left, and I didn't hear another word he said for the rest of the evening. Just nodded and smiled whenever I saw his mouth moving.

After we ate, we walked the marathon back to the bank parking lot and got in his piece of a car. When he turned the key in the ignition, nothing happened. His eyes widened.

He looked at me and turned the key again. Not a sound. "Sorry, it's been doing this a lot lately." He pulled a tool box out of the backseat. "It'll just take me a second to get it started."

Lisa was right. I vowed this would be the last time ever I was caught without my car. I pulled out my cell and called Nicole. Thankfully, she was only about ten minutes away.

He was still tinkering under the hood when she pulled up in her Mercedes. I got out and walked around to the front of his car. "Thanks for the evening, Kelvin. You take care."

"You're leaving?" He looked at Nicole's car, looked at me, then back at her car.

"Uh, yeah." *Be nice, Michelle.*

"What about me?" He wiped his black hands on his jeans.

I stepped back, hoping he wasn't planning on touching me. "Don't you have someone you can call?"

"Oh, it's like that?"

"Like what, Kelvin?" *You knew this broke-down piece of junk would probably leave us stranded when you suggested we take one car.* What was I supposed to do, call him a cab and pay for it?

"You think you could help me out with a cab?"

I didn't bother to answer. Just walked around to the passenger side of Nicole's car.

"You're leaving for real? You gon' leave a brother hanging?"

The only bad part of this was that I would have to see him around church occasionally.

He continued to rant, "I can't believe this. You like all the rest. I'm sick of all you Black women who think . . ."

I got in the car and slammed the door as the curse words started flying.

Nicole looked over at me and started to say something.

I held up a hand. "Just drive, girl. I can't even talk about it right now."

She looked at Kelvin's three-toned car, chuckled and pulled off. "Umm, umm, umm. Girls' night can't come fast enough."

I leaned back and closed my eyes. *Okay, God. I tried. It was horrible. Can you send me my perfect man now? Just send him to ring my doorbell . . .*

thirteen

It was a good thing we had the next girls' night at Vanessa's. Nobody else had enough floor space for everyone to be rolling around laughing when I shared the details of my date with Mr. Cheapo.

Vanessa held her side, trying to catch her breath, Angela laughed and coughed until I thought she would choke to death, and Lisa kept screeching for me to stop before she peed on herself. And Nicole? She turned bright red. I was scared her eyeballs were gonna pop out of her head. Of course, I embellished the story and made the whole thing sound worse than it had to. I figured I needed to get some pleasure out of it.

When I got to the part about his car, Nicole stopped laughing long enough to validate the fact that the car was indeed maroon, yellow, and blue.

"So, I think that counts as enough for the next three weeks." I waited for everyone to stop laughing and get back on the couch.

"What do you mean?" Lisa wiped her eyes. "You don't want to go on any more dates?"

"Did you hear anything I just said?"

"I know it was bad, but you have to keep trying. You can't stop now. You're just getting started and already, you've topped me." Lisa erupted into a fresh set of giggles. ·

Vanessa said, "Even though she's being evil, Lisa's right. You have to get back out there."

I folded my arms. "Yeah, whatever."

Vanessa continued, "No. Really, Michelle. In fact, you have to promise to go on another date within the next week."

"Within the week? It took me all this time to get this one. Where am I supposed to meet a guy to go out with by next week?"

"You can find a guy," Angela said. "You're Miss Social."

I could tell they weren't going to let me out of it. I suddenly had an overwhelming need for something sweet and was glad Angela had baked chocolate chip cookies for us. I reached over to the coffee table and grabbed the largest cookie on the plate. "Okay, enough about me. Lisa, let's hear about your fiasco for the week." The only thing I could do was change the subject and hope they'd forget by the end of the evening.

Lisa was all too ready to tell her story. I was beginning to think it was fun for her to shock us with how bad her guy encounters were.

"Remember the guy I told you about that I met on eHarmony and we hit it off? The journalist guy?"

"The guy that broke up with you by text message?" Nicole started laughing again.

Vanessa frowned. "I think I missed that one. Catch me up."

"Well, I met this guy on eHarmony." Lisa rolled her eyes like she was beginning to wonder if it was a worthwhile investment. "And he seemed cool. We emailed back and forth for a while and had similar interests. When I felt like he wasn't a lunatic, I gave him my number, and we talked on the phone a few times. We were really feeling each other, and for the first time since this whole madness started, I felt like I might actually have a nice date."

"Uh-huh." Vanessa nodded and picked out the smallest cookie on the plate.

"For real this time," Lisa said emphatically. "We like the same music. Same movies and television shows. He writes for a newspaper, I work for a magazine. He's a Christian and really into God. We had some really good spiritual discussions and after a couple of weeks, we decided to meet. He lives in Macon—not too far—so we made plans for him to come here like six weeks ago.

"Well, you know me. I got my hair done and bought a new outfit and planned where we were gonna go for the weekend. And then at work on Friday afternoon, I pick up my cell and notice that I have a text from him. Five messages, to be exact."

"Five messages?" Vanessa asked.

Lisa nodded. "I read the first one. He says he can't believe this happened but there was this girl his cousin had introduced him to a month prior. The first time he met her, he thought God told him she was his wife, but she dumped him. She called him the night before and told him she felt like she missed God—next message—and she had a dream about him and God showed her they were supposed to be together. He didn't want to disobey God since He told him that they were to be married on the first date and then God gave her a dream—next message—that he knew it was God for them to be together. And so even though it seemed like I was wonderful and we had hit it off, he had to heed the voice of God and date—next message—this woman. And he was sorry to have to break it off this way and hoped there would be no hard feelings and he knew God would send me—next message—the perfect man in His perfect time."

Vanessa's mouth was locked open. "He sent all that in a text?" She looked around at all of us, stifling giggles.

"Not one text." Lisa sucked her teeth. "Five texts." Lisa reached over to the coffee table and turned the plate around, examining the cookies, probably looking for the one with the most chocolate chips. She finally picked out two and slid the plate back to the middle of the table.

"So, fast forward to the present. I get a text two days ago, and I don't recognize the number. It says, *Hey beautiful lady. How are you?* So, of course, my curiosity gets the best of me, and I answer and text, *Fine, who is this?* This nut has the nerve to write back, *The love of your life—Randy.* Girl, I almost threw the phone. I texted him back and said I was busy on a shoot. He wasn't worth a minute more of my time."

"I know that's right, girl," I said. "I can't believe he had the nerve to even contact you."

Lisa sucked her teeth and rolled her eyes. "So, I didn't even think about him. This afternoon, I get this text from him saying he's going to be in town this weekend and he'd love to have the opportunity to meet me. I texted back, *Hmmm, things didn't work out with that other girl, huh?* He writes back, *No it didn't. How did you know?* Now y'all know I'm trying to get delivered from the spirit of sarcasm, but he took me there. I wrote back, *I'm prophetic. The Lord showed it to me by divine revelation.* This nut writes back, *Wow you really are prophetic. That's amazing. Godly and beautiful. What a combination.* I just stared at the phone. Couldn't believe he could be that dumb. So, then he sends another text. *So do I get to meet you this weekend, lovely woman of God?*"

"No way in the world. Are you serious?" I asked.

"Girl, yes. I just wrote back, *No, I'll be spending my weekend with my wonderful new man of God.* Then I blocked my phone, so he couldn't call or text me anymore. God's gonna have to forgive me for lying."

We all laughed.

I wondered when Lisa would get tired of it all. If I'd had so many bad experiences, I'd shut it down and start praying for God to make me a eunuch.

"So, Angie, how's Gary?" Vanessa asked. "Is he coming, or are you going this weekend?"

"I'm going down there. He has to work late tomorrow, so it's easier for me to travel."

Angela's glow was blinding. I thought we were

going to have to put a veil on her, like the Israelites did with Moses.

"Where do you stay when you go down there?" Nicole shivered and pulled a blanket around her shoulders, snuggling back into the couch. "Does he put you up in a nice hotel?"

"Well . . . um . . . the first few times I stayed in a hotel, but the last time, I stayed in his guest room." Angela munched on a cookie. "We both figured there was no sense in spending all that money since we spend so much of our time together anyway."

We all sat silent for a few minutes.

Finally, Vanessa said, "Angela, do you think that's a good idea?" She got up to adjust the thermostat. Sometimes she overdid it with the air conditioner.

Angela shrugged. "It's not like we're doing anything. He sleeps in his bedroom. I sleep in the guestroom. It's really no different from the hotel, if you think about it."

"No different from the hotel? Instead of miles, you're sleeping within feet of the man you're in love with?" Vanessa said gently.

"We're not going to do anything," Angela said.

Lisa asked, "You don't get tempted?"

"Not at all. I've waited this long. I'm not gonna mess up now."

"How do you know?" Lisa asked.

"Because I'm not. We're both committed to waiting until marriage. And, yes, we talked. I told him I was a virgin and that made him feel even more committed to us not doing anything."

Was it me, or did Angela seem a little too defensive? "Yeah, but even if you're committed, that doesn't mean you're above temptation. You're still human, Angela," I said.

"I'm not like that. I don't get all hot and bothered like you guys do. I guess 'cause I've never had sex. I mean, I enjoy kissing him and all and snuggling and being close to him. We even slept in the bed together one night because we fell asleep watching a movie, and nothing happened."

"You slept in the bed with him?" Lisa, Nicole asked together.

Angie put a hand over her mouth, like she hadn't meant to let that slip out.

Vanessa put a hand on Angela's shoulder. "Sweetie, you're playing a very dangerous game. Gary is a grown man, and even though he may have every intention of waiting until marriage, you can't put yourself in that kind of position. You're asking to fall."

Angie shrugged off Vanessa's hand. "We're not going to fall. Gary is godly, and I'm godly. I'm a virgin at forty-one. Doesn't that count for something? Why don't you guys have any faith in me?"

"It's not a matter of having faith in you, Angie," I said. "It's understanding the flesh and our natural urges. Especially a man's urges. It's human nature. If you play with fire, no matter how careful you are, you eventually get burnt."

Vanessa chimed in, "Please, sweetie, you've got to hear us on this and trust that we know what we're talking about. I think we've all found ourselves in compromising positions. And no matter how much we loved God and how saved we thought we were, it wasn't enough to keep us. You can't take it for granted that you won't do it. Because when you're the most vulnerable or even when you least expect it, things happen. You don't want to live with that kind of regret. After holding off this long, you should experience the joy of waiting until your wedding night."

Angela sat quietly for a few minutes. "I hear you guys, but I assure you, there's nothing to worry about. Sometimes I even wonder if I have a sex drive. I feel love for Gary, but the sex thing? I feel nothing. There's no burning or sweating or lusting like Michelle's always talking about. And Gary is a perfect gentleman."

"How about we all chip in and pay for your hotel?" Nicole suggested.

"You guys don't have to do that. It's really not about the money. I just want to be with him. I've never been in love like this before."

"Exactly why you don't need to be staying at his house," Lisa said.

Angela got up and walked toward the kitchen. "Stop worrying. I'm not gonna do anything."

The four of us let out a collective sigh. I knew we'd all be sending up some serious prayers because Angela's head was like a brick. And like my daddy always said, a hard head made a soft behind.

Angela came back with a liter of Coke and some cups.

I remembered the awful feeling the first time me and my ex slipped. I felt like dirt. Worse than dirt. I didn't want to go to church. Didn't want to pray. Didn't want to face God. The shame was crippling. And in spite of the shame, we did it again. And again. And again. I couldn't seem to stop. And he didn't even try. Which is how I ended up married at twenty-one.

And Angela thought she was immune to it. That sex demon that took over your life when you gave it half a chance. That awful thing that made you put on your sexiest lingerie and end up at his apartment when you knew you needed to take your butt home. Then, somehow, you ended up in the bedroom or on the couch, and somehow your clothes came off, and next thing you knew, you were filled with regret that you had messed up yet again.

I shook my head.

"What, Michelle?" Angela almost spat the words at me.

I pursed my lips and shook my head again. "Nothing, sweetie. Nothing at all." Seemed like all we could do was sit back and pray, hoping for the best.

And be there to help Angela put things back together if things went wrong.

fourteen

I didn't escape the last girls' night meeting without promising them I would try at least three more dates before I gave up. I don't how they got that promise out of me. Angela started talking about how wonderful it was to have a date every weekend and how Gary had started hinting about spending the rest of his life with her. Vanessa took over with some spiritual psychobabble about pressing in when we want to retreat, and Lisa finished me off with old- maid jokes.

So, I encouraged myself in the Lord and went on the prowl for more dates. Even though things turned out bad with Kelvin, I decided it was safest to stick with guys from the church.

One of the guys that served in the homeless ministry with me had always been a little friendly, and I figured he was worth a try. Any guy concerned about the less fortunate had to be pretty godly, right?

After our latest trip to a downtown women's

shelter, I struck up a conversation and flirted a little, and it wasn't long before he asked me out.

I decided to try the movies again. As I had found out with Kelvin, if I didn't like him, at least I could lose myself in a good movie and then the date could be over. And this time, I wouldn't let the date drag on after any hints that things were gonna go south.

Once again, we met at Stonecrest Mall. Thomas was leaning against a pole waiting for me. Outside the church setting, he had a different look. A different swagger. I didn't like it.

"Hey, Michelle. Boy, do you look good." He started a lame LL Cool J impression, licking his thick lips.

"Hey, Thomas. Good to see you, too." I couldn't think of another thing to say. So, I smiled and stood there watching him lick his ashy lips. I started to offer him some Chapstick, but I didn't want to share. No telling how much slob he had built up on those lips of his.

We headed toward the theatre. The line was a little long, so I had no choice but to talk to him for a few minutes. I wanted to tell him to wipe off the white stuff gathering at the edges of his lips. I almost gagged at the thought of him trying to kiss me at the end of the night.

He looked up at the movie choices and times. "You know, I was thinking, instead of seeing *Meet the Browns*, how about we go see *Iron Man*?"

I really didn't want to see *Iron Man*, but decided to try to be agreeable. "I guess, if that's what you want to see."

"Well, I only want to see what you want to see."

I forced a smile. "I told you what I wanted to see."

He licked his lips, disrupting some of the white crust. "I know, but I didn't want to see that. I figured you might want to see *Iron Man*."

"Sure, Thomas. That's fine." Now I couldn't even use the deliciously gorgeous men Tyler Perry always seemed to find to star in his movies as a distraction. *God, just let this end, please.*

"Yeah, but only if you want to see it."

My only solace now was that I was going to have another funny story to share on girls' night. "Honestly, I really want to see *Meet the Browns*, but if you'd rather see *Iron Man*, that's fine."

"I want you to be happy."

"Then take me to see *Meet the Browns*." We were almost at the front of the line.

"Okay. Okay." He stood there for a second. "Wow, I really don't want to see *Meet the Browns*. Are you sure you don't want to see *Iron Man*?"

It's a sure sign that a date isn't going well when you start to imagine what it would feel like to have your fingers gripping the man's throat.

"You know what, Thomas? I have a great idea. Why don't you go see *Iron Man*, and I'll go see *Meet the Browns*."

"But then we won't be on a date."

"Exactly."

He stood there pondering that for a second. "Will I still have to pay for yours then?"

And with that, I simply turned around and walked back to my car.

* * *

And then there was Derrick from the youth ministry. He seemed like a godly enough guy from our brief interactions with the kids. After the last youth ministry meeting, I did my usual batting my eyelashes and giggling at non-funny jokes, and next thing I knew, we were on a date.

He took me out to dinner at The Cheesecake Factory. He was the perfect gentleman, opening doors and pulling chairs, like his momma had taught him well. He was also cute, with nice white teeth and dimples. Kinda reminded me of Jason. He did the conscientious Christian-guy thing, forcing himself to look at my face every time his eyes instinctively wandered down to my body.

"This is a nice place. How often do you come here?" I looked at the menu to pick a mid-priced item. Another one of Lisa's rules.

"Only when God leads me. I try to make sure in everything I do and everywhere I go, I'm led by God."

Okay . . . the first sign. Hopefully he wasn't serious. I laughed a little, but realized he wasn't telling a joke. He seemed to be purposefully looking away from me, making me wonder if I had something in my nose. I thought I looked extra cute tonight—had even worn a V-neck top that gave up a little cleavage.

Second sign . . . when the food came, he grabbed my hand for prayer. "Father, in the name of Jesus, we bless this food, Father God in the name of Jesus. And we pray that you cleanse it of all impurities, Father God in the name of Jesus. We declare that it is blessed and that it blesses our bodies with health and life, Father God in the name of Jesus. We curse any curses on this food and bind any curses that may have been imparted into it by the hands that prepared it, Father God in the name of Jesus. We declare that any voodoo or witchcraft that anyone in the kitchen may be participating in to bring curses into our lives does not affect us, Father God in the name of Jesus, and we curse the curse and plead the blood and declare it has no effect on us, Father God in the name of Jesus."

I peeked out of one eye at his face, intense with his mealtime intercession. You never knew what was inside of someone until you spent ten minutes with them. Only then could you get an inkling of how warped they might be.

As he continued on in warfare over our dinner, I hoped it wouldn't be long before I could partake of what had to be the most blessed, curse-free chicken I would ever eat in my life. I had to wonder what brought him to this point. Had some girl worked some roots on him in his past?

I tuned back into his prayer just in time to hear him say, "And I rebuke the spirit of perversion. You foul demon, you will not tempt me. I curse you and plead the blood over my life and my purity. You will not cause me to fall tonight. I curse you, spirit of lust. You foul demon of sexual impurity, I curse you. Satan, the Lord rebuke you. You will not draw me into sexual sin." He dropped my hand like it was hot and drew back. He looked at me like I was Jezebel herself.

"Michelle, I am sensing a strong spirit of perversion here. I'm not sure if it's you or if it's someone in the restaurant, but I want to serve the devil notice that I will not fall into sexual sin tonight. I rebuke it in the name of Jesus and declare that the blood of Jesus is covering my life."

I flagged down the waitress. "Can I get my food to go?"

Then there was Larry. Should have known better than to let Erika set me up with someone who she knew would be "perfect" for me.

I had decided that with any new guy, we would meet for coffee first, and then if I didn't like him, I didn't have to sit through a whole dinner or a whole movie. He met me at my car a few doors down from the Starbucks in downtown Decatur. He was nice-looking. Nice chocolate brown with a shiny bald head, nice broad nose and strong chin. Maybe tonight would be a better night.

After we shook hands and went through the nice-to-meet-you routine, we started walking down the street and he grabbed my hand. "I hope you don't mind me holding your hand. I like to show my ladies affection."

I tried to not be too abrupt when I pulled my hand away. "That's sweet, but I'd like to get to know you better first." *And I don't know where your hand has been.* I looked longingly at my car, wanting to dash back to it, get in and go screeching down the street. *Just coffee, Michelle, and a new story for the girls.*

So we ordered our coffee and sat in those comfortable armchairs in Starbucks. We didn't get too far into the small talk before I started to wonder what it was about him that made Erika think I would want to go out with him. He bantered about his years working at the post office and all the stress that went with that line of work.

As he droned on and on about stuff I had no interest in, I remembered Angela asking about dating a guy without a college degree. It wasn't about being snotty about his level of education. It was more a matter of him not having anything to talk about that I wanted to hear.

When it came time for me to talk about what I did, he listened intently, then said, "Wow. That's intimidating. You're really successful. That's really intimidating for a guy like me."

Strike two. Time to go ahead and get it over with. I asked one of my most important rule-out questions. "So what's your ultimate? Your dream? Where are you trying to go with your life?"

He sat there for a second, blinking, like he had never considered that question.

I sat quietly, waiting for him to come up with something. Even if I never saw him again, maybe my role here was to make him think about destiny and purpose.

"I don't know. Haven't really ever thought about that." He kept blinking with a blank stare.

"Really? Never?" *Sir, you are forty years old. When do you plan to think about it?*

He shrugged. "I guess it hasn't been important."

What could be more important? I wanted to scream at him.

I could tell I had him feeling bad about himself,

so I figured I'd change the subject to something he could brag about. "So, Erika tells me you have two daughters?"

He nodded. "Yeah, but you wouldn't have to worry about them. They both live with their mothers. One in Texas and the other in Kentucky. I haven't seen either of them in a couple of years. They wouldn't be a problem." He said it like I should be relieved.

You haven't seen your children in years?! What kind of deadbeat are you?

I decided to change the subject to give him one last chance to redeem himself, not that there was much chance of that. "So, where do you go to church?"

Erika had gone on and on about how we would hit it off because he was such a spiritual man. Even though I had already ruled him out, talking about God might at least make the rest of this brief coffee date slightly interesting.

"Oh, nowhere. I'm a practicing Buddhist. Like Tina Turner. After I saw *What's Love Got To Do With It*, I knew it was for me." He started chanting. "Na Re Me Co . . ."

I drained the rest of my coffee and stood up. "Whew, shouldn't have had this coffee. My stomach is really bubbling. Hate to cut things short, but I better head home."

He had to run to follow me to my car.

When I opened the door and started to get in, he said, "Call me on your way home. There's something I need to tell you."

Oh dear. Could this get any worse? "What is it?"

"Just call me on your way home. I'll tell you then."

I'd had enough. "We're grown adults. If there's anything you need to tell me, tell me now." *Not like it matters. I will never see you again. Unless, of course, you're delivering my mail.*

He leaned over close to my ear and whispered, "I have genital herpes."

I froze. Did he just say what I thought he said? *Don't react, Michelle. Think. Say something.* "Well, one in four Americans does." All I could think of was this stupid commercial on TV for herpes medicine.

I got into my car as quickly as I could. His announcement not only said he thought there was a chance we'd have another date, but that if we did, he thought we'd sleep together. I knew how to nip this in the bud.

"Since we're making confessions, you should know that I'm celibate and plan to stay that way until I'm married." Certainly that was enough to get rid of him.

"Really?" He stood there thinking for a few moments. "We would have to get married quick, then. Like within six months."

I had no more words. I quickly shut the door and started up the car. As I drove down the street, I reached into the glove compartment to pull out my hand sanitizer. I couldn't believe he tried to hold my hand.

* * *

At our next girls' meeting, I dethroned Lisa as the queen of bad dates. The girls laughed until I thought they would get sick as I told them about Mr. Indecisive, Mr. Super-Spiritual, and Mr. Infectious Disease. I laughed with them at first, but the bad taste in my mouth from each experience took away from the humor.

After all that, I wasn't so sure about this dating stuff. If my bad dates and Lisa's bad dates were any indication of what I would continue to experience, I was pretty sure I didn't want to date any more. Perhaps we needed to come to a scary conclusion.

Maybe guys our age who were single were single for a reason.

I looked up at Angela. She seemed more quiet and withdrawn than usual. I wondered if she was trying to stay invisible because she was afraid we'd get on her case again about staying at Gary's house when she went to Augusta for the weekend.

I couldn't imagine being in her position. If, by chance, I was blessed to meet someone wonderful, I'd have her dilemma. I couldn't imagine trying to stay celibate in a relationship where I was in love with someone. It was hard enough when I was a twenty-one-year-old virgin. What would it be like now that I was a grown thirty-five-year-old woman who was all too familiar with the pleasures of sex? With hormones raging twice a month.

As much as I wanted a man in my life and as tired as I was of fighting the lonely monster and the horny monster, I wasn't sure I could handle any more bad dates. And I wasn't sure I could handle fighting to stay celibate if I did fall in love.

I looked around at my girls. I wasn't gonna tell them, but I was ready to get on the bench in this game. I'd continue to have brief guy encounters just to have something to say on girls' night, but that was about it.

Between you and me, God, I'm through.

fifteen

I looked at the clock on my office wall. It was 7:00 on a Friday night. Angela was in Augusta with Gary, and Lisa had a date with some eHarmony guy. Vanessa was spending family night with the kids, and Nicole was exhausted from a rough week at work. So, I was alone. Friendless. Manless. Dateless.

It was a perfect opportunity to get some work done, so I planned to hole up in my office until I couldn't keep my eyes open anymore. Nicole promised to hang out with me tomorrow after I finished running around and doing errands, and then there were Sunday's activities. So Friday night was the only gaping hole in my weekend I needed to fill.

Jason stuck his head in the door. "I'm about to cut out. Want me to walk you to your car?"

"I'm fine, Jason. I want to get a lot more done before I get out of here. When I'm ready to go, I'll get Hank to walk me." That would give our security guard the highlight of his day. I remembered his gold-toothed smile lighting up the night when I asked him to escort me to my car.

"What are you working on? Need some help?"

Honestly, I did, but didn't think it would be a good idea to be sitting up in my office with Jason late on a Friday night. "Nah. I got it. Just need some quiet time to get my thoughts together. It's hard when everybody's here, popping their heads in my office with questions all day. I get my real work done when everybody's gone." I hoped he would take the hint without being offended.

He didn't. In what was becoming his habit, he plopped himself down in the chair in my office. "Come on, two heads are better than one. Whatever it is, the two of us can knock it out together in half the time it would take you by yourself. Let me help."

What was up with that? Jason was practically begging. "Don't you have to get home to the girls?"

He shook his head, a pained look spread across his face. "Their mom has them this weekend. The whole weekend. She got them from school this afternoon, and I won't get them back until Sunday night."

So that was it. Jason was avoiding being home alone without his girls like I was avoiding being home alone without a man. It seemed cruel to send him away after that. "Okay. If I'm not keeping you from anything . . ."

He shook his head.

"Why don't we take my computer and these files down to the conference room, so we can spread out?"

His eyes brightened like he was glad to be needed somewhere. "Cool. Want me to order in some food?"

My stomach grumbled almost as if on cue. "Yeah, food would be good right now. What do you want?"

He grinned. "I'll surprise you." He disappeared down the hall.

My stomach did a little flip-flop, this time not from hunger. *Michelle, what have you done? Bad idea. Bad idea . . .*

I gathered the files and unplugged the cords from my laptop.

By the time I had everything all together, Jason was back. "Food will be here in about thirty minutes. Is that cool?"

Before I could answer, my stomach let out a loud grumble again. We both laughed.

He said, "Want me to get you a snack from the machine? Doesn't sound like you're gonna make it."

"I'm fine, Jason. I always keep food around." I grabbed a box of raisins and some chips from my desk drawer and followed him down the hall to the conference room. The office was completely empty. Guess everyone else had plans for their Friday night.

I wondered why Jason was desperate and lonely. If what Erika said about men finding a replacement woman real quick was true, he should be out on a date right now. Maybe he was taking time to focus on himself and on his girls. Maybe his recent lingering appearances in my office had nothing to do with being interested in me at all.

"Why are you working late anyway? I'm surprised you're not out on a Friday night with that special someone," Jason said.

Oh dear. So much for that theory.

"I'm focused on my shows right now. God gave me this shot, and I've got to make the best of it. I'm trying to get to senior producer in the next two years."

"You'll get it. There's no one more qualified, and plus, you've got the favor of God on your life. If you don't get it, it's only because He's got something much greater for you."

"Thanks, Jason. I appreciate that." I smiled at him.

He smiled back.

God, help me. "So anyway, this is where I am right now." I powered on my computer, spread out some papers on the table, and we went to work.

After about twenty minutes, the security guard buzzed in to let us know our food had arrived. When the delivery guy walked in with two bags, the rich, pungent fragrance of exotic spices filled the air.

Jason paid the guy, and he left.

I looked in the bags and confirmed what my nose had guessed. "Ethiopian? That's one of my favorites. How did you know?"

"I remembered you bringing in leftovers after you went out one night. You ate it like it was the best thing you ever tasted and kept saying how much you loved it. I figured it'd be a nice surprise."

"How thoughtful. Thanks, Jason." *I'm in way over my head here, God.*

We ate and worked for a couple of hours.

As always, I couldn't help but realize how smart Jason was. His mind was quick, and he had a different way of approaching things. Creative. Out the box. Like me. Every time I got stumped, he'd come up with an answer. If I couldn't figure out something, he would sit and talk to himself for a minute until he came up with a great idea.

"Jason, you're good at this. Have you ever thought of trying your hand at producing or directing?"

He nodded. "I did before I came here. Some friends and I shot a few short films and some documentaries. But when things fell apart with my marriage, I had to get a stable, salaried job. My girls go before my dreams."

"Wow. I didn't know. You're such a help to me around here, I guess I should have known. You're definitely more than an editor."

His cell phone rang. His face lit up when he recognized the number. "Hey, baby."

I stood up to leave to give him some privacy, trying to ignore the sinking in the pit of my stomach. Did Jason have a girlfriend?

He motioned for me to stay. "What's wrong, sweetie?" His face clouded over. "I know, honey, but Daddy—"

It was one of his girls. I let out a breath I didn't realize I was holding.

"I know, sweetie, but Daddy can't—" He rubbed his forehead. "Where's your sister?" His face looked more pained. "Put your mother on the phone." Jason stood up and held up a finger as he walked out the door.

I could hear him say a few more gentle words to

his daughter, then his voice changed. His tone sounded diplomatic at first, but then became a little strained. I couldn't hear exactly what he was saying but knew he was getting upset.

He paced back and forth up and down the hall while still talking.

I finally heard him say, "I won't talk to you about this anymore. I'm hanging up the phone now. I'll be there to get my girls in the morning." He continued to pace up and down the hall for a while, mumbling to himself.

He stopped for a minute, and his tone changed. I heard him still talking to himself, but I could hear him quoting scriptures. His pace slowed. I could hear bits and pieces of the Word coming from his mouth.

He finally came back to the conference room. "Sorry about that. The girls are . . . Latrice is . . ." He shrugged his shoulders and tried to grin. "Baby mama drama. What can I say?"

"Do you need to go?"

He shook his head. "Not at all. Working helps. And I don't need to be by myself right now." He looked at me with those eyes, asking me to rescue him from whatever pain Latrice had just caused.

"Want to talk about it?" *Bad idea, Michelle, bad idea.*

He shook his head. "Nah, you don't need to hear my drama. Let's get back to work."

We tried to work for a while, but mentally, he was gone. I could tell he was worried about whatever his daughter had called him for and mad about whatever Latrice had said. My brain was tired too.

"We should call it quits. We're just going in circles now." I saved the files on my laptop. "Thanks for all your help. If I do make senior producer, I'll owe it to you. We got a lot done."

"You'll get it. You're one of those people who gets everything they go for. I bet your life is exactly what you planned it would be when you were a little girl."

If he only knew. "Not exactly, but I have to admit my life is pretty great." *Except that I don't have my Ken look-alike and two daughters and castle on the hill with my ponies in the stable . . .*

He shook his head. "I wish I could say that right now. I mean, God is good and faithful, and I'm grateful for all He's done for me, but . . ." Jason shrugged. "I never planned to be a thirty-two-year-old, divorced, single father of two kids working a job that's less than my potential and having baby mama drama."

I wanted to reach over and take his hand, but knew better. I shut down the computer.

"Divorced, single father of two trying to fight my way out of debt. That's what I get for marrying a spoiled rich girl and trying to make all her materialistic dreams come true."

Jason, please don't open up to me. Then I'll like you more. I don't need to like you more.

Jason stared off into space. "You know when you're young and you have plans for yourself and you imagine just what your life will look like by a certain age? This is not what I planned. At all."

"I know what you mean."

"Come on, your life is perfect. What more could you want?"

"I thought I'd be married with children by now."
Oh my God, did I say that out loud?

"Really? I thought you were one of those success-oriented women who focuses on their career first and family later."

Ouch. Do I really come off like that? "Why is it that if a Black woman is successful, people automatically assume she's not interested in having a family?"

"Whoa, I didn't mean that as an insult. I'm just saying—it seems like you're committed to your career path. That's admirable."

There was no way I was going to tell him that I focused on my career to avoid the pain of not having a family. "I am committed to my career, but that doesn't mean I don't want a husband and kids." I started gathering my papers to put back into the file folders.

"I guess it's kinda hard to balance the two."

No, it's just impossible to find the right man.

"I guess it's easier for guys. A woman has to be concerned about her career *and* her children. Unless, of course, you're Latrice, who decides to quit her job to stay home with the kids, but she ends up going shopping all the time and spending everything I make and completely neglecting the girls."

I could tell Jason still had a lot of hurt and bitterness about his marriage ending. I remembered feeling like that. Every thought path somehow led back to my ex-husband and how he did me wrong. It took me a long time to release and forgive. I wondered if Jason had started his path to healing yet.

"Sorry about that. I'm working on not letting

what happened get to me like that. It's over and done, and there's no sense in harping on it. I just need to get on with my life and forget everything she did."

I nodded. "Exactly. That's what I had to do with my ex."

"You're divorced?" Jason looked like he was shocked.

"Yeah. You didn't know?"

He shrugged. "It's not like you share any details of your personal life. You're always the consummate professional. Wow. How long have you been divorced? If you don't mind me asking, that is."

"I don't mind. I've been divorced for almost three years. I was married for eleven."

He let out a low whistle. "Whew. Eleven years? That's a long time. You never had kids?"

I shook my head. "No kids."

That was the question people asked when they heard how long I had been married. I knew he wanted to know why, but was afraid he'd offend me by asking.

"I got married when I was young—twenty-one. At first, we decided we were going to wait for five years before having children. I wanted to finish grad school, and he was . . . I guess trying to figure out what he wanted to do. After the five years passed, I started to question whether he was really someone I wanted to have kids with."

Jason winced. "That bad?"

"Yeah. Like I said, we were young. By the time I grew up enough to realize what it took to be a good husband and father, I realized he didn't have it. So, I kept stalling. He really wanted a baby, but I kept coming up with reasons why we shouldn't. I kept taking the pill. By about year eight, I knew we weren't going to make it."

"And you stayed for three more years?"

I nodded. "Yeah. I guess it was the Christianity thing. I thought I wouldn't be saved if I got a divorce. I didn't want to disappoint God. So I stayed and prayed and fasted and hoped and waited. And it never got better. Then he cheated on me and gave me the out I needed."

What was it about Jason's eyes that made me spill my painful life story? I couldn't believe I was telling him all this deep, personal stuff. I realized we were turning a corner and arriving at a place we wouldn't be able to come back from.

He reached over and rubbed my back.

Oh, help me Father. Jason, please don't touch me. Not while I'm all wide open and vulnerable.

I swallowed hard to keep the rest of the story from spilling out. For the last two years of my marriage, I stopped taking the pill because I wanted a baby even if we did split up. I knew the stats for Black women my age getting married again. And of course I couldn't have a child without being married. So I decided to get pregnant and have me a baby. Even if it meant I had to be connected to my ex for the rest of my life. At least I'd have a child.

But I never got pregnant. So now, in the back of my mind, I had this nagging fear that maybe something was wrong with me and I couldn't have a baby. Which was why I wouldn't mind marrying a man that already had children. Just in case.

Jason stopped rubbing my back and leaned his

elbows on the table. "Even though they're going through hell right now, I can't imagine not having my girls. Maybe I'm being selfish, because I hate what they're going through, but they are my world. I guess if I had realized how things were going to turn out, I would have been smart like you and not brought kids into a bad situation. Looking back, all the signs were there that Latrice was a materialistic gold digger. But she was so pretty and so sweet, and I was just dumb and wanted to make her happy. So, I let her make us live beyond our means, getting us—me—in a load of debt. And when I couldn't provide enough for her, she went off and found someone who could."

"She left you with a bunch of debt? You couldn't get it back in the divorce?"

He shook his head. "It would have dragged things out longer, and I just wanted to get over it. Plus, I'm a man. I'm not gonna beg for money from a woman."

"Even if it's her debt?"

He shook his head.

"Does she at least pay you child support? It would at least be a way of getting back all she took from you."

He shook his head. "I wouldn't want child support from her. She doesn't work, so anything I would get would be from him. I refuse to let another man support my daughters."

I could see the heat rising in Jason's face.

"I'd die before I did that."

"I can't imagine what it's like to have your girls around another man."

"I try not to think about it. Because of the way

things ended with me and Latrice, I didn't get a chance to get to know him without hostility. I don't know what kind of man he is, except that he's the kind that steals another man's wife. What if I wake one day to the nightmare that this man has molested my daughters? I'd have to spend the rest of my life in jail." Jason tightened his jaw and clenched his fists. "And it would be worth every day.

"And even if it's not that, every time they come home, they have something new and expensive. Stuff I can't afford and wouldn't buy even if I could. I'm afraid it's eroding their value system. I don't want them to end up like their mother. The guy seems to feel the need to make me feel small. It's not enough that he took my wife. He has to rub my face in it. With his money and flashy cars and crazy expensive gifts for my daughters. And comments about my finances that let me know Latrice has run me down to him like I'm some no-good somebody that didn't give her everything she wanted and needed. I'm a good man and did everything I could to provide a godly home for my family. But it wasn't good enough for her. I never saw the dollar signs in her eyes, I guess. Or maybe she changed over the years. I don't know."

Jason seemed to be lost in thought, as if he forgot I was sitting there listening.

"And I can't blame her entirely. I guess maybe I was like that a little when we first got married. We were both all about chasing success and the American dream. But then I got saved. And she didn't. And my priorities changed. All of a sudden, my life was about seeking first the Kingdom. And she couldn't understand that. I guess more than anything, it was God that made us grow apart. Seems weird to even say that, but the Word says Jesus came not to bring peace, but a sword. Even in the most intimate family relationships. I guess that's what happened to us."

Maybe it wouldn't be such a bad idea to date Jason. He was a good father, valued being a good provider, and his first priority was the Kingdom. Sounded a lot like my list. Not to mention he was fine.

No, Michelle. My heart was causing my mind to compromise. I needed to end this before Jason drew me in even deeper. I looked up at the clock. "Oh, my goodness. Is that right?"

Jason turned around to see the time. "Oh, no. I didn't realize we had been there this long."

It was after eleven. I packed up my laptop, and Jason helped me carry everything back to my office. When we had put everything away, he helped me put on my coat and waited until I had gathered all my things.

"Jason, thanks again for all your help tonight. Like I said, when I get promoted to senior producer, I'll owe you big."

He waved away my gratitude. "My pleasure. It's fun working with you, and it helped me keep my mind off the girls. For most of the evening, anyway." He put a hand on my shoulder. "And thanks for listening. It's cool talking to you."

I must have been blushing. "It was good talking to you, too, Jason."

And just like on the church steps, I guess the

moment had him feeling a little too friendly, and he reached out to hug me.

This time, instead of doing my board impression, I hugged him back. Big mistake. His thick chest, broad shoulders, and strong back were more than I could handle, and I wasn't anywhere near horny monster hormone day.

I heard a grating voice behind me. "Well, well, well, what have we here? Isn't this cozy?"

I whipped around to see Rayshawn standing in my doorway.

sixteen

If I had to guess, from the black Lycra micro-skirt and lace-up hooker boots she was wearing, I'd say there was a pole out there somewhere with Rayshawn's name on it. More than her outfit, the smug I-caught-you look she wore, annoyed me.

"Rayshawn. Hey. What are you doing here?"

She looked me up and down with a condescending glare. "That's exactly what I was about to ask the two of you. I was on my way out for the evening and realized I left my wallet in my office and came back for it. What's your story?" Her raised eyebrow and tapping toe reminded me of my third grade math teacher, demanding an answer to the worst fraction problem.

"We were working on my show." I tried not to sound defensive.

"Working. Is that what you call it?"

"Jason was about to walk me to my car."

"Umm-hmm." She smirked. "Jason, perhaps you'd like to wait for us in the lobby. I need to speak with Michelle for a second."

Jason looked at me like he was afraid to leave me alone with Rayshawn. I gave him a slight nod to let him know I would be okay.

"She'll be fine, Jason. You act like you're afraid something will happen to her if you leave her alone with me. Don't worry, she'll be down in a moment without a scratch on her." Rayshawn raked a long, claw-like nail across her chin.

After he left, Rayshawn sat her butt on the edge of my desk. "So what's going on between you and Jason? Is there something I should know about? Or, better still, that Ms. Carter should know about? No wonder you were so insistent on keeping him as your editor. I wonder if Ms. Carter had known, would she have assigned him to you? I guess we'll find out on Monday."

She grinned, and my blood chilled.

"It'll be nice working with Jason again. He's the best editor in the place. And definitely the sexiest. After Ms. Carter finds out that you guys are kickin' it, I'll have him reassigned to my team. I'll enjoy working with him again. That is what you called it, right? Work?" She winked.

Ms. Carter had a strict, but unspoken policy on dating in the workplace. It was rumored that when she was coming up through the ranks as a producer, women made it to the top by sleeping around—being on the couch, as it was called. Because she wouldn't, she felt like she had been passed over for promotions and wasn't as far along as she could be in television. So she wanted to create a workplace where that wasn't an issue.

Whether that was true or not, I didn't want to take any chances. If I wanted to be a senior producer in her department, I needed to walk the straight and narrow.

"I'm not sure what you think you saw, Rayshawn, but there's nothing going on between me and Jason. We were here working on my shows, and he was giving me a hug before walking me to my car. You're welcome to let your imagination take it wherever you want, but you might want to think twice before you go making accusations to Ms. Carter."

Forget being deferential and kissing her tail. Rayshawn wasn't going to back me up into a corner with her threats. God had my back, and if she wanted to cross me, she needed to understand what would happen if she decided to come up against God's girl.

"You got a lot of attitude for a promo producer. You need to remember who runs this place."

I didn't know if she was referring to her clout as a senior producer, or if she was admitting to her rumored illicit affair with the station owner. I wasn't going to stand here and let her try to intimidate me.

I picked up my bag and started toward my door.

She stepped over to block me. "I don't know what you're up to, but I'm not about to let you push me out of my spot here. You need to stay out my way. And stay in your place."

So, that was it. Rayshawn was concerned that any success I gained was failure for her. She thought I was after her position as a senior producer. I guess in a way I was, but I didn't understand why she thought it had to be me or her.

"Rayshawn, I'm just trying to do me. That ain't

got nothing to do with you." I was so tired of Black folks and the crabs-in-the-barrel mentality.

She stared me down, and for a moment, I saw right through her. The nasty diva attitude, sleazy clothes, and arrogance were all fronts. I looked into her eyes and saw insecurity and fear. Made me pity her for a second. That was what I needed to get through this. To pity her rather than hate her. To find a weak spot I could pray for and that could allow me to love her in spite of.

"Oh, it has everything to do with me. You flash a pretty smile and wag your hips in front of Jason, and he takes a pay cut and switches over to your department. You redesign all our promos like what we had spent months developing wasn't good enough, trying to be all artistic and creative. Then you walk up in the pitch meeting with your oh-so-holy ideas trying to take my job. Playing all innocent and pure—manipulating the fact that Ms. Carter is a Christian and that she thinks this should be TBN instead of BTV." Rayshawn spat those last words like I made her sick. "I have worked too hard to get to where I am for you to come up in here and take it all away."

I stood there, unable to speak.

She stepped close to me and lowered her voice. "What you need to do is get a perm and some decent clothes instead of looking like a hippie reject from the sixties. You need to keep your holy-roller ideas to yourself, reverse whatever spell you cast on Jason and"—she lifted a finger and jabbed me in the chest—"stay—in—your—place." A jab for every word.

Help me, Holy Ghost. I'm trying to walk in love here, but this girl is about to push me over the edge. She 'bout to find out I ain't so holy.

Just as I was about to grab her finger to snap it in two, I swear I felt the Holy Spirit grab my hand. Just as I was about to cuss her out, the Holy Spirit froze my tongue. He opened my eyes and peeled back her mask and showed me who Rayshawn really was.

I looked at the thick layers of makeup on her face, covering up old teenage acne scars and probably years of adolescent teasing. I looked at the short hoochie skirt, revealing too much of her skinny colt legs that extended up to her waist without forming hips. Her plunging neckline ended at a push-up bra, trying to make cleavage out of nothing. The beebees lined up at the back of her neck made me wonder what was beneath her bob-length wig. One would have to work hard to call her pretty.

I looked at this girl and realized she'd probably had it hard. I wondered if she'd ever been in a good relationship with a guy. Had she been rejected by so many men that she felt like she had to control them with sex? Use them to get what she wanted out of life? She probably took Jason's asking to be switched to my team personally. Like he was rejecting her like every other guy. Didn't matter to her that he was married at the time. Or that now, even though he was single, he was a Christian and only interested in a godly woman.

And maybe she wasn't confident enough in her skills as a producer and felt like she had to control and manipulate to get to the top. Like she couldn't be successful without destroying everyone around her.

Once again, I tried to walk past Rayshawn.

She stepped in front of me again. "You act like you don't hear me. So I'm gonna spell it out for you. On Monday, you're gonna tell Ms. Carter you feel two shows is too much and you want to work with Mark and not me. You're gonna tell her that you and Jason are having creative differences and that you want him reassigned to my team. And at the pitch meeting for the spring lineup, you're not gonna come up with any brilliant ideas. Is that understood?"

I guess she took my silence for weakness. Because I didn't break her finger, snatch off her wig and beat her down with a good, ghetto-girl, snatch-off-the-earrings-and-put-on-some-Vaseline beating, she thought her intimidation was working.

"No. It's not," I said.

"You don't seem to understand that I can make your life miserable around here. And if you piss me off too much, I can make sure that you don't have a job here at all. You would not want to cross me the wrong way."

I shrugged and stared at her.

She appeared unraveled that her usual tactics weren't working on me. "What is your problem?"

I guess she couldn't understand why I wasn't screaming or cussing at her, or crumbling in tears like I had seen her production assistants do. She stared at me, not so much angry, but more so puzzled.

"I don't get what you're after."

I let out a deep, exhausted breath. "Nothing,

Rayshawn. I want to do my job and do it well. I want to learn as much as I can from you and everyone else here and produce good television. You're the best producer the station has. You have nothing to worry about."

I guess that was enough to appease her. This time when I started toward the door, she let me pass. She stood there for a second, and instead of walking off like I planned, I waited for her to walk out, so I could lock up. Didn't need to give her access to my laptop or anything else in my office.

She turned and gave me one last glare, more defeated than evil. She left, and I closed and locked my office door. I leaned against the door for a minute, giving her ample time to leave.

When I was sure she was completely gone, I walked slowly to my car.

I knew I was going to have to stay prayed up to deal with Rayshawn. I needed to war against all those spirits tormenting her and working through her to torment everyone else around her. I needed His wisdom and strategies for how to deal with her without letting her walk all over me. But most of all, I needed the Holy Ghost to help me to continue to keep my attitude in check. Because if she put her hands on me again, He was gonna have to step aside so I could give her the beat-down she deserved.

One thing was for sure. I needed to keep things on the low with Jason. He seemed to be a sore spot with her that I didn't need to be poking. I needed to focus on my shows and go back to keeping things strictly professional with him. No more late-night conversations revealing our deepest pains, hopes and fears.

Even though he was perfect—everything on my list and more—Jason Hampton was going to have to be unavailable.

seventeen

We were at Lisa's house for girls' night. I shared with them my experiences with Jason and then Rayshawn, from the previous Friday night.

"Girl, you better watch your back. She sounds like a snake," Lisa said.

Vanessa said, "What she sounds like is an insecure girl who, unfortunately, misuses her destructive habits and power to get her way. I agree that you need to watch your back, but at the same time, don't walk in fear. God has you there, and His favor is on you. She might be able to make it hard for you, but she can't stop you."

Nicole gathered up our plates and took them to Lisa's kitchen sink. "Dang, too bad she has the hots for Jason. He sounds like your perfect man. He's everything on your list and is about as fine as it gets."

I picked up the serving dishes and carried them to the kitchen counter. "Yeah. He's pretty perfect.

But it's too sticky right now. Can't take that chance."
I told them about Ms. Carter's policy and Rayshawn's threats. "So I'm just gonna make myself
forget about him."

"Good luck with that," Lisa said, fanning. "That
man is too fine to forget."

I looked down at my watch. "Where's Angela?
Didn't she say she was coming?"

Lisa looked at the clock over the stove. "Yeah,
she's not leaving for Augusta until tomorrow after
work. I hope she's okay. I'll call and check on her."
Lisa flipped open her cell phone and walked down
the hall.

Lisa returned moments later. "She's on her way.
She wasn't gonna come, but I talked her into it.
She sounded a little down, so I said she needed to
come and let us cheer her up."

"Yeah, she seemed kinda down in church on
Sunday. During praise and worship, she just sat
there in her seat the whole time and kept tearing
up during the sermon." It wasn't like Angela was
one of those loud-praising people, but she usually
participated by singing and lifting her hands with
the rest of us.

We all moved into Lisa's living room and sat
silent for a few minutes—fearing the worst, but
not wanting to say it out loud. We'd wait for Angela to get there and confirm what we already
knew.

About fifteen minutes later, the doorbell rang.
Lisa led Angela into the living room. Angela sat on
the edge of the loveseat and didn't even say hello.

"Angie, you okay?" Nicole asked.

She forced a smile and nodded. No giggles. No glow. She looked around the room at each one of us and burst into tears.

In a split second, Nicole was on one side of her and Vanessa on the other. I knelt in front of her, and we all gave her a group hug. She shook silently in our arms for what seemed like forever.

I knew exactly what she was feeling. We all did. I could almost feel each one of us reliving the first time we fell. The shock, the guilt, the shame. I couldn't imagine what that felt like at forty-one.

Lisa brought her some tissue, and we all moved back while she wiped her face and blew her nose. After a few minutes of sniffles, she finally spoke. "You guys were right. I should have listened." That set her off into another round of deep sobs.

Vanessa cradled and rocked Angela like only a mother could, until her tears subsided.

"I don't understand how this happened," she said in a tear-soaked voice. "One minute we were hugging and kissing, and the next minute I looked up and our clothes were off. It was like a split second. And he kept asking me if he should stop, and for some reason I couldn't get my lips to say yes. And then afterward, we sat there looking at each other like, 'What just happened?' It was . . ." Angela's voice trailed off, and she shook her head in disbelief. "I felt so awful all week. The worst part is you guys told me and I didn't believe you."

Vanessa wiped away the new tears flowing down her cheeks. "No sense in beating yourself up about it now, sweetie."

Angela nodded and blew her nose again. "I kept crying and Gary kept trying to comfort me. He felt so bad. I didn't want to make him feel worse, but I couldn't stop crying. I can't believe this happened."

Vanessa lifted Angela's chin to make her look at her. "Sweetie, I know this is hard, but you can't let yourself get overwhelmed with guilt. The enemy would love to drive a wedge of guilt and shame between you and God and make you feel like you can't pray and you can't talk to Him. The worst thing you can do right now is avoid God. You need to run into His arms and let Him love you. I know you've already repented, so now you just need to let Him love you."

I grabbed Angela's hand. "And don't apologize over and over. You've repented, so accept His forgiveness and move on."

Vanessa cut in, "Yeah, because the way the enemy works is to cut you off by making you feel guilty, and unfortunately, that guilt is the very thing that will make you end up right there again."

Angela's eyes flew open. "Again? I'm not gonna do that again. As bad as I felt all week, there's no way that could ever happen again."

Vanessa shook her head. "Sweetie, listen to me. I know it sounds crazy, but there is a way it could happen again. You and Gary love each other. It's just natural for a man and woman in love to want to express their intimacy. It's actually unnatural, this dance we Christians do of avoiding sex in a loving, committed relationship. And by that I mean, you have to go against everything in your human nature not to do it. I know you feel awful now, but trust me, your body wants it again and again, and if you give it a chance, it will happen."

Angela shook her head back and forth so hard, I

thought she would shake her brain loose. "Never—there's no way I would do that again. And Gary wouldn't let it happen again either. You should have seen his face. He couldn't even go to church on Sunday."

"That's exactly what I'm talking about," Vanessa said. "We fall, and then we let the sin drive us away from God, and He's the only one who can keep us from sinning again. It's this awful vicious cycle. Sin leads to guilt, which makes us move away from God—which opens the door for more sin, which leads to more guilt, which makes us move even further from God and over and over, until we get to the point where He can't reach us to help us out of our sin."

Angela got up and paced across Lisa's living room. "That's not gonna happen. Tomorrow night, me and Gary are going to have a long talk about the whole thing. We'll pray together, and this will never happen again."

Lisa raised her eyebrows. "You're going down there this weekend?"

Angela nodded. "Yeah. We need to talk about it. I left abruptly, and I was hurt and he was hurt, and things have been real weird on the phone all week. I need to talk to him in person, so we can straighten this whole thing out and put it behind us and move on with our relationship." Angela started crying again. "I can't lose him. I love him too much."

We sat there silent. The only sound in the room was the gentle whir of the ceiling fan overhead.

Vanessa finally said, "If you guys need to talk, have him come up here and stay in the hotel, and you guys talk in a neutral place. You don't need to be going down to his house and be alone having this conversation.

"I can't believe you guys think I'm gonna do it again. Don't you see my face? I've cried every day this week. I just need to make sure he still loves me."

Lisa walked over and gently took Angela's hand. "Don't take this as an 'I told you so,' but we did, and you didn't listen. We're trying to tell you what's next, and once again, you're not listening. Please, Angela, hear us. We've all been where you are before, and we know what comes next."

"I can't believe you guys are judging me. I'm not that kind of person. It was a mistake. I knew I shouldn't have come here." Angela picked up her purse and stormed toward the door.

Before any one of us realized what was happening, she was gone. We sat there staring at each other for a few minutes.

Finally Nicole let out a low whistle. "Whew, what was that all about?"

Vanessa let out a breath. "Honestly? It's a spirit of pride making her think more highly of herself than she ought. I guess she had gotten a little self-righteous about the fact that she was still a virgin at her age. She probably judged other people who fell into sexual sin. Now, the same spirit of judgment she had toward them, she's turning on herself. Thinking she was above falling was and, unfortunately, still is her problem."

"Yeah, the Word says pride goeth before a fall. Until she realizes she's a mere mortal with sexual urges like the rest of us, I'm afraid she'll continue to fall," I said.

Nicole hugged her legs to her chest and leaned back against Lisa's couch. "So what's she supposed to do? You know, this male-female relationship in Christianity thing is all new to me. I've never been in a situation where I had to try not to have sex, but I can't imagine how she'll do that, now that's she's done it. Especially with what Vanessa said about the vicious cycle. What's she supposed to do? Not see him anymore?"

We all looked at Vanessa.

Vanessa thought for a minute. "No, they shouldn't break up because they messed up. They love each other. That's why they messed up in the first place. I know he's hinted at marriage. At this point, they pretty much have to move in that direction."

Nicole frowned. "They have to get married just because they had sex? They've only been dating for three months. Isn't that too soon to get married? Didn't we say that Michelle shouldn't have married her ex just to avoid burning?"

"That's different," I said. "We were kids and didn't know anything. Gary and Angela got together under the premise of moving toward marriage. They're mature adults."

Nicole said, "But shouldn't you make sure you get to know that person first? What if there's some stuff about Gary that Angela doesn't know that would come out later that would make it clear that he's not the one?"

We all sat quiet for a few minutes.

Lisa said, "A good friend of mine always had this thing when she started to get know a guy and she thought he might be a possibility. She would go out with him for a while, get to know him, see if he met every requirement on her list. Then she would pray this prayer: 'God, you know me and you know him. You know what the outcome of a marriage between us would be. I trust that you know what's best for me. If he's not what's best for me, bring this relationship to a screeching halt. Get rid of any and every guy that's not your best for me.' She said it worked. The men dropped like flies. And later she'd find out something about them would have been a deal-breaker. Until finally the right one came along. She fell head over heels in love with him, but still prayed that prayer over and over. Instead of him dropping off, they got closer and closer. Finally, one day he said, 'You're trying to get rid of me in the Spirit, and I'm not going anywhere. God told me the first day we met that you were my wife, so you can forget it. You're mine.' They've been happily married for eight years."

We all nodded. I made a mental note to use that prayer, should I ever get up the nerve to date again.

Nicole said, "That doesn't fix Angela's situation. What are she and Gary supposed to do?"

"Once you cross that line, it's difficult to go back," Vanessa said. "They almost can't be alone together for any long period of time. They have to start moving in the direction of marriage."

"So you're saying it's impossible for them to be in a relationship and not keep having sex?" Nicole asked.

"Not impossible, but difficult," Vanessa said."

"It can't be that hopeless. My friend Raquel met her husband and they dated a year and never even kissed each other. And my friend Teresa and her husband dated and got engaged over about a ten-month period, and they never fell. So it's possible."

"Yeah, but they never fell. Once you fall, it's like an addiction."

We all sat there, I guess, pondering the seriousness of it all. If I did ever decide to date again, I'd go from fighting the lonely monster full-time and the horny monster two days a month to a full all-out war with the horny monster. And for real, I couldn't imagine being in love with someone and not being able to have sex with them. How was I supposed to make it?

It was pure torture. Which was worse? Being desperate and lonely and desiring a husband, or having a man and facing the risk of falling and ruining my relationship with God—the most important thing in my life?

It wasn't anything I felt like dealing with, so I solidified my decision to not date anymore.

eighteen

A couple of weeks later, we had auditions for *Indie Artist* at the station. Erika had posted flyers at some of the city's hottest independent artists' spots and put an ad in *Creative Loafing*. I hoped we'd get enough of a showing that we would be able to pick some good acts. If we didn't get enough people, we'd spend a few nights at Apache Café, Sugar Hill, and Café 290 to see if we could recruit some more.

Just as I was about to relax and sip my morning chamomile, Erika rushed into my office. "Oh my goodness, there's about forty people outside already. We'll be here until tomorrow."

"Really? Wow. Okay, is everything set up?" I put down my mug and followed her downstairs to the studio. Sure enough, there was a line flowing down the hall. It was going to be a long day.

Jason, Erika, and I sat in the three chairs pulled up to a table in front of the sound stage. Mark stopped by to say that he'd be in and out, but for the most part, he was leaving things in my capable hands.

After the first three auditions, I realized the day was going to be longer than I thought. I felt like we were Randy, Paula, and Simon during the initial *American Idol* auditions. It amazed me that some of the "artists" were unable to hear that their singing sounded like someone killing a cat. And they didn't have a parent, sister, or friend who would tell them the truth.

After enduring the first two auditions for far too long, I decided that if someone opened their mouth and sounded awful, I'd cut them off quickly. At first, the notion of being mean bothered me, but I decided I was doing them a favor— helping them realize they didn't need to be trying to sing.

We did have some good acts. There was this young girl with a bright red afro named Eva Kennedy that sang a Tina Turner song better than Tina herself. She sang deep from her soul and gave me goose bumps. If she was singing gospel, I would have said she was anointed. Her voice and passion hit me deep in the pit of my stomach. I knew she'd do a great show. Then there was this girl duo— Venus 7, they called themselves—with amazing harmonies and lyrics, and an eclectic style that would fit the show perfectly.

We had a few other promising ones that I wanted to see perform on stage in front of a crowd, to get a better feel for their vibe. There were some that could really sing, but there was nothing interesting or special enough about them that would make a full episode of a show worthwhile.

After a lunch break and a few more hours of "American Idol rejects," and several more stunning performances, I was ready to call it quits for the day. We had at least ten people I thought would work. We could hang out in clubs to find the other three needed for a full season of the show.

I stretched my arms upward. "I'm ready to end it, guys. I'm exhausted and I'm getting a headache."

Erika scrunched up her face. "It wouldn't be fair not to see the rest of the people, though. They've been waiting all day."

"You guys want to finish seeing them without me? If there's anybody good, you can call me back down. Please? I can't take another one."

Jason rubbed my back. "Sure, we got it. Go take a break."

I was going to have to talk to him about his touchy-feelyness. He didn't know how crazy he was driving me. Erika was smirking behind him. I couldn't glare at her like I wanted to because he was looking straight at me.

I trudged up to my office and laid my head on my desk for a second. It was hard to relax because my mind was racing with ideas for the shows. Where we'd tape—whether we'd try to decorate the studio like an eclectic club or tape at one of the spots in Atlanta. How much could we budget for a house band? I thumbed through some of the artists' press kits, thinking about how we'd tell each person's story, to make it compelling.

I stopped for a second and smiled when it hit me. I had my own show. I was doing something I had dreamed of. And if God was faithful enough to make that dream come true, what else did He have up His sleeve? I had a Romans 8:28 moment—somehow deep down, I was sure God was working out everything in my life for good. I knew if I continued to delight myself in Him, He would continue to give me the desires of my heart.

You'll send me the right man one day too, huh, God?

My phone rang. It was Erika calling from downstairs. "Yeah?"

"You gotta come down. This guy is the best all day. You'll love him. He's perfect."

I hung up and let out a deep breath.

When I walked back into the studio, a serious piece of eye candy stood talking to Erika and Jason. I tried not to notice how cute he was, but it was rather impossible. He was gorgeous. Not in that polished, clean-cut way. He had that artistic thing going on. Nice brown skin, eyes that laughed, five o'clock shadow with a goatee. His long locks that flowed down his back were thin and well-groomed. When he turned to me and smiled, I thought I would die.

"Isaiah Thompson." He held out his hand.

I shook his hand and smiled back. "Nice to meet you. Thanks for coming in."

"My pleasure." He held my hand with a firm grip.

We locked eyes for a second, and I knew I was being silly, but it felt like instant chemistry.

Focus, Michelle. This is work. And we're not dealing with any more men. Remember?

He smelled like this African musk oil I had tried one day while shopping in Little Five Points. I remembered sniffing my arm the whole afternoon, thinking about how sexy it would smell on a man. He had on worn Levi's and a T-shirt that read, "Music Is My Life." A guitar was slung over his shoulder.

He went back up onto the stage, and Erika passed me his press kit. I glanced at his bio page. He described his music as folk gospel—not a genre I had heard of before. His influences ranged from Bob Marley to Andre Crouch to Donnie Hathaway. He had been raised by missionary parents all over Africa and South America, which he said colored his music and world view as well. He seemed to be an interesting guy, which would make for a great show.

"Umm, I guess I should play a little something for you?" he said when I finished perusing his info.

"Yeah, that would be great."

He strummed his guitar a little, adjusted the tuning and then strummed a little more. He had beautiful, strong-looking hands. He played a few chords and started to sing. His voice was raspy and deep—caused a little tingle that started from my toes. He sang a chorus about the beauty of God's presence.

When he was finished, I had to work hard to find words. "Wow. Very nice. Thank you. I think you'd be great for the show. I'm looking forward to listening to your CD." I pulled it out of the press kit.

"I can do you better than that. I'll be performing at Apache Café this Friday, so you can get a taste of it live. That is, if you're not busy this weekend. I don't want to be presumptuous in assuming you don't already have plans."

Was he flirting with me? "I'll have to check my calendar."

Erika spoke up. "Her schedule is clear. We'll be there."

He chuckled and smiled.

That smile. I didn't know if it was the lonely monster or the horny monster, but this guy was getting under my skin a little too much, a little too quick. There was this energy about him that filled the room.

Jason cleared his throat. "Well, thanks for coming in. We've got quite a few more people to go, so we'd better keep moving. We'll be in touch with you soon." He walked over to the stage, shook hands with Isaiah and led him to the door.

Erika raised her eyebrows at Jason then turned to me. She pursed her lips and gave me a what's-up-with-that look. I shrugged it off, but did think Jason was a bit abrupt.

Erika picked up Isaiah's press kit and put it in my hand with a devilish grin. "So, what time should I meet you at Apache on Friday night?"

nineteen

On Friday night, I stood in front of my full-length mirror, checking out my outfit for Apache Café. I had on a hip-hugging pair of flared jeans, a black tank top, and a midriff blue jean jacket with leopard print accents I had picked up in the Little Five Points bazaar. I blew out my afro—Angela Davis style—and put a flower behind one ear.

I listened to Isaiah's CD the whole time I was getting dressed. I found myself thinking about his bio and coming up with questions to ask him so I could start writing his show. I was a little concerned that he was a gospel artist, though not in the traditional sense. I could hear Rayshawn's disdainful comments about me being a holy roller, trying to turn BTV into TBN. It didn't matter. He was a great artist, regardless of his genre.

Apache was pretty crowded when we got there. Thankfully, Isaiah had reserved a table for me and Erika. I remembered all too many trips to Apache when I didn't get there on time and had to stand the whole night. Especially for the packed-out Wednesday night jam sessions.

We sat down front, right at the stage. I looked around the club, considering it as a potential taping spot. It had exposed brick walls, crowded tables and chairs in the front, standing room in the middle, and couches in the back. There were abstract original paintings on the walls. It had an artsy ambiance that would be perfect for the show.

I was pleasantly surprised to find that Eva Kennedy, the young girl with the red afro we had auditioned, was opening for Isaiah. I'd get a good idea of what she was like on stage with a band in front of a crowd.

Her four-song set of original music overwhelmed me. I found myself lifting my hands like I was worshipping in church. There was something spiritual about her, in spite of the somewhat risqué lyrics she was singing. I had never seen a more passionate performance. She poured her whole soul into what she was singing, and the crowd loved her. She got a standing ovation and did a quick encore song before Isaiah came on.

When he first came onto the stage, I realized I had forgotten how cute he was. He had on some acid-washed, bummy jeans and a T-shirt that said, "I Sing Because I'm Happy." He said a few words, thanking everyone for coming and went right into the first song.

It was an upbeat song with poetic lyrics that declared each person's responsibility in making change to overcome poverty, war, and other societal ills. I could tell everyone was feeling him on the social consciousness vibe. I was anxious to see how they would respond to the worship, though.

I didn't have to wait long to find out. The next song he sang was the one he auditioned with about the beauty of the presence of the Lord. The atmosphere was electric. It didn't seem to bother anyone that he was singing the name of Jesus. His passion and his voice filled the room and were infectious.

I tore my eyes away from him for a few minutes to see how the crowd responded. Everyone seemed mesmerized, staring or closing their eyes, listening intently.

At the end of the song, he ad-libbed about how being in God's presence brought so much joy, love, life and laughter. I felt every word he said.

Next, he sang a love song about meeting a girl that blew him away, and even though he didn't know her, he couldn't see spending the rest of his life without her. His use of words was beyond poetic. At first, I thought I was imagining things when I thought Isaiah seemed to be singing to me. When Erika nudged me and smirked, I knew it wasn't just me.

He sang a few other worship songs, a couple of love songs, and then a warfare praise song with African rhythms that made everyone dance. He stopped it several times, but people kept clapping and dancing. The guy on the congas kept playing, so Isaiah started it up again and again.

Isaiah finally put down his guitar and took over the conga drums. I thought he did it to end the song, but he started drumming, and the crowd went even wilder.

After about five minutes of showing his skills, he gave up the drums and started to dance. He looked like an African warrior, stomping his feet, jumping, and slinging his locks. His agility and energy had the crowd on their feet.

I kicked myself for not bringing a camera crew with me.

After he finished performing, he came off stage and hugged a few people. He stopped over at our table in the midst of everyone congratulating him on his show. "Can you hang around for a little? I promise I won't be long. I'd like to hear your thoughts before you go."

Erika yawned. "I've got to go, but I'm sure Michelle can stay around for a while."

I wanted to smack her, but smiled at Isaiah. "Sure, if it's not going to be too late. It's already way past my bedtime."

He grinned. I knew I'd be sitting around for the rest of the night if he took that long. I tried to squelch the little pang in my heart, but seeing him perform had gotten to me. I told myself it was the musician magic thing and that I refused to be a groupie.

I grabbed Erika as she stood to leave. "Where do you think you're going? At least stay until he comes back. I know you ain't trying to leave me here all by myself."

She laughed. "Yeah, I guess I better stay to make sure you don't try to sneak out."

"It's the least you could do."

She sat back down and leaned over to say, "So, he's extra sexy and fine, talented, and real spiritual too. Seems like your type."

"Erika, this is business. I'm not gonna date talent."

"You and your excuses. You're determined to end up alone, aren't you?"

Ouch. "No, I just know the importance of being professional."

"Girl, you and your professionalism is gonna make you an old maid. You need to relax your rules a little. God is sending you all these wonderful men, and you keep turning them down."

"Wonderful men—like Larry, huh?" I glared at her.

"You're never going to let me live that down are you? How was I to know the guy had the plague?"

I had to laugh. "Exactly. So, please understand I won't be needing anymore hook-ups from you."

"I ain't hooking you up. Looks like you pulled this one all on your own." She stood as Isaiah approached the table. She shook his hand. "I guess I'll be leaving now. Thanks again for inviting us. I really enjoyed your show."

"Thanks, Erika. Hope to see you soon."

"You definitely will." She winked at me when he turned his head, then made her exit.

He turned a chair around backward and sat down at the table across from me. "So, what'd you think?"

"It was great. You have awesome stage presence. I'm looking forward to shooting your episode of *Indie Artist*."

He nodded and grinned. "Great. Thanks—that's great news." His smile faded. "Oh, one thing though. I don't know what your time frame is like. I'm about to go on a short tour."

"When are you leaving?"

He bit his upper lip. "Tomorrow morning. I'll be back in eight days."

"Dang. That makes things difficult. I wanted to do your show first. I planned to start writing this week and to shoot by next week. I guess I can put Eva first."

"Oh, man! I was first?"

I nodded.

"Well, what would you need me to do to still be first?"

"I basically need to do your interview so I can start writing. We could tape it as soon as you get back. But if you're leaving in the morning . . ." I knew good and well we could tape his show last and still air it first.

He looked at his watch. "I got about eight hours before I leave. I can run down my whole life story in about four hours. It would be a squeeze, but I think I could hit all the high points."

I laughed. He smiled at me, and I felt myself falling. I looked down at my watch. "Do you have any idea what time it is? It's almost midnight."

"I'm a musician. The night is just getting started. Come on, I'll buy you coffee while we talk. If my life story isn't interesting enough, the caffeine will keep you awake."

Go home, Michelle. Interview him when he gets back. "Okay. But you gotta get your whole story into an hour. That's all you get."

"That's impossible. No way you can get to know everything you need to know about me in an hour."

"Your show segment is only a half-hour long."

"I'm not talking about for the show."

Oh, my. I raised my eyebrows. "Is that so?" *No flirting, Michelle. Keep it professional.*

He nodded. "That's so." He looked down at his watch. "The only places open long enough for our four-hour interview are IHOP, Waffle House, or City Café."

"I guess City Café is the closest. I'll follow you there?"

"Aha—the don't-get-in-the-same-car-on-the-first-date rule. Smart girl."

I laughed. "Exactly. And this isn't a date. It's an interview—remember? Meet you there in a few."

I waited for him in the entrance of the restaurant. After we sat down and ordered some dessert, I took out my notepad to remind him of why we were there. I pulled out a pen. "So, tell me about your genre. I've never heard of folk gospel before."

"Gee. All business, huh?"

"Yep. Folk gospel. What is it?"

He chuckled and rubbed his goatee. "I sort of made it up. It's worship music with an acoustic flow to it. It's kinda Bob Marley meets Israel Houghton. I couldn't think of what else to call it."

"Nice." I scribbled a few notes. "Tell me about your journey as a musician. When did you first know you wanted to do music, and what has gotten you to where you are now?"

The waitress bought over a cup of tea for him and ginger ale for me.

He put cream and sugar in his tea. "The best thing that happened to me was my parents being missionaries. I grew up all over the world, and the person it made me is what inspires my music."

I found myself becoming deeply intrigued as he described his love for music since childhood. He had studied African music and rhythms during his time in Kenya and Cameroon in his early teens, then Brazilian drumming and Cuban music as well. Even after he left his parents' house, he continued to travel all over the world, chasing music.

"I was raised in a strong Christian home. My whole life was one big missions trip. It was in Nigeria, under the ministry of Benson Idahosa, that worship was born in me."

He continued on about how his favorite influence in the Bible was King David and how he considered himself a worshipper, warrior, and king as well. He also discussed his frustration with the American church and how their worship was steeped in tradition. "It seems so ritualistic. Rather than trying to pierce the heavens and enter the awesome, sweet presence of God, we're stuck on three praise songs, two worship songs, shed three tears, then get out of the way for the offering."

His voice was low and melodic, soothing—almost hypnotic. "You've never praised until you've danced with all your might to the rhythms of the master drummers in South Africa. You've never worshipped until you've sat under the stars by the waterfalls in Brazil, singing a private love song to God. I try to share all these experiences in my music. So that's why it's folk gospel."

Oh, my . . . .oh, my . . . oh, my. I sat there silent for a while. I couldn't seem to gather enough words together in my brain to form the next question.

The waitress brought our desserts, which gave me a chance to get my mind together.

Focus, Michelle. I know he's cute and well traveled and intriguing and wonderful and godly, but this is work.

He cut a large bite of coconut cake and said, "So tell me about you. I feel like I'm doing all the talking here."

I cut a small bite of carrot cake. "That's because this is an interview. Me interviewing you, remember?" I knew I smiled too much when I said that.

"So, how do I get to know you? You know my whole life story now. It's only fair that you tell me about yourself."

"I don't know your whole life story. There's still stuff I need for the show. So, do you plan—"

"Wow. You're so serious. I guess we're going to have to go out another time, when we're finished with the show, for me to get to know you."

I put down my pen. "Isaiah, please don't take this the wrong way, but this is work. I don't date where I work."

"Really?"

"Really." I said it firmly.

"Too bad. You should rethink that. You might miss something special following that rule. How do you know this isn't a divine hook-up? God sending you the desires of your heart?"

My heart fluttered a little at his using my special scripture specifically about God sending me the perfect husband. I didn't believe in signs, but I also didn't believe in coincidences.

"Because God knows I maintain a sharp line between personal and professional, so He wouldn't send me a divine hook-up that way." *Why was I even entertaining this conversation?* Perhaps it was his smile, or his musky cologne, or the sound of his worship still coursing through my soul.

He rubbed his goatee. "I don't know. You seem like the kind of woman that wouldn't give Him much choice. Your life is probably work and church. Where else do you go that He can send you someone?" His half-grin said he knew he had me.

"You don't know anything about me, Isaiah. How do you even know I'm a Christian? You could be trying to push up on an atheist."

"Nah." He shook his head. "I know better than that. You're a God's girl. Definitely. I can tell by your face when you were listening to my worship songs. Only someone familiar with His presence looks like you look when I'm singing. You're not looking at me. You're thinking about the One I'm singing about." He tilted his head to the side. "Am I right?"

I kept my face blank, so he wouldn't realize how much he was getting to me. "So, do you prefer being an independent artist, or will you be trying to land a record deal?"

His face broke into a full smile, and he laughed real deep. "Wow. Redirect, huh? Okay."

I grilled him with questions over the next half-hour while we finished our cake. I finally looked down at my watch. "Okay. I think I have everything I need to script the show. As soon as you get back, we'll be ready to start taping. By then, I'll have decided if we're going to tape at the studio with an audience or at Apache or somewhere else. We'll also need some nice shots of you in your environment, like at home, playing the guitar, or maybe, at your favorite places where you go for inspiration to write. Think about a couple of spots while you're gone." I put my notepad into my large purse and waved the waitress down for the check.

"So that's it?" He raised his eyebrows.

"No, silly. Like I said, when you get back, we tape your show. Then that's it."

"That's too bad." He nodded like he was sizing me up. "Let me ask this then. If I refuse to do the show, will you go out with me?"

I couldn't help but smile. "Stop playing. You're not gonna refuse to do the show. You don't even know if I'm worth that."

"I have a feeling." He gave me this intense look that made me fidget. "Maybe I can take you to dinner after we tape the show. When it's all finished, you won't have to worry about your rule then, right?"

"Isaiah, don't take this the wrong way. It's not personal. You seem like a great guy. I just can't. I've got too much riding on this show, and I can't afford any indiscretions. Okay?"

He picked up the check and pulled out his wallet. "Okay. I guess I'll have to accept that."

I tried to take the check from him. "You don't have to get it. This was a business meeting."

He held it out of my reach. "At least let me get the check. I really enjoyed talking to you. It's not often I get to spend an evening with a beautiful, godly woman."

"Please." I rolled my eyes. "Like you have any problem meeting women."

"I didn't say I had any problem meeting women. I have a problem with meeting too many women. Bunch of chickenheads trying to sleep with me, even though they just watched me on stage pouring out my heart to the Lord. What I rarely meet, though, are godly women. Especially smart, beautiful ones." He rose from the table. "I don't know. I might have to refuse to do this show."

As he headed off to find the waitress to pay the bill, he turned and said over his shoulder. "You might be a once-in-a-lifetime."

twenty

Over the next week, I spent as many hours as I could, working on *Indie Artist*. Erika and I went to a Harmony in Life show at Sugar Hill and found two more acts to complete the season. I started meeting with the artists to interview them, and we made arrangements with the manager at Apache Café to tape there. That way, I wouldn't have to worry about getting a studio audience and a sound system. We decided to use the house band from the Wednesday night jam session.

I tried not to think about Isaiah, but he kept creeping into my mind all week. For some reason, his CD ended up in my CD player, playing over and over while I was at home. I wondered what it would be like to date him.

I didn't let myself wonder too long. The only thing worst than dating a co-worker would be dating talent. I could hear Rayshawn accusing me of giving my boyfriend a show or even creating the show to promote his career. I didn't need Ms. Carter questioning my ethics or motives.

Nope. He was another perfect guy I would have to put out of my mind because of work.

As well as *Indie Artist* was going, *Destiny's Child* wasn't going at all. Rayshawn always said she was too busy to sit down to do budgeting and scheduling, which made it difficult to even get started. She never had time to approve the script ideas I had submitted to her based on kids I planned to audition from our inner city outreach. And when I talked about holding auditions for the kids, she said I didn't need to worry about that, she'd be finding the talent.

It smelled like sabotage to me. I knew she had some idea cooked up where she would make it look to Ms. Carter like I was the one who missed the deadlines. She would probably say I was too busy working on my other show with Mark and that it was too much to expect me to do two shows anyway. She'd get me fired off my own show and then somehow turn it into her video hoochies brainchild.

I had to find a way to keep that from happening. If I went to Ms. Carter and complained, I would look like a big tattletale and would make an even worse enemy in Rayshawn and some of the other producers. I had already started a paper trail of memos and emails documenting my attempts at reaching out to her. But her answers were strategic in that they shifted responsibility back to me so she could easily say I hadn't met her expectations, and therefore, she couldn't do her part. If I went ahead and did the budget and schedule and started auditions without her, she would say that I was usurping her authority. It seemed like a no-win situation for me.

I finally prayed and asked God how to handle the situation. He didn't say much. I figured it'd be one of those situations that He worked out without telling me the details.

Late one afternoon, Erika buzzed me to let me know Ms. Carter wanted to speak with me. I knew she had been checking on the progress of the shows with all the senior producers. Mark told me he had given her a glowing report about how I was handling *Indie Artist* almost independently with very little input from him. I hoped that would counteract whatever horrible stories Rayshawn told her about *Destiny's Child*.

I decided to arm myself before walking into her office. I gathered my budget and schedule, flyers Erika had made to advertise auditions, and script ideas to take to the meeting. The Holy Spirit would have to tell me how to frame things to where it would be clear I was trying to do my job without defaming Rayshawn.

I walked to her office slowly, praying the whole way. Once again, God didn't say anything; just had that quiet, peace-of-God thing wash over me. Of course, He knew something I didn't know.

I took a deep breath, knocked on Ms. Carter's office door and decided to sit back and watch how things unfolded.

After we exchanged pleasantries, Ms. Carter motioned for me to sit down. I laid my folder in my lap and waited for her to begin.

"Michelle, how are you? How are things going so far with the shows?"

Shoot. She put the ball in my court first. I would rather her come right out and tell me she knew things were bad and give me my ultimatum about how long I had to turn things around before I lost my show. Her fishing forced me to choose my words carefully.

"Things are going great so far. Of course, I've had to deal with the usual challenges, but I feel like things are progressing. In some areas, not as far as I would like by this point, but I understand that's how things go sometimes." Hopefully that was vague enough to punt the ball back into her court.

"Let's get down to it, Michelle. You know I'm not one to beat around the bush. I've spoken with Mark about the progress of *Indie Artist*, and he has nothing but great things to say about you. The most telling is that you're already functioning like a senior producer, taking a lot of initiative and being aggressive about being excellent and ahead of schedule. Unfortunately, that report is completely different from the one I'm getting from Rayshawn."

I started to speak in my defense, but she held up a hand to stop me.

"It doesn't take much for me to figure out why there's such a difference. I know that you're a dedicated worker. Eyeing your budgets, schedule, and scripts from *Indie Artist* lets me know you're more than capable of doing both shows. I know Rayshawn can be impossible to work with. And I know she has no problem with sacrificing the good of the station for her own agenda."

Oh, my. Didn't expect that to come out of her mouth. The obvious next question was, Why did Rayshawn still have a job here?

As if she heard my thoughts, Ms. Carter said, "It may be difficult to understand, but Rayshawn is a very good producer."

Yeah, but she's not a team player. There are other very good producers out there without the drama.

"And quite honestly, my hands are somewhat tied with making certain personnel decisions around here." Ms. Carter looked away and folded her hands when she said that.

What did that mean?

And then it hit me. The rumors about Rayshawn and the station owner were true. Ms. Carter was stuck with Rayshawn, no matter how much she might have wanted to fire her.

Ms. Carter continued, "I was prepared to have a sit-down meeting with the two of you to discuss how best to get your show moving forward. Instead, I got a phone call from Rayshawn's sister saying there was a family emergency and Rayshawn would be out for at least two weeks. I'm not sure what that's all about and, hopefully, will get more information as to exactly when we can expect her back."

I clutched my folder and didn't say anything.

"That means you have a small window of time to get some things accomplished. I know it's a lot to ask, with everything moving on your other show, but if you can get me your proposed budget and schedule within the week, perhaps we can get some auditions scheduled. That would require some extra hours from you, but if you're willing to try, let me know."

I held up the folder. "Here they are."

Ms. Carter furrowed her eyebrows as she accepted the folder. "You've already completed them?"

I nodded.

"Why weren't they submitted to me?"

I shrugged and bit my tongue to keep from telling her.

"How long have they been done?"

"A couple of weeks."

Ms. Carter thumbed through the papers in the folder, briefly reading them. She looked back up at me. "I don't understand why I'm just seeing these."

I slowly let out a deep breath. "Rayshawn hadn't approved them yet, and I didn't want to go over her head. I'm sure you would have gotten to them today if it weren't for her emergency."

Ms. Carter nodded slowly, looked at me, down at the folder, then back up at me again. "Okay. Well, I'm glad they're done." She closed the folder and placed it on her desk. She smiled and looked right into my eyes. "I guess things have a way of working out for our good, huh?"

I smiled and nodded. It wasn't the first time I had noticed Ms. Carter cryptically sneaking scripture into her conversations at the station. "I guess they do. I'll be pushing to get as much done as I can in the next couple of weeks. Should I report back to you?"

"That would be good."

I rose to leave, and Ms. Carter stood with me. "Thanks for all your hard work, Michelle. You have a bright future in television. Continue to be excellent in all you do."

I nodded and smiled. "Thanks."

After I left her office, I couldn't wait to get to Erika and Jason to tell them the news and enlist their help in getting as much done as possible in the next two weeks. I was prepared to put *Indie Artist* aside to get as much done on *Destiny's Child* as possible.

I sat down in my office to take a few deep breaths and try to get my thoughts together when Erika came busting in, red-faced and breathless.

"Did you hear the news?"

"What?"

She closed the door and sat down in my office chair, leaning forward like she had the tastiest bit of gossip to share. "Rayshawn is gonna be out for a while."

"I know. Ms. Carter just told me. We'll get to get some things done on *Destiny's Child* and—"

"Ms. Carter told you? She knew the whole story?"

"No, she said there was a family emergency."

Erika smirked. "Family emergency? I guess you could call it that." She leaned even further forward in her chair to the point I was afraid she would fall out. "Rayshawn is pregnant. By the station owner. He's forcing her to have an abortion. She had a major emotional breakdown." Erika grinned like she was sharing the best news I'd ever heard.

I frowned. "Erika, that's horrible. Where did you

hear that? You shouldn't say stuff like that. I know she's evil, but—"

"I'm not gonna say how I know, but I know it's true. She's in love with him and wanted him to leave his wife. He sent her away somewhere to get rid of the baby and get herself together. He thought she shouldn't work here anymore, but she blackmailed him to keep her job. The only bad thing about it is that she'll be even more terroristic when she gets back. Ms. Carter better watch her back. Rayshawn might use this to try to take over everything."

I held up my hand. "That's enough. I don't want to hear anymore. Even if it's true, it's not anything we need to sit around talking about."

Erika looked at me like I was crazy. "After the way she's treated you and everybody else around here? You should be happy."

"Why would I be happy about that? Can you imagine what she must be feeling? What it will be like for her to have to come back here and work, knowing what everybody knows about her? Why would I be happy about somebody getting their heart broken and having an emotional break-down? I don't care how she acts. She's still a person with feelings, and I know she must be pretty messed up right now."

Erika rolled her eyes at me and sat back in her chair.

"Erika, you have to promise me you won't tell anybody else about this."

Her eyes widened. "Are you serious? Girl, please. Why are you defending her?"

"I don't expect you to understand. Just promise me, okay?"

Erika stood up and stomped toward the door like a little kid whose fun I had spoiled. "Fine, Michelle. Even if I don't tell it, people will know." She gave me a crazy look and left.

I sat staring out the window, processing everything she had said. I remembered seeing the real Rayshawn when we were in my office that late night. I couldn't imagine what she was feeling right now. I didn't even know what to pray. *God, please help her.*

twenty-one

The next couple of weeks were grueling. I worked nonstop, trying to get as much done as I could on *Destiny's Child* before Rayshawn came back. We put tapings for the *Indie Artist* on hold to conduct some auditions. I contacted our sister church in the inner city after hearing about the awesome youth program they had there. One of the youth pastors, Shara Mercer, was excited to recommend to me more than enough kids to tape two seasons worth of shows. I met with a lot of kids and their parents and started writing scripts.

After three weeks, Rayshawn still hadn't returned to work. Ms. Carter approved everything I had done, and we got *Destiny's Child* to the place where we were ready to start taping. Much as I wanted to go ahead and get some shows taped, Ms. Carter recommended I get back to *Indie Artist* and wait for Rayshawn to come back.

The first taping we rescheduled was Isaiah's. Even though he had crossed my mind a lot over the past weeks, enough time had passed that I thought I was free of my momentary infatuation with him. I was ready to get his show taped and in the can, so he could be completely out of my mind.

I smelled him before I saw him. When I entered the studio, that African musk scent assaulted me, and I felt butterflies dancing in my belly. I tried to tell myself it was nervousness about my first real taping, but when I finally laid eyes on him, I knew it was more than that.

As he sat answering the interview questions, on camera this time, I was drawn in—again. Worse than before. He had a magic about him that was irresistible.

After he finished answering questions, he pulled out his guitar and did one of my favorite songs from his CD.

When he finished singing, he came off the stage to where I was standing. "How'd I do?"

"You did great. It's gonna come out good for the show." I had to keep myself focused on the professional, to keep from melting under that smile. "Did you think about where we can shoot you writing and singing?"

He nodded. "You guys can come out to the house. There's a lot of light, great windows and a lake in the backyard. We could get some cool shots there."

I raised an eyebrow. Where did he live? "Okay. I'll have Erika get with you, and we'll set up a shoot. We'll be doing a big show with everybody at Apache for the live performances. She'll get you those details as well."

"Okay. Thanks." He lingered there for a few

minutes, looking at me. "It's good to see you again. When Erika first called me to reschedule, I thought I was getting cut for crossing the line with you. I wanted to apologize if I made you uncomfortable while you were interviewing me. I shouldn't have done that, but I guess . . ." his voice trailed off, and he smiled a little. "I guess you had an effect on me. Made me . . . I don't know. Anyway, I wanted to apologize."

I smiled. "That's sweet. I appreciate it. And we had to reschedule everything to get some things done on another show."

"Good to know. Anyway, see you around."

I nodded.

Jason walked up as Isaiah was giving me another one of those intense looks of his. "All set, man. Great interview. Gotta keep it moving with the next artist. I'll walk you out." Jason extended an arm toward the door to lead Isaiah away.

Isaiah frowned at him for a second, said a quick goodbye to me, and left.

When the production crew and I arrived at Isaiah's house for the taping, he answered the door in a wife-beater and pajama bottoms. I turned to avoid looking at his thick arms and broad, muscular chest.

"Ummm, did you forget we were coming?"

He laughed. "No. You said you wanted it to look natural—how I always write and practice. This is how I do. Pajamas, by the fireplace, looking out at the lake. You want it to be authentic, don't you?"

I winced and nodded. I could feel Erika smirking at my discomfort.

The house was spectacular. Two-story foyer and living room with a huge fireplace and large clear windows with a perfect view of a peaceful lake. It was a great house to be creative in. I would have expected his décor to be more artsy and eclectic than traditional modern, but it was classy. His music career must have been paying off more than I imagined. It was cool how he maintained that starving artist persona. He'd certainly fooled me.

When we started taping, Isaiah was a pleasure to watch. Not only because of his great body—although that was certainly nice on the eye. He was a natural in front of the camera. He made it look like we weren't there. Lost in his own world of music. We got shots of him sitting Indian style, with his guitar in front of the fireplace, singing while looking out the window at the lake. Shots of him lying on his stomach in front of the fireplace with a pencil and paper, writing lyrics.

I put on my director's hat—seeing how my budget didn't allow for one—and orchestrated a few more scenes and we were done. "Okay, Isaiah. I think we have everything we need. You did great."

He gently laid his guitar on the couch and pulled on a T-shirt. He walked us all to the door. The cameraman lingered behind, packing his lights and other stuff.

I held out a hand to Isaiah. "Thanks so much."

He held my hand a little longer than necessary for a handshake. I wasn't quick to let his go either.

I heard Erika's voice behind me. "I'll wait for you in the car."

It was enough to snap me back into reality. I didn't need to be behaving so unprofessionally. I let go of his hand. "See you at Apache on the thirteenth?"

He nodded. "Yeah. See you then."

I followed Erika to the car, feeling his eyes on me the whole way. It was a long walk too, because the front yard was huge—full of beautiful trees and elaborate landscaping. I had to wonder how Isaiah made so much money as an independent artist.

After a long evening of taping artists' performances at Apache, I was exhausted. Tired in a happy way, though. Everyone had done great. We had a wonderful enthusiastic crowd that gave the artists a lot of energy. There were only a few minor glitches with the sound system and one of the cameras, but for the most part, everything went smoothly.

I stayed around until everything was packed up and my whole crew was gone. I sat talking to the manager for a while, but my body felt like a truck had run over it. I knew it was time to lay it down.

As I headed toward the door, I heard a voice behind me. "G'night, Michelle."

It was Isaiah. I tried not to look too happy to see him.

"I thought you were long gone with everyone else." He shook his head. He didn't seem to know what to say.

I didn't either. So we stood there for a few seconds, looking at each other. We both started to speak at the same time. He gestured for me to go first.

"I . . . I really enjoyed working with you. Thanks so much for doing the show."

"Thanks for the opportunity. I appreciate it."

We both nodded.

I turned to leave, and he stepped closer to me. "Can I walk you to your car? It's almost two in the morning."

I nodded, and we headed out the door together.

When we were halfway to the parking lot, he said, "So, maybe next season, after the show has been long forgotten, we can hang out?"

I took a deep breath and shrugged my shoulders.

"I guess that's better than a no. Gives a brother something to hope for."

I smiled.

"Like I said, this might be your divine hook-up. God answering your prayer. How do you know He didn't send me?"

Thankfully, we arrived at my car. I put my key in the lock and opened the door. I turned to Isaiah and gave one last smile. "I don't." I got into my car and started it up. "You take care, Isaiah. I wish you the best."

He stepped aside and let me drive off.

twenty-two

Too early the next morning, the phone rang. I didn't know who could be calling me at daybreak on a Saturday. I picked up the phone and recognized my mom's number on the caller ID. A feeling of shame swept over me as I realized I didn't want to answer. I had been avoiding her calls lately. Very unlike me. My mother and I were the absolute best of friends. She was the coolest mother in the world.

Except that lately, her conversation always ended up at when I was gonna get married and how I needed to stop focusing on my career so much and think about a family. I couldn't make her understand that focusing on my career wasn't keeping me from being married. It was keeping me from being depressed that I wasn't married. It filled in the gaps, passed the time, and made me feel like I was, at least, accomplishing *something* with my life.

"Hey, Mom. What's up?" I hoped she would hear

the sleepiness in my voice and feel bad and offer to call back later.

"Hey, baby girl. I miss you. I haven't heard from you lately. You sound like you were sleep. Hot date last night?"

There was too much hope in her voice.

"No date. Just a television shoot that ended late."

"Working too hard again, huh? I guess that's why there was no hot date. Say hi to your sisters."

"Hey, 'Chelle."

"What's up, Michelle."

The voices of my baby sister, Sheree, and my older sister, Valerie, made me sit up in the bed. This had to be serious. "Hey, guys. To what do I owe the honor of this conference call?"

"Great news, 'Chelle. We wanted to share it all together. We wish you were here with the rest of the family, but I guess a conference call will have to do. I still don't know why you wanted to move all the way over there—"

"Mom, don't start. I know Michelle isn't in the mood for that speech early on a Saturday morning."

Good old Valerie. Always taking up for me. My mom, dad, three sisters, and three brothers all still lived in Houston. All within a thirty-mile radius of one another. I was the one that had to be different and move out here to Atlanta.

"What's the news?" A weird tickly feeling rose up in my belly.

"I'm getting married!" Sheree blurted out.

"Oh, wow! Babydoll, congratulations. I can't believe it. When?"

I tried not to feel sick as my baby sister—twenty-six years old—chattered on and on about her proposal from her long-time boyfriend. What kind of sister was I? I was supposed to be happy for her. *God, deliver me from the spirit of jealousy. Or, at the very least, help me fake it through the rest of this conversation.*

"And we're gonna get married in July, the weekend of the family reunion. That way, everybody will already be in town."

Thanks, God. Really. Thanks. I hadn't planned on going to the family reunion. I was an emotional wreck the year before. Everybody, and I mean *everybody* in my family, was married with children. And my family was huge. Not only were all my sibs, except Sheree, married with at least two kids apiece—all my cousins were married with children. Cousins much younger than me were bringing their husbands and young kids. Younger cousins I used to babysit. Whose diapers I had changed.

And my old uncles had no sensitivity whatsoever. I cringed remembering the conversation at the family barbeque in my grandmother's huge backyard out in the suburbs of Houston.

"Well now, gal, whatcha waitin' on? Seems to me like you oughta be tryin' to find some nice fella to settle down and start a family with. Had a perfectly good one, but you got rid of him. Although I guess he wasn't perfectly good if he didn't give you no babies." Uncle Charlie chewed on his signature toothpick. Ironic, seeing he had very few teeth left.

"Charlie, you may not blame that fella for that. Mighta been her. She probably told him she wanted to wait." Uncle Billy sat across from me at the large picnic table. His wide frame took up almost the whole bench.

Uncle Charlie waved away mosquitoes in the hot July air. "I know it don't make no sense for her to be gettin' up in years and she ain't got no man and no chilluns. Ain't natural. What you gon' do, gal? You gon' find you a man soon and have some babies?"

Uncle Billy used a washrag to wipe off the everpresent sweat beads on his forehead. "Leave that girl alone, Charlie. Maybe she jus' different from the rest of the family."

"Different?" Uncle Charlie's mouth fell open, revealing too much of his toothless gums. "What you mean? Funny? You ain't funny, is you, girl? Is that why you moved to Atlanta?"

"Charlie, I told you to leave that girl alone. If she is funny, she ain't gon' tell you. Leave her be." Uncle Billy leaned in and peered at me over the top of his glasses. "Is you funny? You can tell me." He whispered like it would be our little secret and cut his eyes at Uncle Charlie to let me know I didn't need to worry about him.

"No, sir, Uncle Billy. I ain't funny." I tried to work up a real smile. What I really wanted to do was cuss them both out and tell them to mind their business.

I looked down the table at my grandmother. She

didn't play that. Adults were to be respected and revered. No matter how ignorant they were or what came out their mouths. "I'm sure when God sends the right man, I'll settle down, get married and have some kids."

I looked around for my father. He would save me from the evil uncles. My eyes finally rested on him at a table across the yard with a card slapped on his forehead, talking trash at a spades game.

I excused myself, ran to the house, and up to my grandmother's bedroom. After crying my eyes out on her huge antique bed for a while, I looked around the room at all her family pictures from over the years. My family prided itself on its rich heritage. We could trace ourselves back to slavery.

The highlight of the family reunion would come later when we would all gather around my grand-mother for her to tell stories about where we came from. About where our great-great-great grandfather came from in Africa. She would look at each of us, from every generation and stress to us the importance of keeping the family going. That long after she was gone, we should continue to gather every year. To love and support one an-other. To tell our children and children's children about the importance of love and family.

I would sit close to my daddy while the rest of my brothers and sisters were spread out across the yard with their children sitting close to them. Making sure they took in the stories, took in my grandmother and her strength.

* * *

"So, 'Chelle, you'll do it?" Sheree's breathless excitement pulled me back into the conversation.

"Huh?" Oh, dear. What did she just ask me to do? *Please, God, not another bridesmaid's dress . . .*

"Be in the wedding? Have you heard a word I've said?"

"Of course, babydoll. You shouldn't even have to ask that. You know I'll be right there." My heart was bleeding. I had to get off the phone. "I am so happy for you, babydoll. I'm glad you guys called me. Tomorrow, I'll call and we'll talk more about it and make plans and all. Right now, I have a shoot to get ready—"

"Wait," my mother interrupted me. "Don't you want to hear the rest of the news?"

"There's more?" I tried to sound as excited as possible. I looked up at the ceiling to let God know I couldn't take one more thing.

"I'm pregnant." This time it was Valerie's turn to bubble over with excitement.

"Oh, my goodness. This is too much." Really. It was too much. "Wow. When did you find out? How far along are you?"

I tried to remember all the questions I was supposed to ask. Luckily, Valerie was so excited that I didn't have to ask much more. She babbled on about morning sickness and being about seven weeks and praying that this one was a girl so she could close up shop. She and her husband already had three boys, and he seemed determined to keep trying until he had a daughter.

"That is so wonderful, Val. I'm sure it's gonna be a girl this time. If not, just dress him in pink and ponytails and tell Terrence you ain't having no more."

Everybody laughed at my joke long enough to give me a chance to think of a few more loving sisterly things to say to the both of them before I made another attempt to get off the phone. Mom had been quiet, but I knew all this news was the perfect opportunity for her to launch into me.

"Well, now, Michelle. It's your turn next, huh? Pretty soon, we'll be hearing from you about getting married and then not long after that, you'll be telling us about a baby. Right?"

My mother was almost begging. You would think with all the sons- and daughters-in-law and grandchildren she had, she would be satisfied and leave me alone. I knew it was just her wanting the best for me. That's what I told myself to keep from getting upset whenever this conversation came up.

"Hopefully, Mom. Long as you keep praying for me, right?"

"Oh, I'm praying, but you gotta do your part. Get out of the house. Stop working so much. Go out to where you can meet people. And don't be so picky."

"Momma, please."

I didn't even have to say it. Both Valerie and Sheree came to my rescue.

"Leave her alone. In God's time. Okay?"

Sheree was considered an old maid for waiting until she was twenty-six to get married. I was sure she had started to endure some of the same badgering I got all the time.

"I'm sorry, baby. I want the best for you. Baby-doll is right. In God's time. Well, I guess we better let you get to your shoot. We'll talk to you more tomorrow? I know you been busy, but we miss you so much."

"Yeah, Momma. I'll call tomorrow."

After saying goodbye, I sat on the side of the bed, staring at the wall for a while. Babydoll was getting married. Valerie was pregnant with her fourth child. There was no escaping the family reunion this year. And the crazy uncles.

As seemed to be my custom lately, I burst into tears and rolled onto the floor next to my bed. I wasn't even hormonal. What kind of sister was I? To cry at such awesome news. To be jealous and wish it was me.

I pulled myself up and went over to my closet. After plowing through stacks of dirty laundry, I got to the back and pulled out my hope chest. Once inside, I retrieved the family album Aunt Ladybird had provided for every member of the family. It was filled with pictures of my grandmother, all the aunts and uncles, all their children and everyone's children's children. I turned to the back and pulled out the family tree her daughter, Bunny, had tirelessly worked on.

I looked at each family. A branch between every husband and wife and then a branch downward for their children. I looked at my parents' names joined together, with me and my brothers' and sisters' names branching out of it. I looked at each of my brothers and sisters with their branches joining them to their spouse and branching downward to their children. Sheree and I were the only ones whose name had no branches. And, come July, Sheree would have her own branch.

I would be the last one. Branchless . . .

I got up off the floor and marched, with determination, into my office. I plundered through a large stack of papers, unopened mail, and file folders from work on my desk until I found it.

Isaiah's press kit. I turned it over in my hands a couple of times. Should I do it? One thought of the crazy uncles taking potshots at me during Sheree's wedding was all I needed. That and the possibility of remaining forever branchless.

I took out my cell phone and dialed his number. He sounded sleepy when he answered the phone. I didn't care. I had to do it while I had the nerve.

"Isaiah, it's Michelle. I was wondering if you wanted to go out tonight."

twenty-three

It took Isaiah a second to answer my question. I didn't know if he was asleep, or shocked by me asking him out. After he got himself together, he said he wanted to plan something special and would call me back later. Of course, I couldn't sleep until he called me back.

When he did, he told me to dress cute and comfortable.

I spent the next couple of hours in the bed, staring at the ceiling, trying to guess where he would be taking me.

Since I insisted on driving my own car rather than letting him pick me up, he called me half an hour before the date and told me to meet him at Piedmont Park.

Sounded cool. A date in the park. I dressed in pink Capri pants, a white cotton tee, and some Keds. It was a nice day outside, but I grabbed a blue jean jacket in case it got cool later.

When I walked up to our meeting point, he was there waiting, leaning against a Hummer. His body was made for the jeans he was wearing. He had on one of his signature slogan T-shirts that said, "No Worries. God Reigns." He gave me a shy smile and a hug. He smelled good too. He had changed up from the African musk to some other musky scent. I lingered in his arms a few seconds too long.

"Hey," he said into my ear before he let me go.

"Hey, back." I pulled away from him before I wouldn't want to.

He nodded toward a large tree down by the lake, gesturing for me to follow. When we got to the other side of it, I could see where he had spread out a blanket and had a large picnic basket.

"I know. Kinda corny and cliché, huh? The whole picnic in the park thing?" he said.

"Not at all. It's sweet. I love being outside and love water. It's perfect." I took a seat on a large cushion he had placed on the blanket. I appreciated his thoughtfulness. After ten minutes of sitting on the hard ground, my butt would have started hurting.

He opened the basket and took out fruit, cheese, crackers, and juice. "Hope you're not too hungry. If you are, we can go for dinner after we leave here."

"I'm good. This should be fine." My stomach was too fluttery to eat much anyway.

He picked up a pear and lay down on his stomach, kicking off his sandals and stretching out his legs. "So, you know everything there is to know about me. Now it's my turn to interview you."

"Interview me?" I gave him a flirty smile.

"Yeah. I need to find out all your deepest, darkest secrets."

I giggled. "Whatever. And I don't know everything there is to know about you. Just enough for the show. There's a lot more I need to know about you if—"

He raised his eyebrows. "If what?"

"If . . ." I bit my lip. "If I'm going to risk losing my job to hang out with you."

His face broke into a smile. "Okay, that's fair. I'll give you the rundown." He sat up across from me and crossed his legs, Indian style. He pulled his locks behind his back. I was sure they had to be hot. "I'm thirty-four years old, never been married, no children. No crazy ex-girlfriends that you'd have to worry about stalking you or keying your car."

"Why are you still single?" I scooted my cushion back close to the tree so I could lean against it.

He shrugged and took a big bite of the pear. "God hasn't sent the right one. I'm looking for someone completely submitted to God. I think two people have a better chance in a relationship if they're both completely sold out to Christ— dead to ourselves, allowing His Spirit to reign in us."

His words sounded familiar.

He continued, "I guess my lifestyle may have something to do with it, too. I'm a free spirit led by God's Spirit, and I go wherever I feel His wind blowing me. That really doesn't work for a relationship."

"What do you mean?" I turned around and studied the tree trunk to make sure there were no bugs in sight. I didn't need anything crawling into my afro.

"Like I said, I'm free. I'm not materialistic at all, and I'm not really attached to anything earthly or worldly. When I meet the right one, I'm going to have to make a lot of changes. It would be big changes, but I'm believing she'll be worth it."

"Not materialistic? Just believe in living large, huh?"

He frowned. "What do you mean?"

I was just about to mention his house and car when my cell phone rang. I was set to ignore it until I saw Jason's name.

"Let me get this real quick." I stood and walked over to a nearby tree and answered the phone.

Jason was at the office editing and had run into a couple of glitches with the audio. I talked him through the problem and then hung up.

"Sorry about that. It was Jason." I made myself comfortable on the cushion again. "He's editing a show and needed some help."

"Yeah. Sure." Isaiah finished off his pear and threw the core into the lake.

"What do you mean by that?"

"Did he know you were going out with me today?"

"Of course not." I reached over to the picnic basket and picked up a huge bunch of red grapes. "Why do you ask that?"

"Because if he knows you're with me, that won't be the only phone call."

"Isaiah, what are you talking about?" I bit into a grape. It was a perfect blend of sweet and tangy.

Isaiah took a cup out of the basket and poured some juice. "Jason likes you."

"What in the world?" I swatted away a fly that was trying to share my grapes. "What are you talking about?"

"Come on. You know he likes you." He handed me the cup of juice and poured himself another. "I thought you guys were dating, until you told me about your not-dating-where-you-work policy."

"You thought me and Jason were dating? Why?"

"Because of the way you guys were vibing during the audition. Because of how protective he is of you. He'll barely let me anywhere near you for more than five minutes."

"Please, Isaiah. You're reading into stuff. He's just running the shoot."

He shook his head. "He likes you. Guys know."

"We've worked closely together for the past couple of years. That's all."

"Okay. Just think about it and watch." He took a sip of juice and pulled out the crackers and cheese. "Anyway, it's my turn to ask questions."

"Okay. Ask whatever you want, but I reserve the right not to answer."

He raised his eyebrows. "A woman with secrets. I love it."

I laughed.

"So why are you still single? I can't believe ain't nobody snatched you up by now."

I took a sip of juice. It tasted like passion fruit or something. "I was married for eleven years. Divorced about three years ago." I hope he didn't ask too many questions. I didn't feel like talking about my ex right now.

"If you don't mind me asking, what happened? That's a long time to be married."

I shrugged. "Short version? We got married young. We both had big dreams and goals for our lives, individually and together. After a while, it became clear that mine were real goals and his were dreams that would always continue to be dreams. He kept hopping from idea to idea, never saw anything through, and never achieved any real measure of success. Other bad things happened at the end . . ." Hopefully he wouldn't press me for more details.

"And since then, you haven't found anyone?"

"I only recently started dating again. I've been through some crazy stuff out there. Enough to make me want to stay single."

Isaiah stared into my eyes. "No, you don't want to stay single. You have too much love inside you to give away to stay single. And you need to be loved and covered. You deserve that. And you have to have some babies. You're not one of those women who's going to end up alone."

I looked down at the ground. He had a way of reading me that was unnerving.

He placed a few pieces of cheese and crackers on a small plate and slid it over to me. "So, what's your ultimate? Your goals, your dreams?"

It seemed weird for him to ask my favorite rule-out question. He listened intently as I got on my soapbox about Black television programming and its effect on the African American community and especially our youth. I told him my dreams about television, movies, and theatre. "The media is one of the most effective means of communicating the

Kingdom. I can reach people who may never go to church or watch Dr. Creflo Dollar, Bishop Eddie Long or Bishop Jakes on television. They might see something in a movie or television show that could change their life."

I went on for a while, with him smiling and nodding the whole time. I knew I was going too long, but he listened like I was the most interesting person on earth.

I finally made myself stop by shoving cheese and crackers into my mouth. I asked him, "So what's your ultimate?"

"My life is all about worship. I want to teach people intimacy with God through worship. I don't want to be an entertainer. I'm not trying to make millions selling records. Not trying to get famous, except for the sake of having a platform to minister the Kingdom. If I can lead one person closer to the presence of God, then I've achieved my purpose here on earth."

It was my turn to nod and smile.

He hung his head for a second. "I guess I've had to change my idea of what success is over the years, and that's where I am now. It was difficult for a while. My brother and sister are real successful by the world's standards. She's a big-time entertainment lawyer. He's a professor at Howard. They've really made my parents proud. I'm not like them. They like to stay in one place and like working for the system. I think it was the way we grew up, living from place to place all over the world. They prefer stability. I guess I'm more like my parents. More free- spirited and sold out to ministry than attached to material things."

"I think you're successful. Success is not about having a profession according to society's idea of success. Success is doing what you're called to do and being happy doing it. You should never apologize for that."

He smiled and lay back on the blanket, staring up at the sky. "Thanks, Michelle."

I lay back and stared up at the sky, too. He inched over closer to me. It felt funny being horizontal next to him. It wasn't like he was doing anything, but the feel of his muscular arm against mine and the occasional brushes of his leg against me started a little heat to rise. It was shameful, but it didn't take much for me. I tried to focus on the nature around us.

A hot summer breeze waved across us, and the trees rippled in response. I heard ducks on the lake squawking at each other. I laughed inwardly, remembering my last experience with ducks on a lake. Thankfully, the St. John's Wort had worked its magic on me over the last couple of months, and except for an occasional freak-out moment, my mood was much more stable on my hormone days. It hadn't done anything to deal with the horny monster though.

The thought of tussling with him later made me sit up.

Isaiah looked up at me. "You okay?"

I nodded and scooched away from him a little.

He sat up and pulled out his guitar. "I've been working on this new song. Want to hear it? Here it go." He chuckled. "Really. Let me know what you think."

He strummed a few chords on the guitar and

began singing. The words about being in the secret place with God touched a special place in my soul. He sang about the secret place being the safest place where one could get lost in the joy of the Lord. Made me think of snuggling under my comforter with the Holy Spirit, without a care in the world. Isaiah had a poetic way with words that made me almost see what he was singing.

"You like?" he asked after he played the final chords of the song.

"I like. That was beautiful. You're really going to impact a lot of people's lives with your music. It's clearly what you were born to do."

He smiled and bowed his head like I had embarrassed him. If Isaiah ever did come to church with me, there would be no reason to do the worship test. He clearly had an intimate relationship with God.

We sat and talked for a while longer, finishing off all the food in the picnic basket.

As evening approached, a cool breeze from the lake stirred, and the mosquitoes started to gather. I let Isaiah know it was time to go. I wasn't trying to get bit.

He walked me to my car. I wasn't ready for the evening to end, but I was sleepy from the night before and needed to get some rest before church in the morning.

"So, will I see you again? Soon?" Isaiah asked.

I nodded. "Yeah. I think I'd like that."

His face broke into a big grin. "Good. I'd like that too."

He gave me a hug. I felt myself melting in his arms. I knew I stayed there too long, but my affection-starved body wasn't trying to let go. He kissed me on the cheek and slowly pulled away from me.

He held the car door open for me and waited until I got in and shut the door behind me. He leaned down into the open window. "Thanks, Michelle. I'm glad you called. Call me when you have time, and we'll hang out again."

When I got home, showered and got into bed, I knew my attempts at sleep wouldn't be any better than they had been earlier that day. I couldn't stop thinking about everything Isaiah had said. The song he sang. His passion. How I felt safe and secure in his arms. How sweet his kiss felt on my cheek. I wondered for a minute about all his talk about being a free spirit, not attached to the material world, but that contemplation got lost in remembering how his arms felt around me.

I finally drifted off to sleep at one in the morning with the overwhelming question looming in my mind. Was Isaiah the one?

twenty-four

With all that had been going on at work, it had been weeks since I had spent any quality time with my girls. I basically worked all day and fell into bed every night. I saw them at church on Sundays, but had to leave right after to either write, edit with Jason, or catch up on some sleep.

We decided to go out to dinner after church on Sunday. I was still a little sleepy from my late-night taping on Friday and then being up all night thinking about my date on Saturday, but I missed them and needed some girl time. And I couldn't wait to tell them about Isaiah.

Lisa, Vanessa, Nicole, and I sat around a table at Houston's in Buckhead. Angela had been missing in action from church for about two months. Lisa had been calling her almost daily. At first, she answered and didn't talk much, but lately, she hadn't answered at all. We were all worried but didn't know what to do.

Lisa, Vanessa, and Nicole watched me intently as I told them about Isaiah, from his first audition up to our date the day before. I wondered if I was glowing like Angela used to.

I stopped talking for a minute when the waitress brought over our meals. "I think he's rich, or at least, very well-off. Now, you guys know me. I'm not a gold digger, but dang—it helps, you know?"

Nicole held up a hand to interrupt me for a second and bowed her head to bless the food. We all prayed for a few seconds, then I launched right back into my Isaiah story.

"I hope I don't sound materialistic, but it would be wonderful to be financially secure. Completely different from being with my ex, where I was responsible for everything. It would be cool not to have to work so hard. Maybe take a break from work and create some pilots for my show ideas."

"Wait a minute, girl. You just met the man, and you're already married, and quitting your job? Slow it down." Vanessa cut off a large piece of her steak and took a bite.

"I'm not talking about marrying him. The thought crosses your mind when you're getting to know someone. You look at everything about them to see if they match what's on your list. He's definitely godly. Definitely financially well-off. You should see his house. It's fabulous—out there in Sandstone Estates in Lithonia. And he drives a Hummer. Like I said, you guys know me and I'm not materialistic, but it's nice to have nice things. And he's talented and shares my love for music and the arts. He's sweet and affectionate. And he gets me. He can read me like a book—like God gave him the key to my heart. What more could I ask?"

"A lot more. A bunch of questions for sure." Nicole poured a huge dollop of ketchup on her fries. "Number one, how does he afford his house and car as a musician? I've never heard of him before, so he can't be that big."

"I don't know." I grabbed a fry off her plate. "I didn't ask him for a breakdown of his financials. It was a first date."

"Girl, something ain't right. You sure he ain't selling drugs or something?" Nicole swatted my hand away when I tried to reach for another French fry.

Lisa was distracted, barely participating in the conversation.

"Lisa, are you with us? What's wrong?" I asked.

"I'm worried about Angie. This is the seventh Sunday in a row she's missed church. Something must be really wrong."

"I think we all know what's wrong." Vanessa scooped the butter out of her baked potato and pushed it to the side of her plate. "She'll be okay. When she forgives herself, she'll be back. Just keep praying for her."

"Yeah, but what if something is really wrong? Don't you think we need to check on her?"

"You said you've been calling and she won't answer the phone, right? What else can we do?" I looked at my salad, then at Nicole's huge burger and fries. She made a face that said don't even think about it.

"We should show up at her house. She might be mad at us, but we'll have to take that chance." Lisa looked at her watch. "We should go when we leave here. Even if she went to Augusta this weekend, she'd be back by now to get ready for work tomorrow." Lisa looked around the table at us. "You guys with me?"

We all looked at each other and nodded. She rushed us through the rest of our meal, and we were on our way.

Lisa rang the doorbell while the rest of us stood hiding by the garage. We figured Angela might be more likely to answer if she only saw one person standing there. We'd come out after she opened the door.

Lisa cupped her hands around her eyes and peered through one of the small windows framing the door. She called out to us, "The television is on, and I can see Bishop Jakes preaching. I think I see her head on the couch. She's either 'sleep or ignoring me." She rang the doorbell again and again and stood there waiting.

After a few minutes, she banged on the door and yelled, "Angie, if you don't let me in, I'm going to make a scene, and all your neighbors are gonna be out here wondering what's going on."

A few seconds later, Lisa banged on the door some more, screaming, "Open the door. I'm not going anywhere." Her voice escalated until I was sure someone would call the police.

Finally, the door opened, and Angie stepped out in a bathrobe. "Have you lost your mind? What is your problem, making all that noise out here?" She looked from left to right, I guess, to see if any of her neighbors had noticed. She finally stood with her hands on her hips in front of Lisa. "You couldn't call first? What's your problem?"

Lisa's mouth fell open. "I've been calling you for weeks. You won't answer your phone. What's *your* problem?" They stood facing each other off for a few minutes.

Then Angie's shoulders slumped and started shaking. Lisa pulled her into her arms and held her while she sobbed. Vanessa, Nicole, and I came out of our hiding place and joined Lisa with a group hug.

Angela pulled back for a second when she felt the other arms around her. As she looked into each of our faces, she cried harder.

We ushered her into the house. It was a wreck. Angela was normally borderline obsessive-compulsive about keeping her house clean.

Lisa and Vanessa pushed blankets and crumpled tissues off the couch and sat down with Angela between them. Nicole and I moved books off the loveseat and sat down across from them. It looked like Angela had pulled every spiritual self-help book off her shelf.

Vanessa spoke first, "Sorry for showing up unannounced, but we were worried about you. We hadn't seen or heard much from you since that last time at Lisa's house." She cradled a sobbing Angela in her arms and rocked her. "Sweetie, you know we love you. Whatever is going on, we're here for you. There's nothing bad enough that should separate you from your best friends and God."

Angela cried harder.

Nicole got up and muted the television. Bishop Jakes was whooping pretty loud, and it sounded weird mixed with Angela's sobs.

Vanessa rubbed her back. "Sweetie, tell us what's wrong."

Angela sniffled. She accepted a tissue Lisa offered her and blew her nose. Her whole face was swollen. "You guys were right. I should have listened. I messed up. Again and again and again." She sobbed harder.

Vanessa continued rubbing her back. "Angie, we understand how you feel. But you have to find a way to forgive yourself. God has already forgiven you. You need to receive it and His joy and come back to church. Ask Him to help you get back on track."

Angela shook her head. "You don't understand. I messed up real bad."

Lisa pushed Angela's hair out of her face. "We do understand, honey. We've all been there."

Angela shook her head again. "No, it's worse than that." We could barely hear her next words because of her choking sobs. "I'm . . . I'm pregnant."

None of us could move or speak. The only sound in the room was the quiet buzz of the muted television and Angela's ragged sobs. She looked around the room at each of us—stunned into silence—and cried harder. "What do I do?" She said it over and over.

Vanessa came out of her momentary shock to hug Angela. "Shhh, sweetie, it's going to be okay.

We're here for you, and we'll walk through this together."

Nicole, Lisa, and I stared at each other, eyes open wide. It was every church girl's worst nightmare. I remember the few missed periods before I got married that terrified me down the aisle. I was sure we'd each had our own share of pregnancy scares.

When Angela quieted down, Vanessa asked her, "What did Gary say?"

Angela sniffled. "That he loves me and wants to marry me. And that even though this wasn't the timing and the circumstances he had imagined, he knew from the first time we talked that God had sent me to him and that I was his wife. He said it was up to me whether I wanted to get married as soon as possible or wait awhile."

Lisa patted her back. "That's wonderful, Angie. See—God is going to work this all out."

Angela shook her head. "This wasn't the way I wanted things to happen. I wanted to have a happy, beautiful wedding day—now everything's going to be rushed and covered with a cloud of shame. I've waited all my life for this, and it's not going to be wonderful like I wanted it to. This is so embarrassing."

"It doesn't have to be, Angela. You both have to forgive yourselves and let God heal your hearts. I agree this isn't the ideal way, but it is what it is and you've got to make the best of it. The good news is, he loves you and wants to marry you—and not because of the baby. And you love him. And you guys are going to be happy together. Everything's going to be fine."

Lisa clapped her hands together. "Now I get to plan a bridal shower and a wedding and a baby shower. We're going to have some wonderful parties over the next few months."

Vanessa patted Angela's stomach. "And you're going to have a beautiful, healthy baby and a wonderful husband."

A few tears slipped down Angela's face. "How can you guys be so happy about this? I'm pregnant at forty-one, out of wedlock. This is not a happy situation."

"Sweetie, it's not a matter of it being a happy situation," Vanessa said. "It's a matter of making the best of the situation. You can't afford to be depressed about it. You have a baby growing inside of you who can feel everything you feel. It's time to get up off the couch, dry your eyes, and move forward. You got a lot to do in the coming months. And whether you decide to get married now or later, everything's about to change. And lying on the couch won't get you anywhere."

Lisa said, "And you've got us. We're here to walk through the whole thing with you. Whatever you need us to do."

Nicole looked around the living room. "Yeah. And we're going to start by helping you clean up this mess." She walked into the kitchen and opened the refrigerator. "Oh dear, and we need some groceries to feed our baby."

For the first time all afternoon, Angela smiled. "I love you guys. Thanks for being here. Sorry I haven't—"

"No need to apologize." I held up a hand. "We're here now. And that's all that matters."

We spent the rest of the afternoon cleaning and getting groceries. Vanessa cooked a few meals for Angela to eat all week. Nicole made Angela shower and wash her hair. Lisa blow-dried and curled it for her. And we joked, laughed, and loved on Angela for the rest of the day.

twenty-five

On Monday morning, Erika greeted me with the bad news that Rayshawn was back at work. Terrorizing anyone anywhere near her.

"It's like she's lost her mind." Erika closed my door after doing her usual looking left and right to make sure no one was lurking nearby. "Before, she was snaky and devious. Now, she's downright crazy. I'm not gossiping or being mean. I'm trying to let you know. Whatever you do, stay out of her way."

"I'll be fine, Erika. I'm sure she just feels the need to let everybody know she's back and in control. It'll blow over in a couple of days."

Erika stepped closer to my desk. "I don't think you're hearing me. This isn't Rayshawn's usual evilness. She's lost it. Word is, she's trying to take over the production department."

I shrugged. "I ain't worried. God's got me."

"I hope so. Put in some prayers for me and everybody else while you're at it. Especially, Ms. Carter. They've already had words this morning."

"She had words with Ms. Carter?"

"I'm trying to tell you. She's crazy."

Without warning, my door flew open. "Who do you think you are?"

It was Rayshawn. Looking crazier than Erika could have ever described. She had on a blinding-red pant suit that looked two sizes too big. Her wig was crooked, and her thin eyebrows were accentuated with thick, angry pencil lines.

Erika and I stood there staring at her. She glared at Erika until she slipped behind her out the door.

"I asked you a question. Who do you think you are? Going over my head? Making all those decisions and getting things approved without my signature? I told you before, I run things around here. I told you to stay in your place. I turn my back for one second, and you stab me in it. You think you're so great? So beautiful? So in control? Everybody likes you? I tell you what." She marched over to my bookshelf and started pulling books onto the floor. "You need to get you a box and start packing. You're out of here. Your services are no longer needed at BTV."

"Rayshawn, what is your problem?" I didn't get too close to her. I wasn't sure how close to the edge she was, and I wasn't taking any chances.

"My problem? You're my problem. Or you *were* my problem. But my Michelle Bradford problems are about to end. Today."

"What's going on, guys?" Jason walked into my office. Either Erika sent him to rescue me, or he'd heard the commotion.

After seeing Rayshawn snatch a few books off

my shelf, he looked at me with wide-open eyes. He walked over to me and put a hand on my arm.

I shrugged it off and shook my head. I knew Jason was a sore spot with Rayshawn and didn't need him being touchy-feely in front of her while she was three shades of crazy.

Rayshawn smiled when she saw Jason. "Looks like your boyfriend is just in time to help you pack." She looked him up and down. "You can get ready to move back to my suite when you're finished." She turned on her heel and left.

"What was that all about?" Jason started picking up books and placed them back on the shelves. "Are you okay?"

"I'm fine."

I had to admit I was a little shaken up. Unlike my last confrontation with her, I had no desire to give Rayshawn a beatdown. My grandma taught me you don't fight crazy people. You can get killed like that.

Erika popped her head back in my office. "Ms. Carter wants to talk to you." She saw the books on the floor and came over to help Jason with the mess. "You go ahead. We got this."

I nodded and left. I rushed to Ms. Carter's office to see what was going on. Did Rayshawn really have the power to fire me?

The look on Ms. Carter's face when I walked in made me even more worried. She didn't have her usual quiet confidence. "Have a seat, Michelle. I don't know if you've heard, but Rayshawn is back and is . . . somewhat upset."

"Somewhat upset? She's lost her mind. She just fired me."

Ms. Carter's smile was strained. "She mentioned that she was going get rid of you."

I frowned. "Can she do that?"

Ms. Carter took a deep breath, and I felt a sick knot in the pit of my stomach. "She's got the station owner against the wall. She's threatened a sexual harassment case against him and says she has his wife's number on speed dial if he crosses her in any way." She gave a weak laugh. "Hell hath no fury . . ."

"Miss-es Car-ter," I said slow and drawn-out. "Does Rayshawn have the authority to fire me?" I wasn't in the mood for her double-speak or cloaked scriptures.

She let out another deep breath and folded her hands on her desk. "I'm afraid she might. She's decided that she should be the VP of programming. I received a phone call this morning, and although it wasn't said directly, I think I'm being moved over to the marketing department."

"Marketing? What are you talking about? They're going to turn this station over to Rayshawn? You know exactly what'll happen. We'll end up with shows about video hoochies, pimps and hoes, and who knows what else. You're going to let that happen?"

Ms. Carter leaned forward, her lips drawn into a thin line. "What exactly do you expect me to do, Michelle?"

I could tell I had offended her. I didn't care. "Do something about it. Fight back. You don't want to be in marketing. You're supposed to be the VP of programming."

She shook her head and laughed. "You're young

and idealistic. You have no idea how this business works. I'll be fine in marketing. And I'll retire in five years."

"You won't have a job to retire from because this station will go completely downhill with Rayshawn at the helm. You know that. I can't believe you're going to let her roll over you like that."

She folded her arms and narrowed her eyes at me. I refused to be moved. If I was gonna be fired, I was going down fighting. And I knew just the strategy to use.

"What if God placed you here at this station to take it in the direction He wants it to go? What if you're called for such a time as this?"

I could tell I got to her. She looked down at her desk. I could almost hear her thinking.

After a few moments of silence, she looked up at me. "What do you expect me to do?"

"Ask God what to do and go fight. If it's His will for us to be here, He'll fix all this. If not, then I don't want to be here. Do you? Do you really want to market video hoochies?"

She shook her head and exhaled. "I don't know. This could . . ."

I knew she was thinking that if she fought, she could end up with no job at all.

She stood up and gestured toward the door. "Why don't you take a few days off until this all blows over?"

I stood. "You're sending me home?"

She held up her hands. "Just for a few days until I can sort this out. I need to meet with the other VP's and, hopefully, with the other two station owners."

Was she saying that to appease me? Was she trying to get me out of her face so she could pack up
her stuff and move over to the marketing department?

"I promise, Michelle. I'll do everything I can. I'll
call you when I know the outcome."

twenty-six

When I got down to the parking lot, I sat in my car, stunned. *Did I just lose my job, God?*

I pulled out my cell phone and tried to reach Nicole. She was in a meeting, and her secretary promised to have her call me back later. Vanessa was in with a client and couldn't talk either. Lisa was in the middle of a shoot. Angela wasn't in any position to hear about my problems.

I felt alone. I tried to pray, but didn't even know what to say. I needed a hug and for someone to tell me it was going to be okay. Before I knew it, I had dialed Isaiah's number.

He answered on the first ring. "Hey. You miss me already, huh?"

I giggled. "Yeah, whatever." I let out a deep breath. "You busy?"

"Not at all. What's wrong?"

I spent the next few minutes spilling my guts to Isaiah about the whole Rayshawn situation.

"Where are you?" he asked.

"Still at work. Sitting in the parking lot."

"Meet me at the house in fifteen minutes."

"Give me thirty. I want to go home and put on some comfortable clothes."

"You mean I don't get to see you looking all sexy in your work clothes?"

I giggled. "Don't play with me. See you in a bit."

It didn't make sense how much better I felt all of a sudden.

I drove home and changed into some jeans and a T-shirt and quickly got back into the car to go see Isaiah.

When I pulled up at the house and rang the doorbell, Isaiah opened the door and pulled me into his arms. His hug seemed to take away all my anxiety, fears, and frustrations about what was about to happen next in my life.

I pulled away from him. I barely knew this guy and didn't need to be letting him comfort me like that. "I can't believe this happened. I don't even—"

He held up a hand. "We'll talk about that later. Come on. Let's go have some fun."

He led me to the garage and helped me climb up into the Hummer.

"Where are we going?" I asked.

"To have some fun. Didn't you hear me?" He pulled out of the garage and wheeled down the street.

"Where?"

He frowned. "Tell me you're not one of those women who has to know everything all the time."

I laughed. "I'm a producer. We're control freaks."

"I'ma need you to dig up your spontaneous side and relax."

I decided to chill and give in to whatever Isaiah had on his mind to cheer me up. Before I knew it, he was pulling into a parking spot. I glanced at the sign on the door he had parked in front of and frowned. "An arcade? Why did you bring me here?"

"Because when I finish beating you at Pac-Man, you'll forget all about your job troubles."

My mouth fell open. I couldn't help but laugh. "You think so?" I looked him up and down. "Please. In your dreams."

When we walked into the arcade, it took me a second to adjust to the flashing lights, loud music, and shooting, crashing, and beeping sounds.

The Pac-Man game was being held hostage by two belligerent-looking teenagers, but Ms. Pac-Man was free and clear. Isaiah had no idea what he was in for. It was my favorite game as a teenager. I beat him so bad, it was shameful.

Next, we played this interactive dance game, and he impressed everyone in the place with his fancy footwork. I had to let him get his ego back after the Ms. Pac-Man thing, so I let him beat me on the race car driving game. We finished up with a few games of pool.

Next, Isaiah took me out to a ranch his friends owned in Ellenwood, to ride horses. Who knew horseback riding was difficult? Either my horse didn't like me, or there was some skill to it I couldn't seem to master. I finally got on the horse with Isaiah, and we had a great time riding.

We went back to the house, and he told me to go home, shower, change and come back in an hour. He said he had one more place to take me.

When I got back, we got into the Hummer and set out for another adventure. We drove up to a huge mansion in Buckhead.

I began to wonder who Isaiah was. All day, he had great favor everywhere we went. At the arcade, he seemed to be best friends with the owner, and the guy gave him this funny coin-key thing and we played all the games for free. At the horseback riding place, we rode for hours, and the guy refused to let Isaiah give him any money.

And now we were sitting outside a mansion, in a Hummer.

When we walked in, once again, Isaiah got a warm reception. There were about eight people there, sitting in a large entertainment room. They all had the same artsy-fartsy look Isaiah had. Dreads and afros, T-shirts with slogans, worn jeans, hand-crafted jewelry. A few of the people sitting around had guitars.

One girl, wearing a long flowing skirt, a tie-dye top and large silver hoop earrings, was painting at an easel. Another guy, with long thick dreads, had a large African drum between his legs. A few people were scribbling in notebooks, and one was typing on a laptop.

The house was gorgeous with beautiful dark hardwood floors, high ceilings and large windows. It was decorated modern art deco with art, masks, and sculptures that looked like they came from all over the world.

"Guys, this is my friend, Michelle. Michelle, this is everyone."

They all laughed. Everyone came up and introduced themselves to me one by one. They were a blur of names and faces. One girl had so many piercings, she looked like she hurt. A girl with a Mohawk afro eyed me up and down while shaking my hand. I wondered if she had a thing for Isaiah or whether they had dated in the past. It looked like it cost her everything to give me the strained, fake smile she plastered on her face. And when she lingered for a few minutes and looked like she was about to say something, Isaiah came over and struck up a conversation with her.

The painter girl must have witnessed the interaction and sauntered over to where I was. "Don't mind Sanitha. She wants Isaiah, and he don't want her. She's harmless though." She looked me up and down too, but more so with curiosity. She held out a hand. "I'm Naya. It's good to meet you."

I shook her hand. "Michelle. Good to meet you too."

"You hungry? We got a spread in the kitchen. Everybody cooked." She beckoned for me to follow as she sashayed into the kitchen. Her almost-bald, natural cut was perfect for her heart-shaped face and huge fawn eyes. She handed me a plate. "Mostly everything is vegetarian. There's wine or juice if you want."

She stood, watching me fix my plate. I felt like she wanted to ask me a question. I smiled at her. "What?"

She laughed. "Nothing. Isaiah's never brought a girl before. In fact, I've never seen him with anyone. If he weren't so into God, I would have started to wonder." She picked up a carrot off a vegetable tray. "You must be something special. You a singer?"

I shook my head, heaping my plate with hummus and raw vegetables. "Television producer."

Her eyes lit up. "Oh, you're the girl doing that independent artist show?"

I nodded, wondering what else Isaiah had said about me and what his relationship was with this girl.

"Don't believe a word she says about me. It's all lies." Isaiah came in from the entertainment room, smiling. He hugged the girl. "Hey, baby sister. How are you?"

"I'm good." She looked at me and back at him. "She's beautiful—inside and out. Don't mess up." She gave Isaiah a kiss on the cheek and left the room.

He laughed. "You okay? I see you found the food."

"Yeah, Naya took good care of me."

He walked over and peeked into the entertainment room. "Hurry up and come back in. You don't want to miss anything."

I finished piling my plate with some fried plantains, black beans, and brown rice, grabbed a cup of juice and joined Isaiah in the other room.

He scooted over to share a seat with me on an ottoman. He pulled out his guitar and started strumming some chords. The guy on the keyboard joined in, as did the other guy on guitar. The guy with the African drum added a nice rhythm.

The impromptu jam session went on for hours. At times, people joined in to sing, making up lyrics as they went along. Other times, different people on the instruments soloed. They stopped between songs to laugh and talk. Naya danced her cute little self all over the room. I thought she would pass out. I could tell she had studied dance.

I kicked myself for not bringing a camera. This would have been a perfect addition to my *Indie Artist* show.

And then it hit me. I might not have an *Indie Artist* show. I might not even have a job. I let out a deep breath. Isaiah had done a good job of distracting me. I hadn't thought about it all day.

He must have felt my sigh. He stopped playing guitar, leaned over and squeezed my leg. "You okay?"

I put on a smile and nodded. "Yeah, this is fun. I was thinking how great this would be for the show, but then I realized . . ."

He looked into my eyes. "Everything is going to be okay. I promise. You'll have your show and many others after it. You're gonna run that station one day. And if not that one, your own. God is going to make you the queen of Black television because you have His heart." He rubbed my back.

I leaned my head on his shoulder. "Thanks, Isaiah." I felt my heart tumbling. It scared me. I hadn't felt that in a long time, and I knew it was too early to be feeling it.

Everyone gave me big hugs like I was part of the family when we were leaving. Nobody else seemed to be leaving, even though it was almost one in the morning.

"How long will they stay there playing and singing?" I asked Isaiah as he helped me up into the Hummer.

"They all live there. It's sort of like an artist commune. The house belongs to Nigel—the guy on the keyboard. He used to be a big corporate America investment banker. He made a huge chunk of money and retired and came back to his first love—music. He loves to support young, starving artists. Anyone he selects can stay there as long as they need to, as long as they're producing art on a daily basis."

"That's a cool idea." I let my window down to enjoy the brisk night air.

"Yeah. Nigel's great." Isaiah rubbed my arm. "You had a good day?"

I sighed and nodded. "Yeah. A great day. You made me forget. Thanks."

"My pleasure."

We drove back to the house listening to a Bob Marley CD. I fell asleep listening to *Redemption Song*.

I woke up as Isaiah pulled into the garage.

He walked me out to my car. "You gonna be okay getting home? I shouldn't have kept you out so late. I would let you crash in the guest room, but I know you're a church girl, so you'd say no."

I smiled. The weird thing was, I didn't want to leave. He made me feel so safe and peaceful, yet giddy inside. I thought of Angela talking about not wanting to be far away from Gary and understood. Of course, the next thing that popped into my mind was that she was pregnant.

"You're absolutely right. I better go. Thanks again, Isaiah. I had a great day."

He gave me one of those hugs. I buried my head in his chest and tried not to think about Rayshawn, BTV, and Ms. Carter. I let out a deep breath and relaxed further into his chest. I felt like I could stay there all night, but knew I had to let him go before I decided that sleeping in the guest room would be okay.

When I pulled away, he grabbed both my hands and bowed his head. "God, I thank you that Michelle is Your daughter and You're a good Father who takes care of His children. I thank You that she has nothing to worry about because You've already got it worked out. I thank You that You show Yourself mighty on her behalf and move swiftly to straighten this situation out.

"'Cause your perfect will to prevail. I thank You that You're removing everyone that stands against You and Your Kingdom purposes and that You elevate those that represent You and Your interests. Give Michelle the peace that surpasses understanding, so she won't waste a moment in worry. Take her to a new place of faith and dependence on you through this situation and give her a divine revelation of Your love for her. In Jesus' name."

He kissed me on my forehead. And then my right cheek. And then my left cheek. And then a soft, sweet kiss on the lips. And then he pulled me into another hug.

I kissed his cheek and leaned my head against his shoulder. We both sighed at the same time and then laughed.

"I better go." I pulled away from him and opened the car door.

"Yeah, you better." He stood back as I got into the car, then closed the door behind me.

Before I left, he said, "God is going to work this out quickly. Don't even bother to look for another job. You're going back to BTV with a promotion.

Until you get the phone call, relax and have fun, okay? No worries."

I eyed him to see whether he was being encouraging, but he had such a conviction in his eyes, I took it as a word from God. I nodded. "Okay. No worries."

He grinned. "I'm making myself available to show you the time of your life until you go back to work. Call me when you wake up."

I smiled and started up the car. "Good night, Isaiah. Thanks again."

twenty-seven

Of course, I called Isaiah as soon as I woke up. And, of course, we hung out again. In fact, for the next few days, we were almost inseparable.

On Tuesday night, we went to the jam session at Sugar Hill, then stayed out until about four in the morning at IHOP, talking. I slept most of Wednesday. Then he cooked dinner for me at his house, and we went to the jam session at Apache and stayed out until about three in the morning.

On Thursday, I caught up on sleep until early evening, and then we went back to Nigel's house for another jam session. Everywhere we went, Isaiah was well-loved and knew everybody. We got in free everywhere, and the bartenders wouldn't even let him pay for our sodas. He performed each night, and I felt myself falling further and further.

On Friday afternoon, after recovering from another late night out, I sat in the middle of my bed, trying to sort out my feelings. It seemed too easy for Isaiah to stroll into my life, just like that, and be the one. I needed to talk to God about it. We hadn't talked much over the past few days. I realized spending so much time with Isaiah had me spending less time with God.

"So, God, what do you think of Isaiah?"

After I said it, it seemed like a dumb question. I could imagine God saying, "He's my son. I love him. What do you think?"

I rephrased my question. "What do you think of Isaiah for me?" I thought of the prayer Lisa said her friend had prayed. "God, I really like him a lot. But you know him, and you know me. I ask that if he's not Your best for me, that You reveal it. Bring this thing to a screeching halt. Expose whatever it is I need to know about him to realize he's not the one. If he is the one, make us grow closer and closer. In Jesus' name." I thought about Angela and added one last thought. "And if he is the one, please show me how to keep it holy. My relationship with You is more important than anything, and as much as I want to get married and have babies, it's not worth losing You."

I lay back on the bed. He didn't say anything. Of course, with me feeling so giddy and mushy, yet scared and confused inside, it would be difficult for me to hear anything if He did talk. I had to trust that the circumstances would work out.

I tried to pray about my job, but it was another one of those times where God didn't answer but I felt His peace. Isaiah's words flooded my spirit. It wouldn't be long before I had my job back with a promotion. "I hope that's true, God. I hope I haven't been foolishly falling in love when I should have been looking for a new job."

A week wouldn't hurt though. After the financial devastation of my divorce, I had lived poor for a while so I could save money. I planned never to be desperate and broke again. I could live for a good six months without working.

I awoke about an hour later to my cell phone ringing. It was Erika's office line. I answered it quickly. "Yeah, girl. What's up?"

"You lazy bum. You sound like you were 'sleep. Get up, get dressed and get here. Ms. Carter wants to talk to you."

In less than an hour, I walked into Ms. Carter's office. Quite unlike her character, she greeted me with a hug. Her confident smile was back. She gestured for me to take a seat.

"Michelle, I have to say thank you. You challenged me to do the right thing, and I really got to see God in action. Like you said, He worked everything out for our good and for the good of the station. I will continue as VP of programming, and everything will go forward as planned with the fall lineup. I won't go into the particulars, but know that Rayshawn is no longer a part of BTV."

My eyes widened.

Ms. Carter nodded. "I trust you had a good little vacation, because it's time to get back to work. I hope you're up for the added responsibility, because I'm going to have you finish your shows as senior producer. Mark will answer any questions if you need him to, but for the most part, you're on your own. Think you can handle it?"

"Yes . . . yes, ma'am . . ." I couldn't believe it. Exactly what Isaiah said was unfolding before me. "I can handle it."

"Good. Well then, get to work. You're four days behind schedule." She smiled and stood to shake my hand. "Michelle, thanks again. I learned a lot from you challenging me to seek God's will. I know He's got a great future planned for you. Who knows, you may be the one to take my spot when I retire in five years. Imagine how big the station will be by that time. Like you said, for such a time as this . . ."

I smiled. "Thanks, Ms. Carter. I appreciate Him giving me such a great mentor to learn from." She gave me another hug, and I left her office.

When I got to my office, Jason was there waiting for me. He gave me a big hug. "Welcome back. It was weird being here without you."

What was it with everyone and the hugging today? "Thanks, Jason. Glad to be back."

"Congrats. I heard the news. I told you it wouldn't be long."

Erika came rushing in. "Hey, girl. Or should I say *senior producer*?" She gave me a hug. "Girl, we missed you. You must have been doing some serious praying. I'm glad God listens to you. Maybe I need to give you a list of things to pray about for me."

I laughed.

Jason's cell phone rang. He frowned. "It's my daughters' school. I'll be right back." He answered the phone on the way out of my office.

Erika sat down in my office chair. "Okay, I know you hate gossip, but this is good gossip. Did you hear what happened?"

"Ms. Carter told me that everything is as it should be. She'll continue on as VP, I'm being promoted to senior producer, and Rayshawn is no longer here."

Erika shook her head and rolled her eyes, obviously annoyed by my lack of information. "Girl, Let me give you the whole scoop. Ms. Carter and the other VPs got together and decided they needed to get rid of Rayshawn to keep the station from going straight to hell. They scheduled a meeting with the board and the other station owners and told them what was going on. They decided that Rayshawn's relationship with the station owner was jeopardizing everything we've all worked hard for. They met with the station owner and convinced him that his lack of judgment was a risk to everything they had planned the station to be. They strongly recommended that he sell his interest in the station and move on to avoid legal proceedings."

Erika leaned forward in the chair like she did when the gossip got good to her. "And he agreed. He's usually an arrogant, stubborn man who doesn't like to be told what to do, but he signed the papers without putting up a fight."

All I could do was nod.

"So, yesterday, Ms. Carter called Rayshawn in and told her she was no longer needed at BTV. Girl, she lost the last little piece of mind she had left. Security had to drag her out kicking and screaming. The only reason she didn't get arrested was Ms. Carter told them not to."

My mouth fell open.

"Yeah, girl. It was crazy." Erika was obviously pleased that her gossip was getting a good response. "Here's the real kicker. Do you know what made Ms. Carter set up all the meetings in the first place?"

For some reason, I felt the need to prove to Erika that I knew something about something. "I talked to her before I left and told her to fight the changes Rayshawn was trying to bring."

"That might have been part of it, but there was more." Erika popped her head out the door, looked right and left and then shut my door and sat down. "Like I said, this is good gossip. After you got sent home, Jason got upset—mad really. He went to Rayshawn's office and got into it with her real bad. I've never seen him like that. Can you imagine Jason yelling? Anyway, she ended up grabbing him and trying to kiss him or some madness like that."

My eyes widened.

"Yeah, girl. Completely crazy. Jason marched to Ms. Carter's office and told her about it and all the times Rayshawn tried to sex him up in the past. He said that if something wasn't done about her, he'd be filing sexual harassment charges against her. Then he got together with some of the editors and producers, and they all decided that if Rayshawn took over, everybody would walk out all at once. There was no way we could have shows ready by fall, and the station would go down. You should have seen him."

I was floored. Jason had risked his job to save mine? Knowing he had two daughters to feed and debt from his ex-wife hanging over his head? It was more than saving my job, though. It was about saving the station.

"Erika, how do you know all this stuff? Do you have every office in this place bugged?"

"Girl, don't ask me about my sources. If I tell you, I have to kill you."

We both laughed.

"Well, girl, we better get back to work. We got some days to make up," I said.

"Yes, ma'am. I's getting to it. Congratulations, Michelle. And thanks."

"For what?"

"For being a good example. Watching the way God works things out for you makes me wonder if I should try to do better. You know, be a Christian and pray and go to church and all that stuff. If it works for you, it might just work for me. God knows I can use some changes in my life."

I hugged her. "He's got you, Erika. More than you know. And you're welcome to come to church with me anytime. Let me know."

"I will," Erika said as she turned and left my office.

Jason came back in. "Sorry about that. Cameron's teacher called. She got sick and threw up all over the place. I hate to cut out now, but I need to go pick her up."

"Sure, Jason. No problem. And thanks. Erika told me what you did. I think you're crazy, risking your job like that, but I'm grateful that you did."

"Yeah, I guess all your talk about changing Black television has gotten to me. I couldn't let it go down like that. No telling what kinda stuff we would have been producing with Rayshawn in charge. And I didn't like the thought of working here without you. We need you."

I felt my face turning red. "Thanks, Jason. I hope Cameron is okay. Call me if you need anything." Not that I would know what to do with a sick child.

"I will. Thanks."

After he left, I sat at my desk for a few minutes. *God, You never cease to amaze me. Thanks. I promise I'll make You proud.*

I picked up the phone to call Isaiah.

When he answered, he said, "I see you're calling me from your office phone. I take that to mean God did exactly what He promised."

"Yep. It happened just like you said. You're speaking to the newest senior producer at BTV." I explained how everything went down. Without thinking, I told him about Jason's part in it.

"I told you he liked you."

I couldn't tell whether he was amused or annoyed. "It wasn't about him liking me, Isaiah. It was about the station. He didn't want to work for Rayshawn and watch the station go downhill."

"Okay. If that's the way you see it. Anyway, congratulations. I'm proud of you and happy for you. I knew God would work it out. I'm glad I got some time in with you when I could. You'll be working overtime now, huh?"

"Yeah, things are about to get pretty busy. I'd still like to spend time with you, though. Maybe late tomorrow afternoon?"

"Can't tomorrow. I'm moving."

"Moving?" I got up to close my door then sat back down at my desk. "You sold your house?"

"My house?" He laughed. "That's not my house. You thought that was my house? No way."

"No way? What do you . . . it's not . . ."

He laughed again. "I guess I should have explained. It's my sister's house. I was house-sitting for her while she and her family are in Nigeria visiting my parents. They've been gone for a month and didn't want to leave their house empty. They have enough room for me to stay there when they get back, but me and her husband don't get along. He thinks I'm a bum that doesn't want to work and support myself. He's always making some cracks about me living off people."

My head was spinning. "So that's her house? And her Hummer?" I winced as I realized I sounded like a gold-digger.

"Yeah. I can't believe you thought they were mine. I told you I wasn't a materialistic person attached to stuff like that. Why would I say that if I owned that big house and that obnoxious car?"

"I wondered that myself. It didn't seem to fit." As a sinking feeling settled into my stomach, I remembered my prayer that morning. "So, where are you moving to?"

"Nigel's place. The house I took you to in Buckhead. He's been trying to get me to move there for months, but I wouldn't because Sanitha was staying there—the girl with the Mohawk you met. She's leaving for New York and is moving out this weekend. So God worked things out for me perfectly because my sister and her family will be back Sunday evening."

I sat there silent, processing everything.

"Michelle?"

"Yeah, I'm here. I'm . . . just thinking . . ."

"That's why I told you about my lifestyle on our first date. You seemed okay with it. Is this a problem?" He sounded worried.

"It's not a problem. It's . . . not what I expected."

"I see. You thought I was some rich musician with a huge house and fancy car. Does this change things between us? I'd still like to see you. I'm enjoying getting to know you."

"I'm enjoying getting to know you too, Isaiah." Erika buzzed my other phone line. "I need to take this call. I promise I'll call soon. Or you call me when you're finished moving, and we can get together."

"Okay." He sounded hopeful again. "We'll talk about this more when I see you. Okay?"

"Yeah. That sounds good. Talk to you soon."

twenty-eight

Isaiah must have been nervous about our conversation, because he called and sent text messages several times the rest of the day, and the
next, asking if we could meet to talk. When he
called for the millionth time Saturday evening, I finally answered the phone.

"Hey, Isaiah." I tried to tell myself that I ignored
all his calls because I was busy, and not because I
was no longer interested in him because he was
broke.

"You answered. I wondered if you had written
me off for good."

"Been crazy busy, getting back into the swing of
things at work." I sat at my desk in my messy office at home, thumbing through a script I was
working on for a *Destiny's Child* episode. I hated
bringing work home but needed to get the show
moving.

"Oh. I'm glad to hear that."

I didn't say anything.

"So, I still want to see you. To talk." He sounded

hopeful and defeated which made me wonder how many times he had been through this with women who initially fell hard for him then balked when they found out about his financial situation.

"You said you were moving today, so I didn't think it was good for you."

He chuckled. "Yeah, well, moving for me is not a big deal. It's not like I have a lot of stuff. Just clothes, books, and instruments really . . ." His voice trailed off like he wished he hadn't shared that information.

"It's late now. How about tomorrow after church?" I planned to spend the whole day working to get *Destiny's Child* to the point where we could start shooting. "I need to work most of the day, but I could squeeze in an hour or two after service."

"I'm being squeezed in, huh?" He tried to laugh, but his voice sounded sad.

"It's not like that, Isaiah." I decided to lighten things up. "In fact, this is your fault. You're the one who prayed for me to get my job back with a promotion, so now I have to pay the price for it."

"My fault, huh?" His laugh was a little brighter. "Okay. I'll take that. What time is service over?"

"I'm going to early service so I can have most of the day to work, so about ten thirty. Where do you want to meet?"

"Uh . . . well . . . I left my sister's car at her house, so . . . uh, unless you want to pick me up to take me somewhere, we should probably meet here at Nigel's."

"Oh." My silence said everything.

"Is that okay?"

I could hear the embarrassment in his voice. "Sure. No problem at all. I think I remember how to get there." *You don't have a car. How lame is that?* "I'll be there at ten thirty. Eleven at the latest."

"Cool. Looking forward to seeing you."

"Yeah . . . uh, me too, Isaiah."

Lisa agreed to meet me for early service. I hated going to church alone. I knew better than to ask Nicole. There was no way she was getting out of bed early enough on a Sunday morning to get to 8 o'clock service.

Lisa met me at our usual section in the middle. We sat chatting for a few minutes—mostly her pointing out cute guys—when I felt a tap on my shoulder. I turned around to see Jason standing there, flanked by his two daughters.

"Hey, what are you doing here?" I said without thinking.

"Why do you always ask me that when you see me at church? Do I act like that much of a heathen at work?"

I laughed and stood to hug him. "Of course not, silly. I forgot you told me you'd been coming to early service." I looked at his daughters. "And who are these two gorgeous girls?"

The younger one hid behind his legs and peeked out at me.

He nudged her to come from behind him. "This is my baby girl, Cameron. And this . . ." He turned to the older daughter. ". . . is my big girl, Candace."

Pride filled his voice, and he stuck out his chest. "Girls, this is Miss Michelle. My friend from work."

Candace held out a hand to me. "Nice to meet you, Miss Michelle." She pulled her sister from behind Jason's leg. "Be a big girl and say hello, Cameron."

Cameron peeked out from her hiding place long enough to wave and to flash me a snaggle-toothed smile and went back behind her father. Candace rolled her eyes and shook her head.

Both girls looked exactly like Jason. Like their mother only served to carry them for nine months, but they took all his genes. Their clothes were color-coordinated, clean and freshly pressed. They wore matching shoes and earrings, and even their ribbons and hair bows matched. The parts in their hair were a little crooked and their braids a little uneven, but it was clear that Jason was efficient as a single dad.

"I see Cameron's feeling better."

Jason nodded. "Yeah. After I picked her up on Friday, she didn't have any more vomiting. Their mom was supposed to pick them up for the weekend, but with Cameron sick, they ended up staying with me." He reached down and smoothed a few stray hairs into Cameron's ponytails. "Seems like we're catching a stomach virus one Friday a month lately."

I nodded, catching what he was implying.

"We better grab a seat before it fills up in here. Good to see you."

Lisa, who had pretended not to be eavesdropping on the conversation, stood and gestured down our row. "We have three seats here with us. Every-where else looks pretty full."

"Oh. Okay, thanks." Jason looked at Lisa. "Nicole, right?"

She looked surprised. "I'm Lisa. Nicole was the other friend you met."

Jason pointed for the girls to step over me and Lisa to the seats next to us. He sat between them. Cameron sat in the seat next to me.

Jason leaned over to explain. "I have to keep them separated during church. They become little giggleboxes if I let them sit next to each other."

I nodded.

Cameron stole a glance at me with her big pretty eyes. It was like looking into Jason's eyes, and I felt myself getting lost in them, like I did his. She turned away from me and tried to wedge her-self behind Jason's back.

"Why you acting all shy, Cam?" He pinched her little legs and looked over at me. "When she gets warmed up, you can't get her to stop talking."

Jason opened his book bag and pulled out two children's Bibles and handed one to each of the girls. He took his daughters' jackets, folded them and put them under their seats.

When the lights dimmed a little to indicate that praise and worship was about to start, Lisa leaned over and whispered in my ear. "Cool, we can do the worship test." She rubbed her hands together.

I rolled my eyes at her. "You're hilarious."

She winked. "Watch him close, girl."

Not only did Jason stand for praise and wor-ship, the girls stood with him, without any coaxing. Jason sang, lifted his hands, and knew all the words to all the songs.

I wanted to kick Lisa for elbowing me the whole time.

The girls also clapped and danced. Candace sang the chorus parts in a loud little-girl voice. Cameron danced in circles and sang a few words every once in a while.

When praise and worship ended, we all sat down. The girls sat quietly through the announcements. When it was time to take up offering, both girls pulled out their little purses and took out a dollar. They reached for the seat back in front of them to get an envelope. Cameron handed hers to her father to fill out, while Candace wrote her name and address in large letters on hers.

When Pastor started to preach, Cameron tapped Jason on the shoulder. He leaned down for her to whisper in his ear. He picked up the book bag and pulled out a coloring book, crayons and a Ziploc bag full of Cheerios and gave them to her. He pulled out a pink notebook and marker and handed them to Candace. She reached into the bag and grabbed a box of raisins. I had wondered why Jason needed such a large bag for church. I guess, if I had kids, I would've known.

I was so busy watching Cameron do a good job of coloring within the lines, I barely paid attention to the sermon. She tapped Jason every once in a while, and he'd look down, admire her artwork, then go back to listening to the sermon.

After about twenty minutes, Cameron's eyelids drooped, and her head started to bob. After a few more minutes, I felt her little head land on my arm. She was knocked out.

Jason was too caught up in the sermon to notice. After a good five minutes, she let out a snore, and he looked down at her leaning against me. His eyes flew open. He mouthed the word *sorry* and started to pull her off me, but I shook my head. "She's fine," I whispered.

He shook his head like he was embarrassed, but I smoothed back her hair to let him know she was okay. She snuggled into my side and let out a sigh. I coulda sworn I felt my poor ovaries cramping.

When it sounded like Pastor was about to end the sermon, Jason handed the book bag to Candace, and she put her notepad, marker, and empty raisin box in it. One by one, he handed her Cameron's book, crayons, and half empty Cheerio bag. She put them and the children's Bibles into the book bag and zipped it shut. Jason patted her leg.

After the benediction, he gently picked a sleeping Cameron up from my lap and lifted her in his arms. Candace covered Cameron with her jacket and put on her own, picked up the book bag then nodded at Jason. Lisa and I moved, so they could step into the aisle.

As they left, Jason turned and whispered to me, "See you at work tomorrow."

I nodded and waved goodbye to Candace.

She said, "Nice to meet you, Miss Michelle," as she hoisted the book bag over her shoulder.

After they left, Lisa turned to me. "Oh, my goodness, his girls are beautiful. And they're so well-behaved. Girl, they had me rethinking my 'kids are a deal-breaker' rule. And he's such a good daddy. They were clean, and their hair was done all cute, and everything matched. Girl, ain't nothing sexier than a man taking good care of his children. Except, of course, a man worshipping. Speaking of, he passed the worship test too. Did you see him with his eyes all closed, hands lifted, singing his heart out to the Lord? And not only him, but you can tell the girls like church too. Did you see them filling out their tithing envelopes? I bet his house is clean and he can cook. I don't know what your problem is, Michelle. He's perfect."

I held up a hand to stop Lisa's flood of praise for Jason. "Please, Lisa. I can't think of Jason like that."

"You mean you don't like him?"

"I didn't say that. It's just . . . I can't talk about it." I looked at my watch. "I gotta go."

"You're going to work right now? We could go for brunch first."

"I have to meet Isaiah. To talk."

Lisa looked at me and shook her head. "Girl, you got too many men for me."

When I rang the doorbell at Nigel's, Isaiah opened the door almost immediately. He stood for a few seconds with his hands shoved in the pockets of his jeans. His head was slightly bowed and his smile not as big as usual. When he reached out for me, his hug didn't feel the same. I didn't know if it was me or him. He seemed to put the same affection into it, but now, that safe, secure feeling was gone.

"Hey," he said.

"What's up, Isaiah?" I hoped I didn't sound too abrupt. Apparently I did, because a pained look came into his eyes.

"You okay?"

I nodded. "Was up late working on a script, and I need to spend the rest of the day working on stuff." I smiled. "Guess I had too much fun while I was off." I figured I'd give him a little something.

He smiled back. "Yeah, that's what happens when you spend too much time with Isaiah." He led me through the foyer and up the stairs and down a long hall. "Glad you got your job back though. I told you God was going to do it."

"Yeah. He did exactly what you said. Thanks for your prayers and for helping me stay in a place of peace through all this. I appreciate you being there for me." I followed him into his bedroom.

"But . . ." He looked me in my eyes.

"But what?" I averted my eyes and looked around. It was a narrow room with a twin mattress on the floor. Bags of clothes lined the wall. Some were in plastic bins.

"But now?"

I shrugged. "I don't know. You kinda threw me for a loop." I looked around at boxes of books and CD's lining the other wall.

"And it matters that much? We have a great time together. I feel like there's something special starting between us. But because I don't have a fancy house and luxury car, you're no longer interested in spending time with me? How can it matter that much?"

"I guess I'm trying to figure that out." I walked

over to a wooden chair by the window. "I'm at a certain place in my life right now where..." I looked out at Nigel's large, tree-lined yard. "Let me be honest. I'm thirty-five, and my heart's desire is to be married and start a family. So as much fun as we have and as good as we may be together, we're in different places right now. Different goals and different priorities."

"Why do you say that? I want to get married and have a family too."

"Okay, then maybe the same goal, but different time frames." I sat down in the chair, staring out the window.

"What do you mean by that?"

I turned to look at him. How could I explain it without insulting his manhood? "I mean, I'm looking for someone who's looking to be married in the near future." He still looked puzzled. "Remember you said you'd have to change your lifestyle a lot when you met that special someone?"

"Yeah. And I can do that. I won't travel as much. Obviously, I can't spend three months in Europe and six months in Africa and wherever else the wind blows me if I want to have a family. I'm willing to change all that. I've traveled enough to last a lifetime. Meeting the right person and settling down would be worth giving that up."

"Okay." Certainly, that wasn't the only lifestyle change he thought he'd have to make. I hated to have to spell it out for him. "And where would we live, Isaiah?" I gestured around the room. "Here at Nigel's? Would we share a car? Would I be responsible for all the bills? How would that work?"

He let out a long, defeated breath like I had

punched him in the chest. "Oh. I see." He sat down on the mattress and pulled his guitar onto his lap. "When we talked that day at the park, you sounded like you understood. That's the only reason I let things go this far. I know everyone's not up for the way I live."

I shrugged my shoulders. "I'm not sure I understand the way you live."

He strummed a few chords on the guitar. "Think about it. My parents are missionaries. They live their life based on people's generosity, and they're able to do the work of the Kingdom because of it. They sacrifice the *normal* life—having a house and car and so-called stability—and pour out their lives for the sake of others and for the sake of the Kingdom. And their fruit is great. They've impacted thousands of lives, if not millions. That's what I've known. How I've always lived."

He raked a hand through his locks. "You've seen me in Atlanta chillin' and being a bum. But if you went with me on my next trip to Cameroon, you'd see the real me. Sometimes I lead worship in church meetings daily—services with thousands of people that last for hours where the presence of God falls and people's lives are changed. I pray for the sick, help build houses, and dig wells. Sometimes, I take my guitar to the hospitals there and play for people dying without hope—without Jesus. And they get saved. And sometimes they get healed. I visit the orphanages of hundreds of children who've lost their parents to AIDS. And I play with them, sing with them, dance with them and then teach them about Jesus. You mean to tell me that my life isn't meaningful because I don't have a million-dollar house and a Hummer?"

"No," I answered. "Not at all. That's a very meaningful life. Very beautiful and fruitful. One you shouldn't give up for me or any other woman. It's who you are and what you're called to do. God should send you a woman who's willing to be out there in the trenches with you. Digging wells, building houses and ministering to the children in Africa. I'm just . . . I'm not that woman."

I added, "And it's not about a million-dollar house and a Hummer. It's about a certain degree of security that I'm used to having. I'm the kind of girl that needs a house and a car and some consistent form of income to feel secure. You need the kind of girl that doesn't."

He stood and walked over to the window where I sat. "Okay, so we could still hang out then. I really enjoy spending time with you, and I know you enjoy spending time with me."

"Isaiah, I'm too old to be hanging out for the sake of hanging out. My heart's desire is to be married and have children. And if that's not where this is going, then . . ." I put a hand on his arm. "And honestly, if we kept hanging out, we'd probably fall in love. And one of us would end up compromising the life we're called to live. I can't forsake my destiny, and I can't ask you to give up yours."

He nodded. "Okay." He rubbed his goatee and pressed his lips together tight. "Okay. Well . . . I guess that's it then."

"Yeah. I guess so."

He led me back down the hall, down the stairs

and to the front door. He gave me one last hug, kissed my cheek and then held me again. Tight. He let out a deep breath then let me go. "Bye, Michelle."

I gave him a little wave and walked down the steps to my car. As I drove off, I waved again. "Goodbye, Isaiah."

As I drove away, I wasn't sure how to feel. I was sad because I had put my heart out there one more time and it turned out he wasn't the one. I was grateful to God that He quickly answered my prayer about bringing things to a screeching halt. As bad as I felt, I knew it would be ten times worse if I had spent a lot more time with Isaiah. He had crawled up in my heart real quick.

My only hope was that if Isaiah was so wonderful and he wasn't the one, then God must be planning on sending me something better.

twenty-nine

"**T**his one's nice." The girls and I were seated around Angela's dining table, looking through bridal magazines. I held the magazine up for everyone to look at a simple, yet elegant bridesmaid's dress. Angela had decided to go ahead and get married before she started to show. She wanted to be married when she delivered the baby and didn't want to walk down the aisle with a huge belly. Which meant we had a lot of planning to do in a very short time.

At first, Angela said she wanted to have a small ceremony at the courthouse with Gary and two witnesses. We convinced her to go ahead and have the wedding she'd dreamed of and waited all her life for. Vanessa had been working with her on getting over the guilt and shame, while Lisa inundated her with bridal magazines. Between the two of them, Angela decided she deserved a ceremony.

Gary's pastor agreed to marry them, after they went through premarital counseling sessions for couples in "special" circumstances. Angela couldn't accept the idea of getting married at our church. Even though she was feeling better about everything, she still struggled with embarrassment.

"Look at this wedding gown." Angela held up a picture. "It has a princess cut, so even though I'll have a little belly, it should still fall right." She was almost glowing again. I wasn't sure if it was the pregnancy or because she had finally made peace with her situation.

"So the Hummer and the house are his sister's? And he's dead broke?" Lisa asked for the third time since I told them the latest and last chapter of the Isaiah story. As excited as she was to be planning a wedding, she couldn't get past my tidbit of news.

I nodded again. It had only been a week since I said goodbye to Isaiah, and I missed him terribly. Missed his smile, missed his music, missed his hugs. And I missed having a "him" in my life. Even though we had only been hanging out for a few weeks, I had gotten used to someone being there for me.

I was back to being desperate and lonely again.

Nicole flipped through the pages of her magazine. "I knew something wasn't right. At least he wasn't selling drugs. I'm glad you found out before you got too deep off into him."

"Yeah, me too," I said, although I wasn't sure I wasn't already too deep.

"That must have been a hard decision to make." Vanessa said. "He sounded really wonderful, and sounds like you guys had great chemistry. Was it difficult to give him up?"

"Yes and no. I mean, he's a great guy. Sexy, talented, and completely committed to building the Kingdom. But number two on my list is *financially secure*. And he's anything but that. It's like the lady from the singles ministry said. Set the important things on your list and don't compromise because you're lonely and horny or because some guy sweeps you off your feet."

"Yeah, but it's like you're sacrificing love for the sake of money. What if he's your soul mate and you're letting him go because he's not rich?" Angela said, as she tore yet another wedding dress picture out of the magazine and added it to her stack of "possibles."

"Girl, I've walked down that road before. That idealistic fantasyland that believes love is all you need. Money matters. For eleven years, I carried the financial weight in my marriage. I can't do that again. I want a man that makes enough to support us—or at least, most of our expenses."

Nicole said, "You know financial problems are one of the leading causes of marital discord and divorce. I can't remember which wins out, that or adultery. Point is, being broke is almost as bad as or worse than cheating."

"Plus, it's a matter of destiny." I finished the magazine I was flipping through and reached for another. "You should have seen the passion in his face when he talked about his missionary work in Africa. I can't ask him to give that up. It's clear that's what he was born to do. My destiny is expressing the Kingdom through television. If I married him, either I'd have to give that up for him to drag me all over Africa, or he'd have to give up his destiny and probably lose his mind staying in one place—in a nation he's not called to. I believe that when God brings my husband, our destinies will line up perfectly. In fact, they should be so intertwined that when we come together, our marriage will help us both reach destiny together."

"Speaking of, what's up with Jason?" Lisa held up a picture of a bridesmaid dress for us to see.

"Yuck," I said. "Too much lace and frills. Looks country. And what do you mean, speaking of?"

"Speaking of destinies lining up perfectly together so you can take over film and television for the Kingdom. You and Jason's destinies match perfectly. What's going on with you two?"

"Nothing. There is no *us two*. We're still co-workers. And with me getting this promotion and being right up under Ms. Carter, there's no way."

"Okay. If you say so." Lisa pressed her lips together like she wanted to tell me something but didn't think I'd listen.

"So what's up with your love life, Lisa?" I had to change the subject. I didn't need to be thinking about Jason like that. I had done a good job of keeping my feelings for him under wraps lately. "We haven't had a good story from you in a long time. No dates?"

Lisa flipped through a few pages in the magazine. She finally got up and walked over to Angela's cabinet and pulled out a package of Oreo cookies.

"Oh, my. That bad?" Nicole asked.

Lisa nodded and stuffed a whole cookie into her mouth. She opened the refrigerator and pulled out some milk. She held up the carton to ask if anyone wanted to join her for cookies and milk.

I nodded. Chocolate might help fill the Isaiah-size hole in my soul right about now.

Vanessa shook her head. "No, thanks. I'm actually pretty happy right now."

Nicole said,

"I'm happy too, but I'll never pass up Oreos. Bring it on."

Lisa brought over glasses for everyone except Vanessa and set the package of cookies in the middle of the table.

"My love life is non-existent. I feel like I'm doomed. Like it's gonna be that way forever." Lisa poured glasses of milk for each of us. She opened a cookie, licked off the cream and dipped each half in her milk. "Maybe I'm not supposed to get married. You think God wants me to stay single?"

Vanessa pushed the cookies out of Angela's reach as she was trying to grab one and handed her an apple from the fruit bowl on the table. "I wouldn't say that. I think if you have a desire to be married, then it's pretty safe to say that God doesn't want you single. He's a loving God and wouldn't torture you with a desire He doesn't plan to fill."

"Then why can't I find anybody?" Lisa whined.

"You might want to look at that ten-page list of yours." Nicole smirked. "You're looking for someone who doesn't exist. I think when you let that go and come back to the real world, God will be able to send you somebody."

"So, you're saying I have to settle?" Lisa pushed a whole cookie into her mouth and took a swig of milk.

"I'm just saying no man is as perfect as the man you've created on that monstrous list of yours.

You're not even that perfect." Nicole gave Lisa a worried glance and pulled the cookies away from her.

"Why do you think your list is that long and . . . unrealistic?" Vanessa asked.

"Oh, dear. Are you about to psychoanalyze me? Should I get on the couch?"

"No. I just think it's worth looking at," Vanessa answered. "You're upset because God isn't sending you anyone, but yet you have this list that pretty much makes it impossible for Him to send you someone. You have to ask yourself why."

Lisa reached for the Oreos again. She pulled out a cookie and munched on it with tiny bites. "I've been in some bad relationships in the past. I've had my heart broken more times than I can imagine. And I don't want to ever go through that again. So, I figure if I pick the right guy, that won't happen. And to pick the right guy, I need to list all the qualities he needs to have and all the qualities he absolutely can't have. If I settle, I'm liable to get my heart broken again, or end up in some dead-end relationship."

"Yeah, but with the list you have, you're never going to end up in a relationship at all. Guaranteed," Nicole said.

"I have faith that God can send me everything on my list. I believe my perfect guy is out there." Lisa shrugged.

Nicole, Vanessa, and I shook our heads.

"Maybe you should do what I did." Angela cut a slice of her apple. "Tell God you're not sure what you want, but you trust that He knows what you need and to send you His very best."

We all turned to look at Angela.

"That's what you did?" Lisa asked. "You didn't have a list?"

"Nope. And Gary is beyond what I could have ever asked for. Which explains me not being able to keep my hands off him." Angela giggled.

We all laughed with her. It was good to see her able to joke about her situation.

"Humph. That's a dangerous prayer," Lisa said. "But if it'll have me married and pregnant in less than a year, maybe I should try it."

Angela's mouth fell open, and she turned bright red. "Ha, ha, ha, Lisa."

"If you pray that prayer, make sure you ask God to help you keep the reins on the nine years of pent-up passion in your loins," Nicole said.

"Okay, that's enough jokes at my expense," Angela said, flipping absently through another magazine. "I know you guys are jealous. You all secretly want to be accidentally pregnant, planning your shotgun wedding."

We all laughed.

"Oooh, look at this one. It's perfect." Angela tore out and held up a picture of a beautiful wedding gown with a princess cut, elegant lace at the sleeves and hem. We all oohed and aahed.

"It's perfect, Angie. You're going to be such a beautiful bride. I'm so happy for you." Lisa leaned over and hugged Angela. They held on to each other for a few moments.

"I'm going to miss you guys so much. I can't believe I'm going to be so far from you."

Angela had decided to move to Augusta. It would be much easier for her to find a job at the

Medical College of Georgia and to sell her house here than for Gary to find a job and sell his house.

"Girl, two hours ain't no distance. We'll be up and down the road every other weekend," Lisa said.

"Plus, you're about to get married and have a baby," Nicole said. "You ain't gon' be thinking about us."

Angela shook her head. "No way. You guys mean everything to me. I've never had friends like you. If it weren't for you all, I'd still be on the couch surrounded by snotty tissue, about to lose my job. And now . . ." Angela held up the picture of the wedding gown she chose. "I'm happy again. About to have a dream wedding to marry the man of my dreams, and we're gonna start a beautiful family together."

"Awww." Lisa motioned for us all to get up and surround Angela. "Group hug."

We all hugged Angela and each other until Nicole finally said, "Okay, enough mushy stuff. You guys know I can only take so much."

We all laughed.

As I drove home that evening, I thought about Angela—giggling and glowing again. Even though it wasn't under ideal circumstances, she was about to be living my dream. Married with child.

I decided to pray her prayer. *Okay, God, I relinquish my right to choose. I give up my list. You know exactly what I need. Send me your best.* I paused for a second and added, *Soon, God. Soon . . .*

thirty

Over the next few weeks, I barely had time to think about being desperate and lonely. Or about the wonderful man I was trusting God to send. Work consumed my entire life. My faithful assistant, camera crew, and I traveled all over metro Atlanta, filming B-roll of artists in their creative places. We had some real cool settings—a courtyard on top of a building with a great view of the Atlanta skyline, a flower garden in the Arboretum, Piedmont Park by the lake.

We also spent hours in the inner city—some of the worst neighborhoods—shooting gritty scenes of our destiny kids. In their homes, schools, and places they liked to hang out, where kids their age had no business being.

Jason went with us on a few shoots, and I got to see his true talent. He was amazing as a director and knew how to handle the camera better than our seasoned cameraman. He had an eye for setting up shots that were unique and creative. After reviewing the footage he shot, I convinced him he needed to go on all the shoots with me because his scenes had extra flavor that was artistic and eclectic.

Which was great for the shows, but not so great for my aching heart. The more we worked together, spending hours and hours doing what we loved, the more desperate and lonely I felt.

Seeing him work out in the field made him come alive. It was one thing to see him sitting at a computer for hours in the edit suite, but behind a camera setting up a perfect shot—staging camera angles and getting the lights just perfect; knowing exactly what time of day the sun would be just right; knowing what colors would work best in what lighting—he was brilliant.

Jason was the right blend of authoritative, yet considerate on the shoots. Everybody liked and respected him. He worked well with our destiny kids, even when they drove me crazy. He knew how to talk to the young guys, and I knew all our girls secretly had a crush on him.

I kept realizing more and more that he was everything on my list and then some. I couldn't shake the image of him and his daughters. They say you can tell a lot about a man by how he treats his momma. I say you can tell even more by the way he cares for his children.

The more I saw of Jason, the further I sank. I tried to tell myself it was because of losing Isaiah, but I knew I'd been drooling over Jason long before Isaiah came and went.

And to make matters worse, after we finished shooting, I had weeks in the edit suite to look for-

ward to—just the two of us—for hours on end.
Talking, laughing, creating . . .

It was going to be torture.

For the first week, I tried to keep everything serious. He kept finding ways to make me let my
guard down. I'd start off all businesslike, and before I knew it, he had me laughing my head off. We
took breaks and had long conversations about
everything. Spirituality, music, movies, our ideas
for documentaries and television shows, and anything else we could think of.

Even though we were having fun, both of us
seemed driven to get the shows done, so we
worked long hours, often late into the evening.

Jason's mom was visiting for a whole month, so
she'd pick up the girls from school, and get them
fed and bathed. Jason left in time to spend "Daddy
time" with them, then tuck them into bed.

I felt guilty for keeping him from his girls and
his mother, but he said whenever his mom was
around, the three of them ignored him anyway. He
insisted we get as much done as we could while
she was in town because he wouldn't be able to
keep those hours when she left. I told him we had
plenty of time even without working the long
hours, but he seemed more pressed than me to get
the shows finished. When I asked him why, he said
it was best to stay ahead of schedule because you
never know what might happen.

After his mom left, we went back to regular
hours. When it was time for Jason to leave every
evening, we both lingered in my office or in the
edit suite until the last possible moment. If the

girls stayed too late in after-care, he got charged by the minute, so by 5:15 P.M. every day, he grabbed all his stuff and went racing out of the office.

One day, at about five o'clock, while we were in the middle of editing a shoot, Jason kept looking up at the clock. I finally said, "You should go. We'll finish this tomorrow."

"I hate stopping when I'm in a good flow. I think I'm gonna take the tape with me and finish it at home tonight."

"How?"

He started shutting down the system. "I recently set up my own edit suite at home. I've done a lot of freelancing over the past six months. Do you mind if I finish this tonight?"

"I guess not. If you run into any problems, you can call me and I'll try to give whatever input I can over the phone."

"Okay. Or . . ." He pulled the tape out of the deck. "You could stop by, and we can finish it together. If you don't mind. I mean, if you don't have anything else to do. I mean, if that's okay with you. I mean, not that you don't have anything else to do. But I mean, if you want to." He shoved the tape in his book bag and stood there waiting for me to answer.

I could feel the heat rising in my cheeks. *He's inviting you over for work, Michelle, not out on a date. Chill.* "Umm, okay. I don't have anything to do. I mean, of course, I have stuff to do, but it would be good to get this done. I mean, since we were in such a good flow and everything. I mean, yeah—we can work on stuff tonight."

He nodded. "Okay, cool. I mean, cool that we can get this finished. You know, because it would be good to go ahead and get it done."

"Okay," I said.

"Okay," he said.

We stood there looking at each other like we weren't sure what we were supposed to do next.

I'm sure God was looking down at both of us, shaking His head. He'd elbow Jesus and ask, "What's wrong with these two goofballs?"

Jesus would shrug and shake His head in agreement with God that we were absolutely pitiful.

I finally looked up at the clock. "You better go."

"Huh?" He gave me a blank stare.

"The girls?"

He shook his head quickly. "Oh, yeah. The girls. Yeah. I better go get them."

He headed toward the door of the edit suite. "I'll text you directions. Give me about an hour to get them settled and get dinner on. You should have dinner with us. I mean, if you want to. I mean, you don't have to, but since I'm cooking and all, you might as well. I mean, you know . . ."

"Sounds good, Jason. I'll be there in about an hour."

He smiled and started down the hall. He called out to me, "Okay, see you in about an hour. Come hungry."

Of course, it wasn't ten seconds before Erika flew into the edit suite. "He'll see you in about an hour? What's that all about?" Her eyes were wide with excitement.

"I really think you do have bugs set up everywhere in this building." I reached a hand under the table in the edit suite, pretending to be checking for bugs.

"Come hungry? Are you and Jason going out to dinner?" Erika looked like she was going to pounce on me if I didn't give her some answers.

I started down the hall to my office. She was close behind. "Michelle, stop playing. What's going on with you and Jason?"

I grabbed her arm and pulled her into my office, looked both ways and shut the door. "Are you crazy? Why did you say that all loud in front of everybody?"

"Girl, ain't nobody paying me no attention. My gossip sources are out in the field or out sick today. Nobody else cares. And, besides, if you woulda told me, I wouldn't have to be all loud about it. Are you going to dinner with Jason? He finally asked you out on a date? I knew it. Just a matter of time."

"We're not going on a date. I'm going over his house so we can finish editing the show we were working on. He's cooking dinner for the girls and said I might as well eat with them. That's all. Don't be making something out of nothing."

Erika's shoulders slumped and she looked a little deflated. "Is that all? I thought something was finally happening between the two of you."

"Sorry not to have any new gossip for you, girlfriend. It's just work."

"Wait a minute." Her eyes lit back up. "He invited you to his house? Around his girls? That's a big deal. You might not realize it, but Jason is really saying something with that."

I started packing my bag with a couple of scripts and some snacks, just in case Jason wasn't a good cook like Lisa had predicted. "Girl, please. Like I said, don't be making something out of nothing. I've met his girls before. At church. It's not a big deal. In fact, if he doesn't mind me being around them, it means he doesn't like me like that. He wouldn't bring me around his children if he thought about me that way." My stomach sank as I realized the truth of what I'd said.

What started as an excuse to get Erika off my case slammed me in the face. Jason must not think of me as more than a friend, if he didn't mind me being around his girls. He was the kind of father that wouldn't introduce his girls to a love interest until he was near 'bout ready to propose.

I had been reading the signs wrong. The flirty conversations in the edit suite all those late evenings. The admiring look in his eyes when we were on a shoot together. The constant touchy-feelyness when he thought I needed comfort or encouragement. He was just being friendly.

And the dinner invite tonight? He only wanted to get the show done.

My movements got slower as I pushed a few final things into my bag. Maybe I should call and cancel. I was silly to think Jason liked me. He only thought of me as a co-worker and a friend.

I probably wasn't his type. I remembered a picture of him and Latrice on his desk when he first transferred to our department. She was red-boned with long, permed hair and a gorgeous face. In the picture, she was facing forward, but her body was sideways. She was petite in every way, except she had a huge black-girl butt, accentuated by a tiny waistline. She was even prettier and shapelier than Nicole. And she was dressed all prissy in a suit, stockings, and heels.

Why would I think he would be attracted to me? Brown-skinned, nappy afro, and dressing like a Bohemian every day.

"Whatever, Michelle."

I had almost forgotten Erika was in the room.

"I can't wait until tomorrow morning. You have to tell me how it goes."

"I'm sure there'll be nothing to tell."

Erika bopped out of my office and started humming that stupid wedding march. "Da da da dum. Dum da da dum."

I wanted to throw my stapler after her.

thirty-one

I pulled up at Jason's house about an hour and a half later. I had spent twenty minutes in the parking lot, dialing his number to call and cancel, and then hanging up. Then I drove to my house, planning on calling to cancel after I was in my pajamas, eating a bowl of cereal. I was just about to take off my work clothes when he texted me the directions with a note at the end. *Hurry up, the girls are hungry and we're waiting on you to eat.*

I reasoned that I couldn't keep his girls starving. I dashed back out to my car, trying to kill the giddy feeling in my heart. *He doesn't like you like that, Michelle. He's your friend and co-worker. This is about work.*

It wasn't enough to keep me from breaking a few traffic laws to get there.

When I rang the doorbell, he opened the door, looking at his watch. "What happened?"

"Sorry. I got caught up at the office." Great. I just had to tell an office lie to someone I worked with, who knew I could have left five minutes after he did.

"Really. What happened at the office?"

Shoot. *Think, Michelle.* "I . . . well, Erika . . ."

"Who's that, Daddy?" Candace poked her head out the door. "Hi, Miss Michelle. We've been expecting you. Daddy, aren't you going to invite her in?"

"Oh. Yeah. Sorry." He stepped aside for me to walk into the house.

Candace rolled her eyes and let out a deep breath, like she was embarrassed that her daddy had no manners.

The house was a modest split-level in an older, but well-kept neighborhood. I could tell Latrice had left him with the furniture, because it was nicely decorated and definitely had a woman's touch. There were kids' toys everywhere. Lined against the walls, in the hallway, in the family room we walked by . . . everywhere. The house wasn't dirty, but definitely a little on the cluttered side.

Jason watched me taking it in. "Excuse the mess. I'm a single dad with two young girls and don't have a housekeeper. I try to keep it at an organized chaos."

"It's fine, Jason." What I was really thinking was that his house was cleaner than mine and I didn't have the kids as an excuse. I was going to have to use my promotion raise to get a housekeeper. Before the week was out. "You have a nice house."

"Thanks. Sorry, but the girls couldn't wait. I went ahead and fed them. You want to fix a plate and come on downstairs?"

I nodded and followed him into the kitchen.

Instantly, I was reminded of my mom's kitchen in the house where I grew up. The décor was homey with bright yellow walls, and a large circular breakfast table with plastic daisies in a large vase. On the refrigerator were several hand-drawn pictures. On one side, the pictures were mostly awkward houses, flowers and people. Each was signed with Cameron's name in large, loopy letters.

The other side was obviously Candace's. There was one picture of a man holding two girls' hands. They all had big smiles on their faces. Another was a picture of a man and said, "I love my daddy" in crooked cursive letters. Another had a man and a girl and said, "I have the best daddy in the world." Yet another said, "Thank you for being a good daddy. You take me fun places and help me with my homework. And when I sick, you make me well." Another had a house with a large sunshine heart over it. All the pictures were stuck to the refrigerator with alphabet magnets.

"Candace is quite an artist," Jason said.

"It's clear that she loves her daddy."

He grinned. "Yeah. That's my girl." He pulled a plate out of the cabinet. "Are you a wee bit hungry or a little bit hungry or a lotta bit hungry?"

"Is that daddy talk?" I laughed. "I'm starving."

He heaped the plate with angel hair pasta.

"Not that much. My goodness." Even though I convinced myself we were just friends, I didn't need to be all greedy in front of Jason.

He took some pasta off and poured spaghetti sauce over the rest then added steamed broccoli and garlic bread on the side.

He poured a glass of apple juice and carried it

and my plate out of the kitchen and down the stairs, nodding for me to follow.

When we got to the lower den, I was impressed by what I saw. Jason had an edit suite similar to what we had at the office, complete with a mini DV deck, a professional playback monitor, and two 17-inch flat-panel computer monitors.

"Whoa, nice setup. I don't see why you ever come in to the office. I'd work from home if I had all this."

"Yeah, but you're at the office, so I have to come there."

He flashed me a grin, and I had to remind myself he was being friendly, not flirty.

"When did you get all this?"

Jason set my plate down on a folding TV table and indicated for me to sit in one of the office chairs. "About six months ago. A friend of mine I used to shoot documentaries with gave me a great discount. It's almost as good as new. I've been freelancing my butt off since I got it." He pushed a button and booted up the computer. "The system has paid for itself and almost all Latrice's debt already. God is awesome. What's that scripture? He gives us the power to obtain wealth."

God help me. He's quoting scripture and working around the clock to support his family. "Wow. How do you do that and raise two daughters and work full-time?"

"I don't get much sleep." He shrugged. "Who needs sleep? It's highly overrated."

I ate a huge forkful of spaghetti. "Oh, my goodness, Jason, this is delicious."

"Yeah, a brother got skills all around. People

say I'm a great catch." He flashed that mischievous grin again.

He's not flirting, Michelle. Just making jokes.

"Yeah, you're pretty all right."

"I guess having two daughters and a drama queen ex-wife makes me not much of a catch at all." Jason slipped the tape into the deck and stared straight at the monitor.

"I wouldn't say that, Jason. Some women don't mind a man with kids. Some might even like it. Especially if they're great kids." I took a sip of my apple juice.

"Really?" He pulled out the dreamy eyes and dimples on me.

"Really." I smiled and looked down at my plate. *Oh, dear. Are you flirting back, Michelle? God, please put a stop to this. Now.*

Cameron came barreling downstairs screaming, "Daddy, Daddy. Candace took my Dora doll. She says it's hers, but you bought it for me." Tears streamed down her face.

Candace came rushing down the stairs after her. "I didn't take her stupid doll. And anyway, she took my Hanna Montana microphone and was singing in it. She left her stinky breath all over it."

Jason looked over at me. "Oh, well. So much for being a great catch."

I chuckled.

He pulled Cameron onto his lap and beckoned for Candace to come near. "What did I tell you guys I had to do tonight?"

"Get some work done," they said in unison. Cameron sniffled, and Candace stuck her finger in her mouth.

"And what are you two supposed to do when you're playing in your room?"

"Share," they said together. Cameron's voice sounded like she was about to cry again.

Jason rubbed her back and kissed her cheek. "And what do I tell you guys when guests come over?"

"Not to embarrass you in front of company," they said together.

Candace smiled, and Cameron covered her mouth to catch a giggle that escaped.

"And what are you doing?" Jason tickled Cameron and poked Candace's belly.

"Embarrassing you," they both erupted into full girly giggles.

Candace ran toward the stairs. Cameron jumped off Jason's lap, and he swatted her little behind as she ran after her sister.

"Sorry about that."

"They're adorable." My heart ached.

"Yeah, those are Daddy's girls. Too bad you didn't get to have kids. I mean, not too bad because of the way things turned out. I mean . . ." He ran his finger across a picture of his daughters taped on the side of the monitor. "Kids are the biggest joy you could ever experience. You're a great person, and you should get to have that joy one day."

I was glad my emotions were finely tuned by St. John's wort. Otherwise, I might have burst into tears. I must have had a disturbed look on my face.

Jason looked at me and winced. "Uh-oh. That was probably a real insensitive guy type of thing to say, huh?"

I nodded and put my empty plate on the TV cart and rolled it away from me.

He turned toward the system and started playing the tape. It seemed crazy that the exact point it started was where a group of our inner city girls were gathered around me. We were all laughing and talking, and I had my arms around two of them. Another held up rabbit ears behind my head.

"See. You're great with kids." He bit his lip and closed his eyes. "Sorry. You mentioned before that you thought you'd be married with kids by now. I don't understand why you're not. I mean, you're a great person, you know. Almost as good of a catch as me."

I guess he threw in a flirt to try to lighten the moment.

"Okay. I'm gonna sit here and chew on my foot that I can't seem to get out of my mouth."

I laughed and elbowed him. "It's okay. I do love kids and pray God blesses me to have some one day. Whether I birth them or whether they come as a package with the man God sends, I believe it will happen." *Oh, God. Did I say that out loud? Now who had their foot in their mouth?*

Jason nodded and focused his eyes back on the screen, a grin forming in the corners of his mouth.

Why were we torturing ourselves? With my promotion, I wasn't about to sacrifice my job. And with his daughters, he couldn't afford to sacrifice his. This was a ridiculous game that could only end badly.

"I like that clip. Go back a little," I said, steering our conversation to the reason we were there.

I would do enough work to say we accomplished something then hightail it out of there. From then on, Jason could edit at home by himself, and I would end the flirty game and touchy-feelyness at the office. I'd had my heart ripped out two months ago and didn't need that to happen again.

Jason pulled the clip and ran through some more tape. "This one's good too."

I could only hope he was having a similar conversation with himself in his head.

We focused on work for a good hour and completed most of the tape he brought home.

As we got close to finishing, Cameron came down the stairs and slid her feet slowly over to where Jason sat. She sucked her thumb and rubbed her eyes with her other hand. "Daddy, I'm hungry. Can I have a snack?"

He pulled her into his lap and rested his head on top of hers, still staring at the screen. "Where's your sister? Did you ask her?"

"She's drawing."

Jason rubbed Cameron's belly, clicking the computer mouse with his other hand.

Cameron rested her head back against Jason's chest, thumb still in her mouth. She reached up to pull on his ear with her other hand. He didn't seem bothered by it.

She sucked her thumb and pulled his ear until her eyelids got heavy. Within minutes, she was 'sleep.

"Works every time," he said softly. "I know I got to break her of this thumb habit. Thinking about using this thumb-sucking deterrent I saw on TV."

I grimaced, remembering my own battles with my mother over my thumb. She used hot sauce with me. I was mad a whole month the first time my mouth got burned. "She'll grow out of it. Give her some time."

Candace padded down the stairs and across the room in some pink footy pajamas. She held a piece of paper in her hand with a drawing on it. Jason held out his hand to receive it, but she pulled it back from him. "It's not yours." She held it out toward me. "It's for Miss Michelle."

I looked down at the paper. It was a picture of a brown woman with a big wavy Afro and a huge smile. The caption at the top read, "Miss Mishel" in big crayon letters.

It was more than my heart could take. "Oh, Candace. This is beautiful. You did this all by yourself?"

She nodded and tried to hold back a smile.

"Wow. You're a great artist. Is that what you want to be when you grow up?"

She nodded and I couldn't help but grin. Looked just like her dad.

"Thank you. It'll go on my refrigerator as soon as I get home." I gave her a hug.

Jason stood up with a sleeping Cameron in his arms and put a hand on Candace's back. "You brush your teeth and wash your face?"

"Yes, Daddy." She rolled her eyes like she couldn't believe he asked her that.

"Okay, time for bed. Say goodnight to Miss Michelle."

"Goodnight, Miss Michelle." She gave me another hug and looked up at my hair. "Can I touch?"

I nodded.

She reached out her hand and touched my hair, softly at first, then her fingers traveled down to the roots. "Your hair is so cool." She turned to Jason. "Daddy, when I get big, can I wear my hair like Miss Michelle's?"

He chuckled and looked at me. "Yeah. Afros are cool, aren't they?" He pushed her toward the stairs. "Come on. Bedtime." He turned to me. "Be right back."

I nodded, but stuffed my papers back in my bag as soon as he got to the stairs. I had to get my poor ovaries home before they exploded.

By the time he came back down from tucking the girls in, I stood waiting by the door with my blue jean jacket on and bag over my shoulder.

"You leaving?"

I nodded. "Yeah, it's late. I feel like I stayed too long."

"No, you're okay. We were making good progress. Don't you want to finish?"

I shifted my bag to my other shoulder. "There's only a little left. You'll be fine without me."

"Oh. Okay. Well. There's something I need to tell you."

Oh, dear. The last time a man told me that, it was about herpes. "What's up, Jason?"

Jason shuffled his feet. "That's why I wanted you to come to the house instead of me trying to say something at the office."

My stomach twisted. This couldn't be good.

"Okay." I braced myself for the worst. Was he getting married and wanted me to organize a camera crew for the wedding? Was he having a secret love affair with Rayshawn and thought I should know? Were he and the girls moving to Nebraska?

He rubbed a hand over his head. "Umm, I know you've been wondering why I've been driving so hard at getting the shows edited so quickly. I know I've been pushing you and taking up a lot of your free time when you should be home or out with your girls or with that special someone or whatever you do when you're not at work. I was hoping we could be finished with everything by the end of the month 'cause I didn't want to leave you hanging. I probably should have skipped the shoots and started editing sooner, but you seemed to appreciate my input, and it had been so long since I got a chance to direct. In hindsight, that probably was a bad choice, but I really enjoyed myself."

I frowned, unsure of where he was going.

"And it inspired me to go after it again. Made me realize God gave me a talent that I haven't been using. You know, when God gives you something, He means for you to use it. And it wasn't right for me to bury my gifts because I wanted to trust in a paycheck. I should have trusted in Him that my gifts would make room for me. But I'm a father and I've got my girls to think about, so I made what I thought was the best choice."

I raised my eyebrows. "Okay?" Was there some hidden message I was supposed to be getting?

"And so anyway, God really used you to stir up my gift by letting me direct the shoots. And it really got me to praying and asking Him what I should be doing. In a way, I guess God used you in my life to get me back on track where I'm supposed to be. And I am really thankful for that. Just like you said

I helped you make it to senior producer, you've really helped me get to the place where I know God ordained for me to be. I've really enjoyed working with you, and I appreciate—"

"Jason!" I put my hands on my head and squeezed. "What in the world are you talking about?"

He puffed out his cheeks and let out a deep breath. "I got a job with Tyler Perry Studios. I'm supposed to start at the end of the month."

My mouth fell open.

He winced. "Sorry. I know this is a bad time to leave you. But I have to do me. This is an awesome opportunity."

"Wow. That's great, Jason. I'm happy for you. And don't apologize. You're far too good at what you do to be stuck in a BTV edit suite. You need to be somewhere big, making big things happen."

He put a hand on my arm, and electric tingles shot up to my neck and shoulders.

"Thanks, Michelle. I'm glad you understand."

"Of course, Jason. This is only the start of great things for you. You deserve it. God is faithful."

"Yeah. He is."

I turned toward the door. There were too many emotions flooding through me. More than my St. John's wort could handle. I was about to lose Jason. I turned back and gave him a weak smile. "I'm going to miss you. I've enjoyed working with you. I mean, I know you're not gone yet, but . . ."

He looked down at the floor. "Yeah. I'm gonna miss you too." He shuffled his feet and put his hands in his pockets. "Unless of course . . ."

My heart flipped. "Unless of course, what?"

He folded his arms and took a deep breath. "Unless of course—"

"Daddy . . ." Candace's voice cut Jason off. "I'm thirsty. Can I have some water?"

Jason's eyes widened and he held up a finger. "Can you wait a second?"

I nodded. My poor heart was beating faster than God created it to.

He dashed into the kitchen and grabbed a bottle of water and dashed upstairs with it.

Within a few seconds, he was back. He exhaled and stood there for a few seconds. He finally said, "What I was trying to say was . . . unless you think—"

"Daddy . . ." Candace's voice rang out again. "I can't get it open. The top's on too tight."

He held up a finger again and gave me a weak smile. He ran up the stairs again.

He came back after a few moments. He put a hand on the stair rail and collected himself. "What I mean is . . . what do you think about—"

"Daddy . . ." Candace seemed to have either the best or the worst timing. "It's too warm. Can you bring me some ice?"

He yelled up the stairs. "Candace, drink some water. Put the top back on and go to sleep. If I come up those stairs again, you won't be happy to see me."

Silence.

Jason ran a hand across his head. I couldn't tell if he was frazzled by our conversation or by Candace.

"She is really blowing my game here."

His game? Oh my. I let out a nervous giggle.

He led me out the front door onto the porch. He left the door ajar, I guess to be able to hear the girls.

He stood, looking up at the sky for a second and finally spoke, "I guess what I'm trying to say is, just because I leave BTV doesn't mean you have to miss me. In fact, I hope to see more of you after I leave there. I mean, not more of you, because we see each other all day every day. I mean, not that I want to see less of you, but obviously there's no way we could see each other all day every day. I mean, well, of course not at first anyway. Maybe later. I mean, hopefully later. I mean . . ." He looked at me with those dreamy eyes, begging me to rescue him from his nervous banter.

"I'd like that, Jason. To see you. I mean, of course, like you said, not every day. I mean, at first not every day like you said, but after a while, maybe then every day. I mean . . . you know what I mean . . ." I bit my lip to make myself stop.

I knew Jason and I were giving God and Jesus a fit. I could see them shaking their heads and rolling their eyes. Either that, or they were rolling around on the throne room floor, laughing at how ridiculous our conversation was. I felt the wind blow across my face and knew they had sent the Holy Spirit down to help us out of the mess we were creating. I felt His peace.

Jason must have felt it too. He took a deep breath and reached out for my hand. "I . . . really enjoy spending time with you, Michelle. We have so much in common, it's crazy. And you're exactly the kind of woman I would have picked if I was saved and knew who I was the first time I got married."

He gestured toward the house. "So you've seen the whole me. My crazy, cluttered house. My girls and my life as a single dad." He fidgeted with my fingers and then strengthened his grip on my hand. "At this stage in my life, I'm looking for a special person—someone I can share the rest of my life with. Someone who loves God with all their heart and puts Him first. Somebody whose destiny matches mine, so we can build the Kingdom of God together. Most importantly, I want someone who would understand that, above all, I'm committed to my daughters." He looked down at the ground. "And is willing to share that commitment."

He looked back up at me and captivated me with those dreamy eyes. For all the wonderful words I should have and could have said at that moment, I couldn't seem to get my mouth to speak. Jason's eyes went from dreamy to that vulnerable look a guy can get that will melt a girl more than anything. And, still, I couldn't come up with one thing to say.

So I slipped my arms around his neck, pulled myself close to him, and let my lips do the talking—without words.

And *dreamy* couldn't adequately express how his lips felt on mine. *Druggy* was more like it. It seemed like his lips were infused with crack and I had just reached a new high.

I made myself pull away. When I looked up at him, his eyes were dreamier than ever, and he gave me that dimply grin.

I had to leave while I could still drive. I floated down the steps to my car, feeling his eyes on me the whole way. I was all butterfingers, and it took me a second to get my key in the ignition.

When I finally got my car started, I gave a quick wave and drove away.

On the way home I said to God, "Okay. I'm not going a step further without asking you this time. You know Jason and you know me. If he's your best for me, then let this thing bloom and grow into exactly what you've ordained it to be. If not, then bring it to a screeching halt." As I said the words, I felt my heart ache. "God, please let Jason be your best for me. I don't think I can handle it if he's not. And give me some sort of sign. Soon, God. So I can relax and not feel all crazy about it."

After I got home, I soaked in the bathtub for a while to relax. I put on some boxer shorts and a T-shirt and crawled into bed.

It took me forever to fall asleep. I tossed and turned, kicked off the covers and threw the pillows on the floor. I was sad about Jason leaving BTV, but happy at the same time.

I relived the kiss over and over. I kept thinking about him and the girls.

Then I got scared about dating him. What if it was like Isaiah? What if I fell hard, and just when I decided he was the one, God showed me he wasn't? I had to trust that God would show me. Soon, this time. Before I fell any further. *God, please send me a sign . . .*

When I finally drifted off to sleep, I had one of those larger-than-life dreams. The ones in Dolby sound and Technicolor where you could feel everything like it was really happening. The kind of dream you knew wasn't from what you ate the night before, but was God communicating directly.

In the dream, I was sleeping in my king-size bed, all alone. I woke up stretching my arms to heaven, thanking God for yet another birthday. The door burst open, and a plastic Ken doll with Jason's face on it came in, followed by two little girls who looked just like Candace and Cameron. They sang "Happy Birthday" and all jumped in the bed and hugged me. We all lay in the bed together for a while, smiling our plastic smiles.

Finally, Jason/Ken got up and said he was taking the girls to school and that he'd be back in a little while. He winked and grinned before leading the girls out the door. And I lay there in the bed waiting for him to come back.

I reached down to rub my hands across my swollen pregnant belly, and my heart filled with joy. And, I promise, I could hear ponies neighing in the stable.

Sherri L. Lewis

Sherri is the *Essence* Bestselling author of *My Soul Cries Out* and *Dance Into Destiny*. She attended Howard University as an undergraduate, then medical school at the University of Pennsylvania School of Medicine.

By day, she "ministers" as the staff physician at a Georgia Department of Corrections' Women's prison. Sherri is co-founder of the Atlanta Black Christian Fiction Writers' Critique Group with *Essence* Bestselling author, Tia McCollors. She is also a member of the American Christian Fiction Writers and founding president of the organization's Southeast Atlanta Visions In Print chapter. She lives in Atlanta, Georgia.

Reader's Group Guide Questions

1. Michelle's story begins with her lamenting over being single and childless at age thirty-five. She asks God to either send her a husband or take the desire away. Is this a reasonable prayer? How should a woman waiting for her soul mate handle the loneliness and desire that occurs in the meantime? What mistakes might she make if she doesn't handle this season correctly?

2. Each of the women in the story is in a different place as it relates to men and relationships. Discuss where they are, the experiences that have brought them there, and which character you relate to the most.

3. In the beginning of the story, Lisa says every one of the women should have a list of what they want in a man. One of the singles ministry speakers says the same thing. Angela said she had no list and asked God to bring her His best for her. Do you think women should have a list when trusting God for a mate? What are the positives and negatives of having a list?

4. What does Michelle mean when she says she wants a man that "feels like God" to her? She says she wants God to send her a husband

who is Him "wrapped up in chocolate." Is this realistic? She also says she doesn't care what he looks like. Is this realistic?

5. During the singles ministry meeting on "Things Your Momma Should Have Told You About Marriage," the guest speakers teach on things they think are essential for a woman preparing for marriage. Discuss what it means to "be prepared," "choose well," and "let God heal your heart after a bad relationship."

6. In the singles ministry meeting, the subject of submission was also discussed. What is submission in marital relationships? Is submission a Biblical concept, or are women today still expected to submit to their husbands? How do the characters' reactions to the thought of submitting to a man compare to yours?

7. Michelle refused to join Lisa and Angela in online dating, stating that it's ungodly. Discuss whether Christians should use online dating services.

8. Michelle is adamant about not going out with Isaiah until she gets the phone call from her family and discovers that her baby sister is getting married and her older sister is pregnant again. How did their announcements affect her decision? How can looking at where others are and comparing ourselves to them positively and negatively affect our actions?

9. The girls often tell Lisa the reason she doesn't have a man is because her list is ridiculous and unrealistic. Is Lisa wrong for trusting God

for exactly what she wants, or should she be willing to settle? What exactly is "settling?"

10. Angela begins the story as a forty-one-year-old virgin and ends up getting pregnant out of wedlock. What were the mindsets, decisions, and actions that caused her to end up as she did? Is it really realistic to remain celibate in a committed relationship?

11. Discuss the reasons that Michelle broke things up with Isaiah? How much should a man's financial status affect whether he should be a potential mate or not? Discuss the concept of two people's destinies lining up and matching, and how that can affect a relationship.

12. Lisa mentions a prayer her friend prayed, asking God to bring any relationship that He knew wouldn't work out in the long run to a "screeching halt." Michelle prays this prayer about both Isaiah and Jason. Discuss the benefits of submitting a potential mate to the Lord before spending a lot of time with them and getting too deep into a relationship.

Urban Christian His Glory Book Club!

Established January 2007, *UC His Glory Book Club* is another way by which to introduce to the literary world, Urban Books' much-anticipated new imprint, **Urban Christian** and its authors. We are an online book club supporting Urban Christian authors by purchasing, reading and providing written reviews of the authors' books that are read. *UC His Glory* welcomes both men and women of the literary world who have a passion for reading Christian-based fiction.

UC His Glory is the brainchild of Joylynn Jossel, Author and Executive Editor of Urban Christian and Kendra Norman-Bellamy, Author and Copy Editor for Urban Christian. The book club will provide support, positive feedback, encouragement, and a forum whereby members can openly discuss and review the literary works of Urban Christian authors. In the future, we anticipate broadening our spectrum of services to include: online author chats, author spotlights, interviews with your favorite Urban Christian author(s), special online groups for *UC Book Club* members, ability to post reviews on the website and amazon.com, membership ID cards, *UC His Glory* Yahoo Group and much more.

Even though there will be no membership fees attached to becoming a member of *UC His Glory Book Club*, we do expect our members to be active, committed, and to follow the guidelines of the Book Club.

UC His Glory members pledge to:

- Follow the guidelines of *UC His Glory Book Club*
- Provide input, opinions, and reviews that build up, rather than tear down
- Commit to purchasing, reading and discussing featured book(s) of the month
- Agree not to miss more than three consecutive online monthly meetings
- Respect the Christian beliefs of *UC His Glory Book Club*
- Believe that Jesus is the Christ, Son of the Living God

We look forward to the online fellowship.

Many Blessings to You!

Shelia E. Lipsey
President
UC His Glory Book Club

**Visit the official Urban Christian Book Club website at *www.uchisglorybookclub.net*